20 Under 30

Edited by

DEBRA SPARK

WITH A NEW PREFACE BY THE EDITOR

SCRIBNER PAPERBACK FICTION
Published by Simon & Schuster

SCRIBNER PAPERBACK FICTION
Simon & Schuster Inc.
Rockefeller Center
1230 Avenue of the Americas
New York, NY 10020

FIRST SCRIBNER PAPERBACK FICTION EDITION 1996

SCRIBNER PAPERBACK FICTION and design are trademarks of Simon & Schuster Inc.

Manufactured in the United States of America

1   3   5   7   9   10   8   6   4   2

Library of Congress Cataloging-in-Publication Data
20 under 30
1. Short stories, American.   2. American fiction—20th century.
I. Spark, Debra, date.   II. Title: Twenty under thirty.
PS648.S5A145   1986   813'.01'08   86-1769

ISBN 0-684-81514-1

Permissions appear on page 271.

Contents

Preface

IN THE PAST TEN YEARS, I've had the mostly happy experience of having people occasionally recognize me as the editor of *20 Under 30*. When I've been in literary circles, the recognition has been, invariably, accompanied by two questions. The first is, why don't I do another *20 Under 30*? And, tangentially, why don't I make the book an annual series? The second question—asked with varying degrees of grumpiness, depending on the age and publishing record of the inquirer—is when am I going to do *60 Over 70*?

So, why not do another collection, especially since this volume has been a success and its authors are almost all still writing and publishing? When people first asked me this, I'd say it was because I wanted to be known as a writer, not as an editor. I had ambitions for my own prose. While this is still true, the real reason is that, for me, the project is an unrepeatable one.

When I began working on the anthology, I was twenty-two. I was in a writing class at Yale, and one of my classmates had won a prize that the college offered for fiction. Encouraged, he'd mailed the story off to *The New Yorker*. He reported back to the class that he'd recieved a note saying, "Yale may like this, but we don't."

"Well!" I'd thought. And then, Pooh-bear style, "dear, dear." I had thought the story one of the best I'd ever read. It was magical and strange, and I resolved to put together a collection of stories like it. And I went around saying I *was* putting together such a collection . . . not thinking, of course, that anything would come of it. I started asking people to make suggestions, started reading literary magazines and then sleuthing through bio notes, trying to guess authors' ages. Every time I "accepted" a story—though the word seemed too grand at the time—I asked the author to tell me about other writers.

Soon enough, I realized I was engaging in the project partially because I could imagine selling other people's work but not my own. I was too shy, too full of self-doubt. This secret motivation had both its philanthropic and its greedy side. True, I hoped to help young writers out, but I also hoped my experience with the anthology would teach me about the publishing world and that I'd be able to apply that knowledge when it came time to sell my own book.

And I did learn. I learned that I was doing everything the wrong way. But by the time I had mastered that lesson, I'd already made my mistakes—failed, for instance, to put an ad in a writing magazine to solicit submissions—and I'd already made a series of personal blunders, not fully aware of the effect my project would have on my new graduate school friends, most of whom, as young, unpublished writers, were eager to be included.

A year after the anthology was published, I had a discussion with Tom Jenks, the anthology's in-house editor, about "moral fiction." I had written something in the anthology's introduction about Tolstoy and moral fiction, and I was coming to believe the exact opposite of what I had written. I was finding it hard not to wince when people mentioned the anthology. Never mind the collection's twenty stories, which I still liked; I felt embarrassed about what *I* had written: my philosophy-major posturing, my breezy claim that aesthetics and ethics could be separated.

"I knew you'd figure that out sooner or later," Tom said.

I was taken aback. "But . . . but why didn't you tell me? I could have changed it." I felt betrayed. He was my editor and a friend. Shouldn't he have prevented me from making a fool of myself?

He shook his head no. It would have been a mistake for him to impose his ideas; what I wrote was what I thought when I was twenty-three and that, given the nature of the project, was significant.

I couldn't duplicate my innocence, my blundering, in a new collection. No doubt I'd make a different set of mistakes, but they wouldn't be the mistakes of early youth. So, no—no more *20 Under 30*s. Not from me. Instead, I have to hope this collection still serves its purpose, and I think it does.

Nowadays, there are plenty of collections of fiction by young writers. Ten years ago there weren't, and *20 Under 30* received attention partially because there were no similar collections available. Back in 1986, when people asked me to characterize the anthology's stories, I always found myself tongue-tied. I'm not a sociologist, and the request seemed to spring from some demand that I—or the work—offer a reading of the youth of the eighties. In the end, my trouble may have had to do with the stories themselves, which weren't, in an overt way, responses to the phenomenon of the decade. Instead, they were stories, ideally expressing the universal concerns of youth, which happened to have been written in the eighties. I suspect it is this ambition to be universal that gives the anthology its staying power. I don't think the same claim can be made about some of the current "Gen X" collections. Perhaps with their very titles, those anthologies brand themselves unfairly, saying, "This is just us, just now," instead of making a larger claim for the sensitive observers and talented young writers of the nineties.

In aging ten years, *20 Under 30* does—like all of us—gain and lose some things. One gain is the picture it gives of the earliest work of writers like Lorrie Moore, Mona Simpson, and David Leavitt, who have considerable national reputations. Though it would be a mistake to say that any of the authors here are no longer doing their "early" work, they have matured, so the collection can inspire would-be writers by acting as an album of childhood pictures, presaging the adult in the slight grimace or off-kilter smile of the youth.

The losses are, perhaps, more apparent. These writers aren't under thirty anymore. Their writing doesn't show us what people in their twenties are producing these days. For a compilation of *that* work, we had best turn to someone in his or her twenties.

Which leaves me without a project. So, *60 Over 70*? It's something to consider. It will be a hefty collection, I imagine—all those stories in one volume, after all; so much life to weigh in.

I just have to wait to start working on it.

—DEBRA SPARK

Introduction

A YEAR AGO, I began to wonder what type of fiction people my age write. This anthology is the result of my curiousity —a collection of twenty stories by writers under thirty. Thirty is an arbitrary age to select and I picked the number more for its neatness than its legitimacy as an age which distinguishes young from middle-aged authors. If the age once separated the single from the married, the childless couple from the parents, or the drifter from the entrenched employee, it no longer does. The authors' ages in the collection range from twenty-one to thirty. They are all Americans. Few are married, fewer still have children. Many are, or recently have been, associated with universities or writing programs. This last fact is an accident and not a particularly happy one. It suggests that the anthology is biased to something other than good writing, though, in fact, it is not. It suggests, too, that I went through academic circles to find the stories, though I did not. My only true criterion for selecting stories for the anthology was jealousy. Any story I enjoyed well enough to wish I had written I included. I would have liked to invent a childless matron who is an expert in "armchair mothering," so I included Leigh Allison Wilson's "The Raising." I envied the imagination that created a desert community in which people are starving for words rather than food, so I chose to use Rand Burkert's "The Stone Inscription of Caleb Pellor."

If the twenty stories in this volume suggest to anyone that young writers tend to write in a certain way, I will be surprised. The stories strike me as quite dissimilar. This is, of course, the anthologist's usual cry: "Very varied! Really! And each one distinct! Not to mention beautifully written!" In this case, I think it is true—a compliment to my jealousy, not my taste.

Generalizations about the nature of a generation's literary tendencies do too much damage to the truth, so I will not make any. None of the stories in the anthology are the work of an immature author, nor are they the kind of stories one tends to accuse young people of writing. There are no teenage suicides in this book, no narrators losing their virginity, no Hesse-esque male youths. Many of the stories, however, are clearly informed by the concerns of a young person in American society. I am thinking specifically of Ehud Havazelet's "Natalie Wood's Amazing Eyes" with its young, not particularly sane, moviegoer/narrator. I am thinking, too, of Emily Listfield's "Porcupines and Other Travesties" in which the female narrator insists that her desires do not mirror the quite specific desires of the desperate single women about her.

If the stories in the book do seem similar in any way, this is more a product of my thoughts about what makes good literature than any trend among young writers. I hold to the definition that Tolstoy, in his "Introduction to the Works of Guy de Maupassant," gives for "that particular gift called talent, which consists in the capacity to direct intense concentrated attention, according to the author's taste, on this or that subject, in consequence of which the man endowed with this capacity sees in the things to which he directs his attention some new aspect which others have overlooked." Often, in the stories that follow, the very subject that the authors pick to serve their vision will be something that an ordinary observer will have overlooked. Young writers tend to have a limited range of experience and their stories often demonstrate this . . . too many tales of family strife, early love affairs, college mishaps. The writers represented here have not had particularly unusual lives. What they do have is imagination which allows them to get past the early writer's excessive dependence on autobiography.

In this book, there is a harmonica named Roy Luther, a dancer intent on perfecting the "attitude" of a grandfather she never knew, snakes that stand on end, a child who believes that she is not of this earth but the planet Dandril. There is, further-more, one man smuggling trinitrotoluene into Dublin, one translator of Rumanian poetry, one dead woman in a Parisian Lavomatic. Lest the book sound like a freak show, I should add that there is also a family with an absent father, a boy with a crush on a young woman, a girl in a bar with man-at-side and fake-ID-in-pocket. In each tale, whether the subject picked is wild and fanciful or commonplace, the vision evidences, as Tolstoy would have it, "the gift of seeing what others have not seen."

I have a few complaints with what is considered the current trend in new fiction and I have indulged them in my selection of stories. In the best stories, I believe that the realizations in the story have the force of a sudden realization for the reader as well as the characters. For this very reason, I cannot stand stories that lament the emptiness of pop culture, TV, fast food. No one needs to read a story to learn this. My objection does not concern the choice of subject matter—one could hardly rule out contempo-rary culture as a fit subject for contemporary fiction—but the simplicity of the vision. Similarly, though twenty years ago it may have been valid to discover, through fiction, that the so-called American dream was a lot of garbage, to read now about this peculiar brand of disappointment is, to my mind, peculiarly disappointing.

Another gripe I have against much new fiction is that it seems not to understand the complexities of conflict. It has a fairytale mentality about how families or couples work. Too often, there is a bad guy in new fiction. While I don't hold that we should understand a Nazi's point of view or get the murderer's side of the story, most of the time the famous other-side-of-the-argument has validity. Sure, sure, in real life, there are nasty parents who snarl "Why don't you get your life together?" to their distraught and pregnant daughter. Yes, there are lovers who suddenly disappear. However, the complexities of the dissolution of the narrator's romantic relationship in Lorrie Moore's "Amahl and the Night Visitors" seems more "real" than stories of straightforward, cruel abandonment. Likewise, in Susan Minot's "Thanksgiving Day" and Mona Simpson's "Approximations," the people who do the hurting are not villains or egocentric fools but people making mistakes, acting stupidly.

My final problem with contemporary fiction is that much of it, by borrowing the language of the very culture in which its characters aimlessly float, by depending on the reader's knowledge of specific advertising schemes and brand names, comes up with witticisms and observations that have as much staying power as advertising schemes and brand names. This causes many contemporary stories to fail the acid test for a good story—however well-crafted, one cannot remember the story after one has read it. I am only jealous of a story with staying power and all the stories in this collection stick with me. I will not soon forget the powerful final pages of Marjories Sandor's "The Gittel" or Robin Hemley's concise story "Riding the Whip." Nor will I forget Bret Lott's plumber who is "just the plumber," nor Kate Wheeler's character Mayland Thompson in "Judgment" who tells his wife he wants to be buried with a fresh young girl to keep him company till Jesus arrives.

A work of art is more than the product of a talented person. To talent, Tolstoy wrote, must be added:

> "1) a correct, that is, a moral relation of the author to his subject; 2) clearness of expression, or beauty of form—the two are identical; and, 3) sincerity—that is, a sincere feeling of love or hatred of what the author depicts."

Tolstoy was certainly wrong about the first condition, wrong, too, in his equation of clarity and beauty of form. When a story allows an author to have a moral relationship to a subject (and often a story does not even admit of such a relationship), the author's relation to the subject is a matter of ethics not aesthetics. As important as the ethical issue may be, it is a separate one and, as such, should not enter into a definition of a work of art. Furthermore, for all but the most rigorous spiritualist, clarity is a necessary but not a sufficient condition for beauty of form. Beauty of form has a sensuous side as well. Still, Tolstoy was right in his insistence on the need for beauty of form and on the need for sincerity. This third condition may be the most important of all, though I do not think of it as a "feeling of love or hatred" as much as the effort to translate one's thoughts and deepest concerns into the language of the heart. The stories that follow succeed by a definition, albeit modified, of a work of art which, I hope, has more staying power than some of the current definitions.

I was familiar with the work of a few of the writers in this anthology before I started collecting stories. Most of the names in the book, however, were suggested by other writers, editors and agents. For leading me to some of the stories in the collection, I thank Doris Grumbach, Robin Hemley, Heidi Jon Schmidt, Scott Raab, Melanie Jackson, Jonathan Dee, Michelle Herman, Tom Jenks and Sara London.

—Debra Spark, 1986

KATE WHEELER

Judgment

WHEN MAYLAND THOMPSON dies he wants to be buried with the body of a twelve-year-old girl. "A fresh one," he says. "Huh! Just toss her in there and let her keep me company till Jesus gets here."

As for his wife, Linda, he'd like her to wait for judgment in a mass grave with all of her boyfriends. He threatens to write their names in his will: two deputy sheriffs, a detective, a railroad switchman, bartenders, motel owners, pavement repairmen, drunks.

"You'll have some real winners to cuddle up to," he tells her. "They're bad enough alive. Just imagine what they'll be like, full of worms."

She holds up a dead mouse by the tail. "There was three of these in the basement. Reminded me of you. Time I get old enough to die, you won't be able to make me do nothing."

His hair turns a shade grayer in the afternoon light. It's just that he wouldn't want her to be lonely either, he tells her.

Her expression is blank, the muscles of her face completely

relaxed. She has Indian blood, and Irish. Once a month, she uses a special wax to remove fine black down from her upper lip.

He's known Linda since she was eight and her mother used to roll with him naked on the musty box spring in the attic. Right on this very porch, he would sit the two of them on his lap, Felicia Biggins and her daughter; they would each put an arm around his neck and fill his ears with tongues. He pinched here and there, gave them sips of Schlitz. The three of them were the talk of Rampart City, Kansas. At least once a week there would be a preacher or a juvenile officer or a member of the Ladies' Benevolent knocking on Felicia's door, until she borrowed Mayland's Goose gun and started to wave it around. That stopped them. She was his kind of woman.

The day she died of the liver, Mayland felt a natural responsibility arise in his heart, so he kidnapped Linda away from her uncle Clyde and the custody girls. Through one moist night he drove, Linda curled snoring beside him, her face stuck to the plastic seat. At dawn, a sleepy Mormon gave him the key to Room 206 of the New Paris Motel outside Provo, Utah. Three weeks he hid her there, feeding her ice and double cheeseburgers. She took two baths a day and watched the TV news in color. She cracked the enamel of her molars and grew plump as a broiler.

They were married, which made Linda the third Mrs. Thompson. He waited six months, until she was of age, before bringing her back to her mother's farm.

Did marriage agree with her? She was as silent and distant as the moon. Each night as she lay under him in bed, she seemed plumper and more mysterious than the night before. By the end of the year, she was pregnant.

Wild with joy, Mayland bought two used pizza ovens at the auction and resold them to buy her a color television set. It had no knobs; he placed it on the coffee table and turned it on for her with a screwdriver. It refused to turn off again, but Linda didn't mind. She watched it for two days straight, changing channels with a wrench, until one morning the tube burned out in the middle of a program. Then she sat up on the couch and announced she couldn't stand the feeling of being overweight. Hitting her stomach with her fists, she walked out into the dusty yard, climbed into Mayland's pickup and drove to town for diet pills. That night, and for two days afterward, blood came out of her in clots that filled Mayland's two cupped palms.

The doctor shook his head. He gave her a shot.

When Linda woke up, she would eat nothing but celery and carrots.

Now she won't let Mayland touch her, so what has he got? A ninth-grade graduate with a magazine figure who sleeps in cotton underwear, and a hundred and twenty acres of her land to take care of. He has done as much as he can, as much as his wife and the farm will let him, but in four years he hasn't scraped together a hill of beans. How much can you do with forty acres of river bottom full of dead trees and another eighty oversprayed? What can you do for a girl twenty years old who can't make change for a dollar?

These days he wakes up, the backs of his legs red from the heating pad, and he has the feeling that there is something he doesn't want to remember. He leaves the house quietly, very early, and goes to talk to high school girls waiting for the morning bus. If he can't get any of them to play hooky he'll spend the rest of the day in town making deals.

In the river bottom, another man's horses graze, standing with their tails to the wind. On the northwest corner of the property, Roy the sharecropper sweats over the broken windmill. Mayland wants to get somebody out there with a metal detector: one of the milo fields is supposed to have been an Indian battleground.

Noon. Linda straightens her legs under the electric blanket. Sunk in the mattress, her body seems boneless. Blue veins show through the skin of her neck; she is no longer asleep.

Behind the toolshed, in a square plot Mayland made by wiring four yellow gates together at the corners, there is a tablet of slate over Linda's mother and a small aluminum marker that says "Baby" but doesn't have anything buried under it. Linda keeps the weeds out, and she's collecting rocks from every state in the union to decorate the graves.

Rummaging in the bottom of the closet, she finds a pair of blue stretch pants and a T-shirt with a silvery photograph ironed onto the front. She dresses, puts on her eye shadow and goes out to stand on the road. The man in the red car sees her from a distance and takes his foot off the gas.

Wednesday Mayland traded a hundred junk cars to the dealer for eighty dollars in cash and a purple boat with an inboard motor. Thursday he traded the boat for twenty dollars and a four-wheel-drive truck that was missing one wheel. Today he is making arrangements with his pal Frank about the metal detector: they'll split anything Frank finds, fifty-fifty.

"It don't matter who holds the title when it comes to something buried more than a foot," Frank says. "This'll be in your name for a change, how do you like that?"

The two men smile at each other across the counter of Frank's Shoe Repair Salon.

"How is that wife of yours, anyway?"

"Oh, you know her," Mayland says. "Pushing the legal limit. And you know me. When the two of us comes to town . . . ."

In that white Lincoln or the blue pickup: Frank knows all about it. "The mothers lock their girls in the closet and they push their sons out the back door."

"You got it."

"No, you all's the ones that's got it." Frank pushes away

the display of rubber heels and leans across the glass. "And you deserve every bit of it you get." He slaps Mayland's shoulder and the two of them laugh. "It's just too damn bad you can't sell the place till she's twenty-one. I hate to see a friend scratching in the dirt like that."

"You bring that machine out and it's finders keepers," Mayland tells him. "Anyway, we'll sell it next year and be in Florida with water skis on our feet."

As Mayland gets ready to leave, Frank says, "I'll remember what you said. If you can sell that dump I'll have a pig roast for you."

"Pigs is free at the 4-H farm. If you go at night."

Walking out in the thin autumn sunlight, Mayland wishes he were in Florida. Some of his children are there, including Junior. The only one of Mayland's kids ever to try to walk the straight and narrow: turns Jehovah's Witness and a week later he gets shot in the head at a rally. Junior's alive, but he'll never be the same. Some things just go to show you, Mayland thinks, they just go to fucking show you.

He decides to check at the bar to see if Linda and the share-cropper are having a beer. But she's not there.

It is too dark to see. There is a smell of frying onions.

Mayland comes up the steps and sees Linda inside, standing in the yellow light of the kitchen, slicing. The tip of her tongue is out, she is concentrating on a potato. He bangs the door and she looks up.

She flicks a strand of black hair behind her ear. "You left the refrigerator open this morning," she says. "I could have drank the spread, it was that runny."

"I want you to tell me where you was this evening and this afternoon."

"Roy came over and we went down for a beer. You said that was all right, Mayland."

Roy the sharecropper, Mayland thinks disgustedly, she's

named eighteen guys after him just because she knows I know she thinks he's ugly. And Roy will usually tell me whatever she says to. But today at six o'clock, Roy told Mayland there was a red car parked all day in the driveway, and Roy didn't know whose it was.

" 'Went down' might be the truth," Mayland says. "But you wasn't at the bar and you wasn't with Roy either."

She smiles faintly at the cutting board. "How come you know so much? You been following me?"

He wants to hit her. "No, it ain't worth my time. I want to know where my three-hundred-dollar ratchet set is and my seventy-five-dollar power saw."

"Ask somebody else. I ain't touched nothing of yours."

"You had somebody over and they took it." He steps closer to her and she shrinks back against the wall, her lips shaking open to show her teeth.

Now she's scared of me, Mayland thinks, damn it. That's all we need for her to think. I never hit a woman in my life. He turns away and walks back toward the bedroom, clicking on light switches as he goes. There are three beer bottles on the table, and an ashtray. As he tears the sheets off the bed, he notices Linda standing in the doorway, watching.

"The trouble with you is that you don't know how to judge people," he tells her. "You might be real pretty, but that ain't going to stop you from getting a disease. You might own a farm, but you'd get yourself in a lot of hot water real fast if it wasn't for me."

"But all my blood relatives is dead except for Clyde, and he hates me because of you."

"I got a lot more dead relatives than you do. That don't mean you can't make something of yourself." He throws the sheets on the floor. "Better make sure them onions don't burn."

She runs back to the kitchen. Look at her, Mayland says to

himself. Pounding through the house like a three-year-old. I guess I can't leave her out here by herself no more to moon over them graves and attract the low-life.

"I got you a job," he says as the screen door slams behind him.

She is standing in the middle of the kitchen, staring out the window. "Somebody ran over that spotted horse," she says. "It's in the road."

"I saw that this morning while you was still asleep." He walks around in front of her, hoping she will say something.

Linda looks down at the floor. Her small bare feet look cold, bluish against the dark linoleum; there is fresh persimmon-colored polish on the nails of one foot. "It screamed," she says finally. "Before the sun came up."

"I'll sell it to the dog food factory tomorrow," he says. "Now listen up. I'm taking you to town at seven o'clock a.m. tomorrow morning. You're going to wash dishes at the cafe for three-fifty an hour."

"You just want to make me pay you back for that saw," she complains. Turning her back on him, she walks past the refrigerator into the living room. "I guess I better get some rest then, huh."

There is nothing in the refrigerator except fifty-two-percent oil spread and an empty cardboard box. The first time he tries to close it, the rubber cord they use to keep the door shut snaps back; the metal hook flies past his ear. He goes in to look at his wife on the couch: she has covered her face with a sheet of newspaper, which blows gently up and down with her breath.

She can sleep more than any human being, until four in the afternoon sometimes. In his opinion, she's still suffering from that brain fever she had when she was two, three years old. At least she reads. She reads the newspaper every day, and she pays attention to the radio.

"There's a man in Colorado who was teaching his dog how

to shoot a gun," she will say, excited. "It picked it up off the table and it fell out of its mouth and onto the floor and now he's in the hospital!"

No way would Mayland let her near his guns. The ones that aren't at the pawnshop are locked in a closet in the basement.

At the table, her mouth full of store-bought chicken, she tells him she doesn't want to go to work in the morning. She'll do something wrong the first hour and then she'll want to quit. He answers that he'll lock her in the woodshed and hustle her to niggers if she wants to stay home.

Linda giggles. "It wouldn't be no worse than nothing to eat but this greasy fucking chicken," she says. "But I tell you what, if you do that, I'll get one of them niggers to kill you and then I'll bury you with a goat!"

"Greasy chicken is your own fault," he says. "You should have asked that guy to take you to the grocery store at least."

Both of them laugh. After dinner, he tries to give her a lesson in case Mrs. Folsom wants Linda to work the register.

"Here's a dollar. Coffee's thirty cents," Mayland says. "Plus tax."

She counts the change in brown coins, big silvers, medium silver, one small silver coin.

"Good," he says. "Now, pie."

She throws the money on the floor.

Her breathing is slow and quiet, her back curves away from him like a train track. He watches her body rising and falling, its edge against the dark. The October moon is cold in the window; a shaft of its light falls across the rumpled blanket, the gray carpet, the gray wallpaper with its gray roses, once pink.

His arthritis is bad tonight; his legs stick to the heating pad. If he touches her now she will roll away, even in sleep. She will mutter in her sleep and roll away.

He tries it anyway. She lets his arm stay for one second and then says, "Quit." For a year now she's been saying he's not her style in bed. It was never good except for once upon a time when she had a couple of other guys on the side, who paid her probably. She was hot for Mayland then. It lasted one month. He didn't understand anything about it, but it was nice while it lasted. Nowadays they have an understanding about sex. She's not jealous about Mayland's little girls and he doesn't ask her questions very often. She will even call the girls' houses sometimes and say she is a classmate when the mother answers.

If you consider the difference in their ages, Mayland figures, if you consider everything together, they are two people who can live with each other.

He'd like it to be different.

It's not as though he is the type to be found on the bottom of the cage with his feet in the air. When he was her age there were women who would pay him fifty, a hundred just to feel his body heat. He rubbed up against a woman eighty and a girl thirteen; he spent himself on a pool table, in church, and in the Sears furniture department.

He used to pick locks with the ace of spades—snap, like he owned the place, that fast. Like he was John Doe, picking up the mail from the mailbox and going inside to read it.

There are at least eight of his sons and daughters scattered over the nation. Rosalinda, his Mexican ex-wife, Junior's mother, still sends him religious postcards from Florida. His first wife, Belinda, is dead. Funny how he ended up with three Lindas. The other two had longer names, but this one's as complicated as half the letters in the alphabet.

"Linda," he whispers.

"Huh?"

"Once for old times' sake?"

She groans. He remembers the horse outside, its brown legs stiff as an inflated toy's.

"A man has his needs," he says.

"I'm trying to sleep, please."

. . .

He stands back and sets fire to a whole book of matches.

It lands on the horse's shoulder. For an instant he can read the words "Purina Feeds" printed in red on the white cardboard. Then there is a thumping sound and a huge yellow flame. It smells terrible, the gasoline and burning hair, and Mayland yells in delight. He sees Linda's white face at the bedroom window, then her white fluttering nightgown as she runs along the driveway toward him.

"See!" he shrieks. The carcass is burning ferociously. Several yards behind it, out of range of his jerking shadow, Linda comes to a stop. Lifting one foot, she shakes a stone from her slipper.

The two of them stand in awe until the burning stops. This happens sooner than Mayland would have liked. In the dark, the dead horse hisses and crackles like a doused campfire. Mayland can tell that only the hide is really burned; but the horse's lips have broken and stretched back horribly, so that its teeth gleam in the moonlight.

Linda covers her eyes. A small cloud of black smoke drifts eastward across the stars. "What did you go and do that for?"

"Saturday night's all right," says Mayland. "That's what we used to say in Texas."

"Texas," she says. "You're out of your mind." She giggles. "Let's go to Texas. Then I won't have to work tomorrow."

"The dump's as far as I guess either one of us is going unless you sell the farm for me in town."

"Guess so."

Later, as they lie in bed staring up at a string of water spots on the ceiling, he feels Linda's fingers brush his shoulder.

"Look," she says. "A crocodile trying to eat a duck."

The water spots on the ceiling. Mayland chuckles, air pushing through his teeth. Thick-fingered, he touches her hair where it lies dark against the pillow.

"That plaster needs to be fixed or it'll fall in on us," he says.

She turns halfway toward him, so that he can see the moonlight gleaming on her teeth, in her eyes. Suddenly he rolls his big body on top of her and kisses her, holding her arms down. She squeaks a little, tries to bite him, but he doesn't give up and soon she is just lying there, staring past his face.

"Fuck you. Fuck you," she says as he begins to grunt. He thinks he feels her spitting. "Fuck you, old man."

A crocodile that ate a duck, he thinks afterward.

The walls of the house dissolve in moonlight.

After some time there is the sound of running water. The radio's digital clock says 6:38. Through the window, the plains are a mild gray-blue; the huge loneliness of the sky is disguised by a thin ceiling of clouds. He has dreamed, he suddenly remembers, that Linda's mother was in the attic calling for cake and ice cream.

His body aches.

Wrapped in towels and a cloud of steam, Linda appears in the doorway to announce that she can't find any underwear. "I guess nobody's going to know the difference."

"I bet you tell six people, time I come get you. I bet you let them look."

"Shut up," she says. "Pig."

"Sorry," he says. Then, "Do whatever you want."

She stares at him.

Ahead, on the road, they can see the dark silhouette. Two buzzards are walking around it in the dust. The birds look awkward on the ground. Linda peers down at the carcass as Mayland drives around, his left wheels almost in the opposite ditch. The buzzards fly up. He accelerates to forty-five.

Linda pulls down the visor and leans her head back on the seat, narrowing her eyes against the sunrise. "I didn't get no sleep at all," she says. "I don't know if I can work today." The muscles of her neck tighten as the truck bumps up onto the highway pavement.

When they reach the café, she won't let Mayland come in with her. He doesn't insist; he watches as she inspects herself in the rearview mirror, tucks her purse under her arm and is gone.

As she walks into the building, she waves at a long-faced young man who is eating an iced doughnut at the window table. Mayland recognizes him as the operator of the truck scales at the Pearsall grain elevator, the half-brother of a fat girl named Minnie who once let him kiss her breasts.

In the window, Linda holds up three fingers. Three o'clock. He makes an okay sign with one hand and she disappears into darkness behind the counter.

The young man's name is Gene, and he changes seats so that he can watch Linda's head and shoulders through the foot-high opening in the wall behind the counter. He orders another doughnut; when it's gone, he wipes his mouth with a napkin and goes to the cash register to ask Mrs. Folsom for a loan of her ballpoint pen.

On a napkin he writes: "Winter coming. Last chance to get out! Meet me at 2 p.m. at Fast Gas, reg. pump if you want a ride to sunny Arizona. Yr pal, G. Friddell."

He folds the napkin and waves it at Linda; he points out the window at a black Pontiac with fiery wings painted on the hood.

Some in jeans, some in Sunday clothes, half a dozen teenagers are sitting on the city park benches near the monkey cage. They smoke, and look Mayland up and down.

"Playing hooky from church?" Mayland calls to them in a friendly tone.

"What's it to ya?" asks one of the girls. Her hair is dyed blonde, showing black at the roots, and it stands out in pointed wings on either side of her face.

"Want some beer?"

The teenagers drift over. They know him, Mayland

Thompson, lives out west of town on Route Six. Mayland invites them out to his place to see the ugliest thing in the world, but first they have to stop at the hardware store to get some kind of pulley rig. The blonde and a red-headed girl sit with Mayland in the cab, along with one of the boys. The redhead's arm is squashed against the side of Mayland's chest. Her name is Diane; Mayland tells her she's a little fatter than he likes them, but he bets she'd be a whole lot of fun if she'd just relax.

He tells them the whole story about the horse: about lying awake in bed, about his old lady cold as a piece of liver out of the icebox until he did something to light a fire under her. They would see it in a minute.

The boy named Fuzzy makes a joke about barbecue.

"We had some of it for breakfast, yeah, but we left the rest for company like you," Mayland says as the carcass comes into view.

"That's the rudest thing I ever saw," Diane observes.

"You bet, honey," Mayland says. He turns the truck around in the road.

Diane stays in the cab, playing the radio while everyone else goes out to sit on the tailgate and look. A tall boy takes out a pack of cigarettes and offers them around. Fuzzy pokes at the carcass with a stick.

"Believe it or not," says Mayland, "that thing right there used to be spotted. A spotted horse. That was even its name, Spot." He wants to put his hands on the blonde, but she is sitting on the tall boy's lap. On her arm is a homemade tattoo, the initials E.G. inside a heart. The horse smiles hugely at Mayland, making him feel uncomfortable. Something ain't right here, he thinks, checking his fly. No problem.

The beer is gone. "Okay, boys," Mayland says. "Time to load up. We've got to take this sucker to the dump."

"Listen, old man," Fuzzy says. "Not so fast." He puts his hands on Mayland's shoulders. "We got our good clothes on, man."

"I was wondering if you'd say that," Mayland says. He smiles slowly. "You can walk back to town if that's how you feel."

Fuzzy's not a bit surprised. "We don't want to start no fight here. Give us ten bucks each and everything's cool. Okay, Grecian Formula?"

Mayland sees all the boys' legs arranged in a loose arc in front of him. One of them could hold my arms and then the rest knock my teeth out, he thinks. I should have seen it coming. "Fifteen bucks for the four of you boys."

"What about the girls? You a chauvinist?"

"Twenty."

It's a deal; Mayland pays in advance: a ten, a five, five ones. The boys take off their jackets, roll up their sleeves. Mayland lets down the tailgate.

In ten minutes the horse is loaded, covered with newspapers and canvas, and tied firmly down.

"You can drop us off at the pinball parlor," Fuzzy says. "Everyone in front this time."

The teenagers sit on top of each other; no one talks. Diane has changed all the button settings on the radio to rock stations. Sharp bones press against Mayland's arm. Once, he is obliged to wave and smile at the driver of another truck, who has pulled off the road to let Mayland by.

Finally they stop across the street from the Balls of Steel.

"See you around, man," the teenagers say as they untangle themselves. They dance through traffic and away.

Two-thirty by the clock on City Hall. A new rattle in the engine. Mayland decides to stop at the cafe on the way to the dump. If Linda isn't finished with work, he'll have a lemonade and figure out what to tell the owner of the horse. He hopes Linda's not going to be mad at him still.

"I bet you can't guess my secret," Linda says as Gene's car reaches eighty miles per hour.

"You ain't got any underpants on."

"You're too smart," she complains. Her bare feet push against the dashboard, her right hand dangles against the window. She starts to tell Gene about her rock collection: she's got a lot from Oklahoma and one each from Texas and Arizona, but none from New Mexico.

"Rocks," he says. "That's a new one on me. Well, where we're going they have all the rocks you want." He laughs. "All the rocks you want."

Mayland never noticed before that the crickets still sing in October. They make a crazy sound in the trees as he stands at the foot of Linda's mother's grave, telling the whole story out loud and asking Felicia for advice.

Yes, he wanted Linda to pay for those tools. Yes, he made her do a lot of things she didn't want to: made rules, gave lessons. Partly he did it because he thought it would have made Felicia happy, partly because he thought Linda needed it. She wasn't smart enough to get along by herself but maybe she knew her own mind better than he did. Maybe she was too old to have a husband who acted like her daddy. About what happened last night, he guesses it was the last straw for her. He can't say why he had to set that horse on fire, but he knows he couldn't stop himself. He couldn't stop himself from rolling over on top of Linda either. He still can't keep from feeling like her husband.

"Tell her I ain't going to chase her down," he says. "If this was the old days I would. But tell her I'm right here. Bring her back if you can." This seems to be the end of what he has to say. His arms hang loose and heavy at his sides. He starts to cry. The crickets keep making their screamy noise. Finally he goes back to the house, careful to step over Linda's curving rows of colored rocks.

Everyone, even the bartender, is out on the sidewalk. The squad car is making a right turn into the parking lot; the siren dies

suddenly, with a strangling sound. The car stops and three Oklahoma state troopers get out.

Grim, pale, silent at the center of a fury of sparks, Linda is
ripping the neon off the front of the Sportsmen's Lounge, by
hand.

No one wants to get close for fear of being electrocuted.

Chrome stripping hangs crazy and twisted from the side of
the black car. Gene Friddell stands under the blue mercury
lights of the parking lot, drunk, telling the trooper it's not his
fault. Yes, he pushed over the chair. Yes, he called her a whore.
But it was only because she kept talking about her dead mother.
No, he didn't slap her, she slapped him.

"The witnesses say different," the trooper says. "Put one
hand on your head. Good. Now the other one." Handcuffs click
twice.

"I got business in Arizona," Gene says.

"Too bad," says the trooper, leading him to the black-and-
white squad car. He locks Gene inside and goes to help his bud-
dies subdue Linda.

The three of them tell her she'll set her hair on fire if she
doesn't stop, but she won't listen. Suddenly they are holding her
arms in a grip she can't break. She goes limp. The troopers call
for another car.

Mayland is at the county jail by midnight with two hundred
dollars' bail money he borrowed from Frank. Linda comes out
of her cell in an orange jumpsuit that flaps around her ankles.
She looks happy to see him.

"It was cold in there," she tells him. "I didn't have no socks."

"You don't look so good," he says.

The jailer gives Linda her clothes and she goes into an
empty cell to put them on while Mayland pays the bail.

"Drunk and disorderly," the jailer says. "Destruction of
property. You got a handful there, mister."

"There's going to be some new rules around the house starting tomorrow," Mayland says, without knowing what they will

be. The jailer tells him that Linda will probably get off with a light fine because it's a lady judge and because of Gene hitting her.

When she comes out in her clothes, the men in the big cell whistle and wave good-bye to her, sticking their hands through the bars. Except for Gene: Mayland sees him reading a magazine at the cement table in the middle of the cell.

Outside, in the parking lot, Linda hugs Mayland. She still smells like beer. "You know what?" she says. "I knew you wouldn't like it when I ran off. I was going to come back anyway in a couple of weeks."

"You should have left me a note," he says.

HEIDI JON SCHMIDT

Shoe

I'VE NEVER SEEN a picture of my grandfather, and in my idea of him, he's not old. I've never seen a photograph, even a poster of a movie star, that can compete with my image of him: very dark in every way, moving powerfully but fluidly, without great thought or care. I believe he's too powerful to be elegant, but that he appears elegant when he wears a suit, that his elegance is assumed with the suit. He's tailored, mustached, composed, a perfect line drawing of a man.

He once designed a famous building, the New York office of the Bank of the Lesser Antilles. He fought in World War Two, was in Paris when the city fell. He grew up in Maine, one of a fatherless family of fourteen, living on potato soup. Somewhere in upstate New York, a town is named for him. These are facts, but they may not pertain to my grandfather. I've heard them or overheard them, but when I repeat them I suspect myself of lying: if I'm talking to an architect, I make my grandfather a criminal lawyer, or a chef. I know that he lives in Sioux City, Iowa, or in Arizona now that he's retired.

I tell people that I'm a dancer, and I usually feel this is the truth. I'm not a ballerina or a chorus girl, but a dancer without the jewels and veils. I study with a well-known master who keeps a studio on the Lower East Side of New York. We lean over, curve our backs, swing our arms loose from our shoulders, jutting one hip upward. We topple and thud to the floor. Taught to consider ourselves substantial, we rarely leap. We move "sinuously—like globs of syrup."

I'm not good at what I do. My muscles are naturally tense. I picture Isadora Duncan wistfully as I flop along with the corps.

We have, as an exercise, to find an attitude for one of our grandparents, to "fit our muscles along their bones." I choose my grandfather. He walks along Gramercy Park, with his pipe. He is wearing a suit. He stops, standing at the wrought-iron gate, holding the pipe just away from his mouth. His other arm is loose at his side. It is evening, and around him everyone is hurrying. They might as well blur. He stands distinct and relaxed, looking away from the street, into the park. Light slants around him, through the tops of the trees.

When I was a child, perhaps six, I found a shoe in my grandmother's closet. She was a schoolteacher, a woman with many small bottles of perfume, and a great number of shoes, all leather, all subdued. Among these was a single shoe, a delightful shoe compared with the others: a high, wedged heel covered in white canvas, stitched all over with glass beads, red and gold and blue. It had no mate that I could find, and it seemed to be a work of art, placed mistakenly, because of its shape, among the shoes.

My mother took it from me before Grandma could see it. Ma's anger has always been cold and terrible. She loses her peripheral vision and sees only the offending act. It is as if she would tear you apart. I stood absolutely silent in front of her, hoping she would overlook me, and she did. She took the shoe straight back to the bedroom, and then she went into the bathroom and took a shower. I climbed up on the back of the couch and pressed my face against my grandmother's window, watching the customers at the deli across the street. When I heard the water stop, I slid down and sat delicately, my feet flat on the floor, a magazine open on my lap.

I am improving the attitude of my grandfather. I think of him in Paris, in uniform. He stands very erect, but easy. My shoulders are loose, one hand rests against the wall in place of Gramercy Park gate, the other is cupped around the space for a pipe. My eyes are absolutely clear, but I don't see the deeply colored leaves that drift in front of me, in the park. He is picturing some scene from the past or the future, no hazy fantasy, but a sharp-edged vision that would precede action, and in which he is entirely absorbed.

One man in the class is lucky. His grandfather was a hunchback. He stoops and each day the hump is more pronounced. His muscles really work. I am amazed at how close he can come to deformity, and how easily he stands up, stretches out, and returns to his own form.

Some months after my mother turned thirty-five, she got a birthday card from my grandfather. It was a "Happy belated birthday" card for a child, with a pastel circus tent embossed on it, signed "Love, Dad," with his name in parentheses below.

"My father had a wonderful sense of humor," my mother said. Then she looked at the postmark. "Chicago," she said, "I wonder if he lives there." She read the little printed poem on the card out loud, but it didn't seem to mean anything special. She put her arms out to me and held me, and cried.

It was that year, I think, that I found the shoe again. At first I thought it was the mate to the one at my grandmother's. I had forgotten the shoe, probably forgotten it the same day I first saw it, but now, discovering it in the back of an unused bureau stored in the cellar, I remembered my mother's face, distorted with anger, returned to composure only after she came out of the shower, her hair wrapped in a towel that gave her the height of a statue. I did not mention it to her this time. I reached into the drawer for the shoe and carried it up to my room, where I stuffed it inside one of my own boots. Knowing my mother's response to it, I waited until I was alone with my grandmother.

"Where did you get that?" she said, when she saw the shoe in my hand. I had never heard her speak so sharply.

"It's just like the one at your house," I said.

"There's only one shoe like that," she said. "Give it to me." She took it out of the room, and when she returned, she was kind and befuddled again, asking if I wanted to help her make caramel apples.

That night, I sat on the top stair and listened to her arguing with my mother. Grandma sounded tired, frustrated. Over and over again she said, "I don't know." Ma's voice was bitter, sarcastic, very low. I could hardly hear it, and what I heard, I couldn't understand.

I searched the shoe stores for a pair like the jeweled wedgie I had found, but there were no wedged heels at all that year. When I finally described the shoe to a saleswoman she went behind the counter and said to the cashier, "Marty, this girl wants a pair of hooker shoes."

I'm at work on the hips, in particular. My grandfather is not a man who would place great emphasis on his hips, I don't think. His shoulders are very sharp, his spine is straight, but his hips are casually at rest. His feet are slightly apart, and his body rises comfortably out of this powerful stance, mannered and elegant in his straight neck, his direct gaze.

My classmates regard me with derisive awe.

"What was this guy, a male model?"

"One of the first," I say, "that's how he put himself through architecture school. It was the Depression, you know."

"Well," says this woman, whose grandmother must have been a potato farmer, from the attitude she strikes, "maybe you should think of him later in life, give him some more character."

She means to be helpful, I know. "He died in World War Two," I say. I don't think of this as a real lie.

"Well, you can't just do a pose. Look how stylized this is." I look into the mirror as she runs her fingers along the curve of my outstretched arm. Maybe he was just a stylized kind of guy. "You've really got to get in there and give us his heart," she tells me.

I strive. I know he stands at the fence. I know he's attractive, intriguing to the men and women who pass him, carrying baskets of bread, sausages, and cabbage. The air is stingingly cool, the sweetness of the decaying leaves is masked by an odor of coffee and diesel exhaust. Two children squeeze through a break in the fence and my grandfather looks above them, outward, making a plan, I think. He's too stiff, too separate. I sag a little and lose him altogether. I want to be stoop-shouldered and cross-armed, to hang my head. It is his ideas, his emotions, that give him his substance. I don't know how to work backward.

When I was sixteen, my boyfriend went away for the summer and came back engaged to be married. For weeks I was despondent. My mother was despondent for me. We stayed up all night watching late movies and I shuffled to school exhausted, got high in the parking lot at noon, giggled through French class and fell asleep in study hall.

One night, in the middle of *Zombies from Beneath the Swamp*, we were picturing the married life of my boyfriend and his fiancée: gray dish towels figured prominently in the discussion. I would get even with them just by letting them live their drab little wedded life. "And," Ma said, laughing, "as a last resort, you can always send her your shoe."

"What?" I said.

We were terribly punchy; she had a pillow over her face and was laughing uncontrollably. She dropped the pillow slightly, so she could see me. "Of course, I don't think *those* shoes would do it." She pointed to my desert boots, drying beside the fireplace. "It should be something a little risqué, preferably something that reveals some toe." She put the pillow back over her face and laughed.

The zombies had gained entrance to the manor house, and the pretty blond girl sat up in bed suddenly, the silk strap of her nightgown slipping over her shoulder as she screamed.

"That's what your grandfather's lover did," she said, "and it worked like a charm. Just the shoe, no message, but my mother didn't have much trouble figuring it out. It's not every day that people send single shoes in the overseas mail."

The girl in the silk nightgown was, by now, a zombie. She still looked pretty to us, but she tilted her head and turned toward the camera and we could see it: her eyes were dead.

"Of course," my mother said, "*she* had the shoes for it. Your grandmother had boots. *Out* went philandering Philip."

"Where did he go from there?"

"Well," she said, "he lived on Gramercy Park for a little while, and he didn't go back to France, but otherwise I just don't know."

"Don't you wonder where he is?"

"Why? Do you think he wonders about me?" She was quiet for a few minutes. Then she said, "I'm sorry I brought it up."

The next night I stayed up alone.

When my parents were divorced and we moved out of the house, I found the shoe again. It was very well hidden this time, in a barrel of old stuffed toys that had long since been turned into mouse nests. I was alone when I found it, and I packed it with my few clothes and books, and took it to New York with me.

. . .

I can't find an attitude for my grandfather. I know it's an attitude, not a pose, I know I'm supposed to look for his heart. We're
not supposed to do research, but I have to resort to it. I find the
New York office of the Bank of the Lesser Antilles: it takes up
three rooms in a hideous blue and white box of a building downtown.

Finally, I take the shoe out with me, to Little Italy, where
I ask people until I find the address of a shoemaker. He lives in
an apartment with beaded curtains, beaded radiator covers, and
a vat of soup in which whole chickens roll in boiling stock. Yes,
he can make another shoe like this. It will cost one hundred
dollars. Beadwork is expensive. I talk him down to fifty-five,
which still means I have to cancel my dentist appointment. As I
leave, he says, "Fifty-five for you only," and pinches my ass quickly
twice, once on each cheek. I don't turn when he does this, but
the next week, when I return to pick them up, I stand in the doorway to hand him the cash, and back all the way to the stairs.

Now that I have the shoes, I have everything. They very nearly
match. The beadwork of the older shoe has a harsh glow; I
imagine there's gold in the dye. The new pigments are too basic,
too exact. I want to run home, but I walk, taking the stairs two at
a time all the way up the six flights to my apartment.

I've never asked again about my grandfather or the shoe. My
mother got one more card from him, at Christmas, years after her
divorce. Its printed message read:

> To wish you loads of Christmas cheer,
> and love that grows each passing year.

She threw it out in a pile of sale announcements and grocery
circulars, and I didn't bother to retrieve it. It was postmarked
Sioux City, Iowa. Maybe he's a salesman. Maybe he's been a hog
farmer all these years. I suppose he's retired now, but I can't
think he would retire to Sioux City, Iowa.

In the center of my room, I stretch my arm out. I'm my grandfather outside one of the Gramercy Park gates, in 1945. It's autumn, and the sky is steel gray, just before dusk. Children play in the park, their coats folded over schoolbooks on the benches. I look out over their heads over the fallen leaves in the park. I wait to feel my muscles drawn into place around some specific emotion. My grandfather looks out over the gate into the network of color and movement that makes up the city, but he sees the horizon of Sioux City, Iowa: uniform and yellowish gray.

I myself see, at this moment, a pair of extravagantly, surpassingly gaudy shoes. I give up on my grandfather and put them on.

They are the highest heels I've ever worn, and the minute I stand in them my body conforms to their dictates: my ankles tilt forward and every other bone leans back to balance them. I stretch my arm out, bring the other to my mouth with the imaginary pipe, and I am indeed a ridiculous figure. I walk confidently in these shoes, taller and more fluid, and I cannot possibly move like my grandfather now. I stand straighter than I ever have, my breasts thrust forward against the cloth of my shirt, my head back, almost thrown back. If I were to laugh right now, it would be a strong but not derisive laugh that I think my grandfather would attend; the laugh of someone who understands what he looks for, and what he sees.

MARJORIE SANDOR

The Gittel

THERE IS A TRADITION in our family that once in a while a dreamer is born: an innocent whose confused imagination cannot keep up with the civilized world. This person walks around in a haze of dreams, walking eventually right into the arms of the current executioner, blind as Isaac going up the mountain with his father. Nobody knows who started this story —my mother used to say it was a second-rate scholar out to impress the neighbors—but apparently there are characteristics, traits peculiar to this person, and two hundred years ago people knew a catastrophe was on the way if such a person came into their midst. Once, when I was a little girl, I asked Papa to name the traits. He said he couldn't; they'd been lost. All he knew was that this dreamer, before vanishing, always left behind a dreaming child, and that sometimes he thought he was such a child.

My father was a modest man; he came to Ellis Island with his eyebrows up, and they never came down. Furthermore he was the kind of storyteller who rarely got past the scenic details, since every time he let his imagination go his children had nightmares for a week. I remember: I was eight years old, sitting with him on the kitchen stairs, my bedtime cup of milk between us. My mother was scrubbing a pot with steel wool, making that sound that hurts the smallest bones in the body, and in the parlor the alabaster lamp had been lit for my grandmother Gittel's yahrzeit.

The lamp looked different than it does now. We hadn't converted it yet to electric, and it glowed pale orange behind the alabaster. As a child I could look at it for hours, imagining miniature cities on fire, or ladies in a golden room. It didn't have the long crack you see running down the left side. My daughter Rachel did that when she was ten years old, running like a maniac through the room and tripping over the cord. She won't go near it now; at nineteen she thinks it's her destiny to break it. She's a little careless, it's true, but nothing some responsibility wouldn't cure. I'm waiting for her now—she said she was taking the 4:30 bus from the city. I've been thinking about things, and tonight, after we eat, I'm going to tell her she can have the lamp when she and Daniel move into the new apartment.

So, where was I? With Papa? Yes, he was looking away from me, at the lamp in the parlor.

"We don't really know when she died," he said. "Not the exact date. But sometimes I wonder—what if these dreamers are common, nothing extraordinary, people you have to fight to recognize as a sacrifice, a warning. . . ." He bent lower, opening his mouth to speak again. Something rough and wet scratched my wrist; it was the steel wool, all soapy, in my mother's hand.

"Don't romanticize, Bernard," she said. "It's common knowledge that Gittel was a selfish woman who should have had the good sense to stay single. Sacrifice, my foot."

Sometimes I wish I were more like her and less like my father. No matter how many questions a daughter had, she knew when to talk and when to keep quiet. Before my wedding, young as I was, she didn't tell me anything. "Why frighten a person unnecessarily?" she said later. Papa was different. He couldn't hide anything from me. It's from him we get the insomnia and the bad dreams—he always left his children to finish his stories in their sleep.

"The Gittel," he used to say, as if she were a natural phenomenon. A little beauty at sixteen, she had red-gold hair to her waist, fine features, and tiny feet. Thank God, Rachel inherited her feet and not mine. Lucky girl. Tiny feet, this Gittel, and a good dancer and musician. The red in her hair and the musical sense came from the Hungarian; the rest was German going all the way back to the seventeenth century, when the Shapiros settled illegally in Berlin. By 1920 the family was in a good position: respected by the new Berlin intellectuals. Of course it wasn't really the brains, but the red-gold hair and the fine noses that made them comfortable. You can bet if they'd looked more Semitic they'd have caught on sooner to the general news.

She was eighteen then. Her father, along with a handful of other Jewish scholars, had been granted a professorship in the University of Berlin, and the family was able to establish itself in a brick house on Grunewaldstrasse, with real lace curtains and a baby grand. Being her father's pet, Gittel took whatever she liked from his library shelves, and sometimes sat with him when a colleague came to visit. Soon after her eighteenth birthday, she came into his study to borrow a book—without knocking, just like my Rachel. She had just mastered the art of the entrance, and paused where the light from the alabaster lamp would shine best on her hair.

"Papa," she announced. "Where is the Hoffmann?"

Shapiro was deep in conversation with a slender, bearded visitor whose trousers, according to Gittel's standards, were a little short. "Read something else," said her father. "The Romantics are anti-Semitic."

"Not Hoffmann," cried Gittel.

The visitor turned. He cursed himself for having put on

his reading glasses, since at that distance he could not see her face or her eyes. He saw hair lit to the color of his own carefully raised flame roses and a brown merino skirt, very trim at the waist. "You enjoy Hoffmann as well?" he asked, squinting.

His name was Yaakov Horwicz: thirty-five years old and a scholar from Riga, Latvia. Like Shapiro he was enjoying the new generosity of his government. For the first time in his professional life he had had enough money to take the train to Berlin for a lecture series: Shapiro's on Western Religions. After the lecture and a three-hour discussion in the Romanische Café, he had received an invitation to coffee in the professor's home.

He was delirious, first to stand in Shapiro's study, then to make the acquaintance of his household. And still wearing those ridiculous spectacles, the cheap frames warped from the weight of the lenses. He took off his glasses for the formal introduction. His eyes, which had seemed to Gittel to be unnaturally large behind the lenses, now had a fine, granular brilliance, like her mother's antique blue glass vase. It was his eyes that kept her standing there, and his eyes that made Shapiro think to himself: he can't help but be honorable. It's not in his veins as a possibility, unfaithfulness. She's young, but better to send her with a scholar than watch her run off at twenty with a young gentile going through his mystical phase.

Professor Shapiro is not to be blamed. I can imagine his concern, for Gittel was famous for her lively behavior with students. A young man would come to the house on Grunewaldstrasse, stand in the front hall, and within minutes a figure in petticoats would appear running down the curved staircase, shouting "Mama, Mama, I can't get the buttons in back!" Mrs. Shapiro was no help either, in the long run. She wore her hair in a neat coil, fastened her own innumerable buttons without assistance, and on top of that made bread from scratch. Just like my mother, she wouldn't let her daughter into the kitchen until dinner was safe in the oven. "You're a little girl yet," she'd say.

"There's plenty of time to learn." I vowed I'd be different with mine. She would make her bed the minute she started to talk back, and help me in the kitchen whenever it was convenient. I wasn't going to make the same mistake.

Mrs. Shapiro got the message from her husband and invited Horwicz to stay to supper that evening. That meal nearly cost them a suitor, for despite the intensity of his vision and the shortness of his trousers, Horwicz had a fondness for table manners, and Gittel's were wretched. She tapped her fingers on the white linen, rearranged her cutlery, and sometimes hummed a phrase of music, as if she were alone in her room. He blushed, torn between embarrassment and desire. She, on her side, glanced at him only long enough to compare his eyes to those of Anselmus, the student-hero of a Hoffmann tale, noting that each time she looked at him, a feverish color stained his cheeks. Gittel hummed and smiled and asked Horwicz if, after supper, he would turn the piano music for her.

Horwicz raised his napkin awkwardly to his lips.

"Go ahead," said Shapiro. "We'll finish our discussion later."

Horwicz had never before turned pages of music for a lady, young or otherwise, and here Gittel sealed her fate. *Turn*, she said, trying out a low, husky cabaret voice. *Turn*. It was easy to obey such a voice. Horwicz imagined going on and on, watching her narrow, lightly freckled hands touch the keys and lift under the lamplight. Her fingers trembled a little; his heart swelled under his ribs, wanting to protect. . . . When at last she released him into her father's study, he had forgotten Western Religions and inquired about Gittel's status. Shapiro was standing by his desk, a book in his hand.

"Tell me about Latvia," he said. "Things don't flare up there the way they do here, isn't that so?"

"That's true," said Horwicz. "The nationals have been very liberal."

Shapiro smiled a small, lopsided smile. "She will be a lovely wife, a delight," he said. "And Latvia is good."

Picture the night Gittel was told of her destiny. They stand in the front parlor, and she turns pale yellow, like a late leaf, and begins looking through her music for something she says she's been missing for a long time. Finally she stops looking and says to Horwicz: "We will live here, in town?" He takes her hands, surprised at the firmness of the thin fingers, the tautness of the palm. The hands don't tremble now.

"I have a house of my own, and a garden," he says. "In a suburb of Riga."

"Mother," cries Gittel. "*Riga?*"

Mrs. Shapiro ushers her daughter from the parlor. Imagine the sounds of their two skirts rustling, and how Horwicz felt watching them leave the room—the upright mother and the daughter, long fingers gripping her skirt. The two men wait in the parlor like displaced ghosts; Professor Shapiro trying over and over to light his pipe; Horwicz holding himself perfectly still, blinking and pale as if he'd just stepped out of his study into broad daylight.

When Gittel appeared in the doorway again her back was needle-straight. She stepped up to Horwicz and held out her hand. "Let me play you something," she said.

"Chopin," muttered her father. "Another anti-semite."

Horwicz escorted her to the piano, where she played for him the Sixth Prelude, her favorite. It's a strange piece: half delight, half dirge. They say he wrote it during a night of terrible rains. A messenger came to his door: George Sand and her three children had been killed in a carriage accident. He kept composing, unable to leave the piano bench. He wrote the last notes in the morning, just as there was another knock on the door, and her voice . . . .

Mrs. Shapiro did not come back into the parlor until Horwicz was ready to leave. She was as gracious as ever, a remarkable woman; I know how she felt. I can see her face, almost as fragile as her daughter's, the eyelids only a little pink, only a little. I admire that woman.

The wedding picture is right there—on the mantel. When my Rachel was small, she used to take it down and touch her tongue to the dusty glass.

"Don't do that," I'd say.

She'd look at me, already the archaeologist, and say, "I'm cleaning it off for you."

Somewhere in her teens she lost interest; she could walk by that picture without even a glance. I can't do that. I walk past and there's Gittel in the dress her mother made for her by hand: a creamy, flounced thing. Her waist is unbelievable. She's tiny, but then the bridegroom is no giant himself. Great mustaches hide his lips, and he's not wearing his glasses. Without them his eyes appear pale and wide awake, as if when the shutter came down he saw something astonishing. I don't know anything about his childhood or bachelor circumstances; why he should have such eyes on his wedding day I can only attribute to foresight. He was like Shapiro that way. So much foresight he couldn't enjoy the wedding cake.

Beside him the Gittel is serious too; only on her, seriousness doesn't look so sweet. Her lips are set tight together, and her pupils are so dilated that her green eyes look black as caves. Rachel used to look at those eyes.

"I don't like her," she'd say. Somehow even a child knows it's not the usual bridal worry that's in Gittel's eyes. Ten years old, holding that picture in her hand. "Mom," she says to me. "Do I have to leave home like her if I'm bad?"

She gave me a nice shock. When had I ever spoken of Gittel leaving home at eighteen? I played innocent. "Who told you that, Rachel?" I asked.

"You talk in your sleep," she said.

She made me nervous then, she makes me nervous now. At

the time, I thought: what good will it do to tell a ten-year-old
that when the time comes, she'll be good and ready to leave
home?

"You're not a Gittel," I said. "Nobody is going to make
you leave home. We just want you to be happy."

She bit her lower lip and big terrible tears dropped on her
T-shirt.

"Rachel, you're breaking my heart," I said. "What's the
matter?"

"It's okay," she said. "I'll go and pack."

Thank God that phase is over—although with Rachel it's
hard to tell. Last month when we looked at that picture together
she laughed.

"I used to have nightmares about her," she said.

I acted nonchalant. "Like what?"

"I don't remember. Big melodramas, everybody in the
world disappearing—"

"Go on," I said.

Then she gave me such a look. "Mom," she said. "All kids
have dreams like that."

"About the end of the world?" I asked.

"Yes."

Sometimes she hurts me with her quick answers. Every family has its stories, why should she deny hers? Besides, she traps
me. She was all eagerness: "Mother, what finally happened to
Gittel?"

What am I supposed to do? If I start to tell it, and she's in a
modern mood, she cuts me off. If she's not, she gets all dreamy
on me. Naturally I start thinking about her and Daniel and their
archaeology studies, and so I say to her, "Rache, tell me honestly
what you plan on doing with those old pots? Read the newspapers, look around you!" I raised her to read the newspapers so
nothing should take her by surprise, and she winds up in the
ancient ruins. Last week on the phone she said to me: "Mother,

I read the newspapers and so does Daniel," and I knew she was biting her lip. It's a bad habit. "I'm coming this weekend," she said, "so you and I can have a talk." I made up my mind right then and there that I wouldn't mention Gittel unless she promises not to interrupt . . . .

Gittel bore her husband seven sons in ten years. Papa was number four, Gittel's favorite because he had his father's eyes and could listen to her at the piano without speaking or tugging on her skirt every three minutes. Sometimes she would stop playing and say to him: "Shut your eyes, Bernard, and imagine that this is a baby grand instead of an upright, and that across from us is a maroon divan, where grandpapa sits reading, his glasses slipping down his nose." Other times she took him into the courtyard and lifted her fine nose into the air. "Smell," she said. "Today it smells exactly like April at home." He listened to her describe where the alabaster lamp had stood in the other house (she had it next to the piano in Riga) and how her mother had given it to her, along with the brass candlesticks, the five handmade lace doilies, and her own key ring to wear at her waist. "A good housekeeper is never without her keys," her mother had said, knowing everything in advance.

Once a week a letter arrived from Grunewaldstrasse, and the family gathered in the parlor to hear Gittel read it. Papa remembered later how his father leaned against the mantel listening carefully to letters that seemed to be about nothing but the weather and fifteenth-century religion. His mother's hands trembled as she read—her voice, too—and sometimes afterward he heard them talking in their bedroom, their voices soft to begin with, then rising, rising.

Gittel captured the little suburb. For months after her departure people talked of how the young mother would be stirring soup in the kitchen and suddenly remember a dream she'd had the night before. Off she'd run to the neighbor's house, bursting in: "Marta, I forgot to tell you what I dreamed about your boy!"

Her friends seemed to love this, especially the burning of the soup that went hand in hand with the piece of news, the almost forgotten dream, the stories about Grunewaldstrasse. It was rare in that time and place to find a woman for whom dreams and stories came before soup, and a miracle that, given her dizzy mind and her husband's library heart, any of the seven boys grew up. "Luck," Papa would say to me if Mother was in the room. "Destiny," he'd say if she wasn't.

He was five years old when his father died. Diabetes: that's where Papa got it, and now I have to be careful too. Gittel was twenty-eight, and after the seven boys she still had her figure and her lovely hair. Papa's memory of her is of a woman in a new black silk dress and fine shoes, hushing a baby. It was at his father's funeral that he began to be afraid of her.

The service was held on a little rise in the Jewish cemetery outside Riga. It was a fine March day, the kind of day when the tips of the grass look caught on fire, and gulls go slanting across the sky as if they can't get their balance. The kind of day where you want to run in one direction and then turn and see the figures of people you've left behind, tiny and unreal as paper dolls. Papa wanted to break out of the circle of mourners and run across the knolls and valleys of the cemetery, all the way down to the shore, where the Gulf of Riga stretched endlessly away.

"Come here, Bernard," said Gittel. "Stand in front of me."

She placed one hand lightly on his shoulder, but every time he shifted his weight, her fingers tightened. His brothers stood all around him: Johan, the eldest, almost ten and already a tall boy; Aaron and Yaakov beside him. Pressed tight to their mother's skirt were the two young ones whose names Papa later forgot, and on her hip, the baby. She stood absolutely still, while around her Horwicz's friends and relatives rocked back and forth. Papa turned once and looked up at her face. Her narrow jaw was marble white, and her eyes, clear and unreddened, were trained on a tuft of grass blowing beside the open pit. People whispered:

"Poor thing, she's in shock. He was everything to her." Only Papa, watching the dark pupils, knew that she was not thinking about her husband. When the rabbi closed his book, Gittel sighed and bent down to Bernard.

"Very soon," she said, "we can go back."

"Back to the house?" said Bernard.

"No," she replied. "Grunewaldstrasse."

For five years no one but Papa knew Gittel's mind. They thought she would pull herself together and become a good manager with all the help she was offered by her women friends. Everybody should be so fortunate; Horwicz's cousins in the city came by often to take the boys out for a drive, and ladies were always bringing hot dishes by. "With seven boys she must be desperate," they said. The neighbors began to wonder, though, how with seven wild boys they would be hearing Chopin and Mozart four hours together in the morning. Certain shopkeepers began to talk. The dishes stopped coming, and the cousins, after a lecture or two, stopped coming to get the boys. "Let her suffer like other human beings," they said. "A lesson is what she needs."

Maybe by that time it was too late for lessons. I suppose she tried. She worked in her husband's garden, coming up with small, deformed carrots and the smallest heads of cabbage imaginable. She sent the three eldest boys to serve one-year apprenticeships in town, and when they came home for the Sabbath they brought her things from the city, and part of their wages. Bernard she sent to school: Bernard, who wanted nothing more than to be a carpenter like his big brother Johan, whom he worshiped for his muscles and his talk of America. Every day after school Bernard went to the carpenter's house to drink tea with Johan, and every day Johan showed him the tin with the money in it. "They say you can't keep kosher there," he'd say. "But otherwise it's paradise."

Home in the evenings, Bernard let his mother caress his face. "You have the eyes of your father, and the brains of mine," she'd say. "He is a great teacher in Berlin, and so will you be, when we go home."

"We are home," he'd say, looking at his feet.

"No," she said. "You wait and see."

Gittel's looks were beginning to go. Her hair was no longer that burnished gold color, although the ladies told her she could fix it easily with a little lemon juice and a walk in the sunlight. But Gittel wasn't listening. She played loud, crashing pieces by Chopin and Liszt, and sent Bernard to do all her errands in town so she wouldn't have to face the helpful remarks of the shopkeepers. When he left for school she sent him with letters to mail to Grunewaldstrasse, which came back marked *wrong address.*

One day a letter came from the Shapiros—with another address, in a district of Berlin Bernard had never heard his mother mention. In the morning, he waited beside her writing table while she finished a letter. Over her shoulder he read: *I don't care if it's smaller, we're coming. People stare at me in the street.*

"I'll be back in a minute, Mama," he said. Upstairs in his room he packed a school satchel and hid it in his closet. He would know when she began to pack up her lamp and her candlesticks.

That night Gittel went to the carpenter's house and wept at his table. "We're running out of money," she said. "Can you keep Johan for another year?" The carpenter was surprised; he knew Gittel's people in Germany were well off, that she could get money any time she wanted. He told people later that his first reaction was to refuse: "Lie in your own bed," he wanted to say, but she looked almost ill. Her lovely skin seemed blue, as if she were turning to ice inside. "All right," he said.

Two days later the shoemaker received a visit, and under the pressure of her tears, offered to keep Aaron for a second year. "He works like the devil," he said later, "better than my own sons, and doesn't waste his money." But telling the story, he shook his head: "It's a terrible thing to see a woman trying to give away her children."

The third boy, Jacob, was finally taken by the Horwicz cousins, though not until they had given Gittel a piece of their minds. Now that Horwicz had passed on, they revered him like a saint. "If our Yaakov were alive, what would he say to all this?" "If your Yaakov were alive," she answered, "would any of this be happening?" She was gaunt and smoky-eyed as a gypsy, and sometimes, in the two weeks that followed, she looked at Bernard with such passion that he ran out of the house and took a streetcar to Johan's, where he stayed till suppertime. Late one night, as he was working in his copybook for school, she knelt beside him.

"Bernard," she said. "Are you still having your special dreams?"

He hadn't been able to remember his dreams for weeks. Instead he heard voices all talking at once: the voices his father had called "demons" because they distorted every word that came into the mind. "No," he said.

"I have," she said, touching his arm. "You are now my eldest son, and we are taking our family home."

"We are home," he said.

"Home," she repeated. "My mother's—"

Something was kicking inside his ribs. Where his heart should be was a small, clawed animal coming loose. He scrambled up onto his chair and stood towering over his mother. "You can't make me," he shouted. "Because I am going to America with Johan and Yaakov and Aaron."

She stayed on her knees a moment, then tried to get up— too suddenly—and swayed forward as she did. Bernard flushed with shame; she looked like a drunk girl clutching the table edge.

"You are my son, and you will do as I say," she said.

The pressure in his chest built higher. He looked at the woman before him, and for an instant, the curve of her nose, the tiny velvet mole beside her mouth, were as alien to him as the landscapes of Asia in his schoolbook. "I don't know you," he cried, closing his eyes against the sight of her hand rushing toward his face.

"Go to bed," said Gittel. "In the morning we will talk."

At dawn Bernard crept out with his satchel and took the first streetcar to the carpenter's house. Every day he waited for the knock on the door, for the sight of his mother and the three children standing on the step, a cart piled high with belongings. The world seemed to him to have closed its mouth; the gulls, the bright grass, the wide and silent gulf—all seemed to have grown bolder in their colors to judge him. A week passed.

One evening Johan came home from work and took his hand. "Come," he said. "I want to show you something." They took a streetcar out of the city and walked down the street to their own house. It was unlocked. Inside the furniture gleamed, the rug lay bright and soft on the floor, and the pots and pans —always before in the sink—hung clean and polished on the kitchen wall. Under the alabaster lamp was a sheet of paper. *To my beloved Bernard I leave my mother's alabaster lamp, her brass Shabbas candlesticks, and the key ring, so that in America he will remember his mother.* The rest of the letter divided up the household items among the other boys. In an envelope they found the deed to the house.

It was the station porter who had told Johan; he was the last person in the suburb to see Gittel and the three children. He said her fingers quivered when she tried to hand him the four tickets to Berlin. He had never seen her up close before, and told people later that she was a little girl. "Magnificent hands, though," he said. "Like a slender man's, strong and nicely shaped. The kind of hands you don't expect to tremble, and she didn't expect them to either. I could see she was embarrassed, so I said, 'Going for long?' 'Oh no,' she said. 'Just to visit my parents and take the children to a magic show.' She put her hands in her coat pockets. 'I'm terrible about traveling,' she said, smiling."

The silence of the world then was different; it wasn't the silence of waiting, but the kind that comes after a mistake, with disbelief caught in it like a maimed bird. The three oldest brothers swore never to allow their mother's name to cross their lips as long as they lived—not even if she wrote and begged their forgiveness, or became ill. They worked hard, and Johan spoke continually of passage costs and departure dates. And Bernard began to dream. He dreamed he was sitting beside his mother on the piano bench, both of them dressed for his father's funeral service. Suddenly she rose from the bench and gripped his arm. "Come with me," she cried, "into the piano where it's safe." Bernard looked out the window. At the door and all the windows of the house stood a hundred men in fine suits, knocking politely. He bit his mother's hand, but she kept her grip, drawing him to her and into the open piano. The lid came down, suffocating . . . .

After school Bernard sometimes went to the station to listen to the porter, who was still elaborating on Gittel's departure: how she looked, how the three little boys clung about her asking, "Will there be an acrobat there? Will there be a fat lady and a thin man? Will they cut somebody in half and make him come out whole?" Every day the story got longer. The porter got better tips, and his tongue lightened as if it were a balance scale tipping in one direction. "Terrible circles under her eyes," he said. "And the children: I swear the youngest knew it was for more than three days—"

Such stories the Gittel could tell you—about strangers in town, or what happened to the neighbors yesterday, or a terrifying dream that would haunt you for weeks, as if you yourself had dreamed it. But when it came to newspapers, she was a fool. Thank God that's not the case with Rachel, although from the look on her face sometimes, and the news of the world, I think: "What's the difference?" She will argue with me about Gittel, too, but newspapers or not, Gittel wasn't thinking about current events. She was sleepwalking, imagining the lovely carpets, the curved staircase, her mother coming down the hall to greet her, her father sitting down to chat with a student.

I should stop the story here. For one thing, Rachel's bus gets in any minute, and the way she walks, she'll be here before I can clear the table of these papers . . . . But I remember how it used to drive me crazy when Papa began to describe the tiniest details of Gittel's traveling dress and people and things he had never seen. He could never get to the end of the story. *Next time*, he'd say, and next time he'd start all over at the beginning, lingering until Mother called us in to supper. Some habits are hard to break, he used to say.

On the train Gittel took her children into an empty compartment, but you know how it is; someone always comes to interrupt your dreams. This time it is an elderly gentleman, the first German she's seen since she got on in Riga. During the first hour of the ride nobody speaks. The children keep their heads lowered, once in a while glancing up at the stranger, who is smart and alternates his gaze between the countryside and his own shoes. You know how the eye roams when you're traveling. Maybe at this moment my own daughter is sitting in the window seat of a bus, a stranger beside her. Any minute he could turn and look at her face and say, "Going home?" The stranger in Gittel's compartment is polite, and Gittel is

busy telling her children about magic shows and lace curtains
and hot potato kugel. "Grandpa and Grandma have moved,"
she says, "but I'll take you to look at the old house. She'll have
a lunch for us, too. A hot lunch."

She has a nice voice, thinks the stranger. He lets his eye
rest on a piece of hand luggage at her feet, and suddenly, coming awake, he sees the name *Shapiro*. He turns pale and leans
forward.

"Frau Shapiro?"

She looks at him, startled, and the children hide their
faces in her coat.

So much goes through the stranger's mind when he sees
the face of the Gittel: a face that cannot shed its innocence,
even when the eyes in it look out the compartment window at
the new red and black flags in the station windows—seen
quickly, because the train goes so fast. The stranger holds out
his hand.

"I knew a Shapiro at university," he says. "I am proud to
say. I am proud."

He holds her hand too long; he won't let it go even when
the conductor comes into the compartment and says: "Pass-
ports, please." Her eyes grow dark with surprise.

"Excuse me, please," she says, pulling her hand away,
reaching into her bag for her passport.

"Wait," he says.

But Gittel, with a nervous laugh, has handed hers over.
She doesn't change expression when the conductor takes a long
look at it and says: "You will report to the Bureau of Immigra-
tion as soon as you arrive. Your passport needs changes."

The conductor is gone. The stranger wants to tell her
something, but her face speaks to him like marble, like a desert
statue that knows either everything or nothing.

What can he do but ask her where she is going, keep her
in conversation until the train comes into the station? So he

asks, and she begins a story. A story about a lovely house, a mahogany mantel, a fireplace, a smoking chimney, a girl who is coming at this moment through the front door, having for once remembered her key; a girl capable, after all, of surprising her mother.

LEIGH ALLISON WILSON

The Raising

O F THE EIGHT MATRONS perched like pigeons around two identical card tables, Mrs. Bertram Eastman was the lone childless woman. Her husband, in whom—she was sure— the fault lay, only confounded this burden she'd borne for thirty years, fixing a funny look on his face every time the subject came up and saying, in a voice soft as solemnity itself, "Spare the child and spare the rod, Mrs. Eastman." But he was like that, a nitwit, and half the time she never knew what he was talking about. Still, being a woman of industry, Mrs. Eastman took up the slack of impotence by becoming an expert on children and motherhood. She was renowned in the gin rummy set, in the Daughters of the Confederacy set, and perhaps in the whole area of East Tennessee, renowned and widely quoted for her running commentary on child-rearing.

"A child is like a new boot," she'd say and pause with the dramatic flair of a born talker. "You take that boot and wear it and at first it blisters your foot, pains you all over, but the time comes it fits like a glove and you got a dutiful child on your hands." What she had missed in experience, Mrs. Eastman overcame with pithy insight; what she lacked as human collateral in a world of procreation, Mrs. Eastman guaranteed with sheer volume. She was a specialist in armchair mothering.

A steady hum of a general nature had settled over the women playing at both tables, punctuated by an occasional snap of a card, but like a foghorn in the midst of a desert the voice of Mrs. Eastman rose and fell in every ear. She was explaining, for the third time since seven o'clock, the circumstances that led to Little Darryl, the Melungeon orphan boy, who would come to live at her house the very next morning. A child! In her own home! She couldn't get over it. Her brain worked at the idea with a violence akin to despair turning upside-down and her hair, from some internal cue, dropped onto her forehead a large, stiff curl that flopped from side to side as if to let off steam. Mrs. Eastman, although not fat, was a formidable personage, stout and big-boned and not unlike the bouncer in a hard-bitten country bar. Mr. Eastman was the tiniest man in Hawklen County. Just yesterday he had come home and told her, out of the blue, that he was bringing Little Darryl out from Eastern State and into their home—one two three and like a bolt of electricity she was a mother. She couldn't get over it.

Little Darryl was thirteen years old and of "origin unknown," a poor abandoned charity case dumped from orphanage to orphanage since the day his faceless mother—unfit and unwed, Mrs. Eastman knew for a certainty—dropped him off in the middle of the canned-goods section of the Surgoinsville A&P. He was discovered beside the creamed corn, eating an unhealthy peanut butter and jelly sandwich. The "origin unknown" part delighted Mrs. Eastman: Little Darryl would be *her* child, sprung as mysteriously and as certainly into her care as a baby of her own making. O, she would make a lawyer out of him, distill the taint of his blood like meltwater. She would recreate the boy in her own image and watch him tower among men in her old age.

"Smart as a *whip*, the social worker told Mr. Eastman," Mrs. Eastman said in a loud, confidential voice. At her table were old

Mrs. Cowan, the Methodist preacher's wife; Mrs. Jenkins, the wife of the Jenkins Hardware Jenkinses; and Mrs. Talley, wife of Hubert Talley, the local butcher. Mrs. Eastman had given each one advice, off and on, for thirty years, from Mrs. Talley's red-headed boy who was thirty years old and no good, right down to Mrs. Jenkins's six-year-old who still sucked her thumb and was a "mistake."

"You said that ten minutes ago, Eloise," Mrs. Jenkins told Mrs. Eastman, "and you said he was a genius before that." Mrs. Jenkins was playing North to Mrs. Eastman's South. "You said he was a genius that wasn't understood and you ain't even met him yet."

"Made him a lawyer already, too," said Mrs. Talley, look-ing calmly over Mrs. Jenkins's shoulder, her lips screwed up in concentration.

"Ida Mae Talley!" cried Mrs. Jenkins. "Put you in the East and straightway you cheat left and right."

"For your general information," Mrs. Eastman said and tossed her curl, like a hook, back up into her beehive hairdo, "for your edification, Little Darryl scored in the 'excessively bright' range on three different tests."

"I am most certainly not cheating," said Mrs. Talley. "I seen those kings three minutes ago."

"God loves all the little children, smart and stupid, black and white," old Mrs. Cowan said with a smile so bright that her lips appeared to retreat back into her gums. She was the simple-minded member of the women's club although, somehow, her children had grown up to be wildly successful bankers and busi-nessmen in the county, as if to intimate that children, even life, were too muddled a factor to control entirely. For this reason old Mrs. Cowan said nothing that was really heard, did nothing that was really seen, and existed in the main as a hand in gin rummy, or as a how-de-do on the Methodist Church steps every Sunday morning. She was incapable of taking sound advice, given in good faith, by even the best of friends. Deep in her bowels

Mrs. Eastman believed her to be the most wicked woman of her acquaintance, the most deceitful as well as the most dangerous, and to hold, somewhere behind her idiocy, a hidden ace in the hole.

"God may be well and good on Sundays," Mrs. Eastman said, leveling her eyes like shotgun bores toward old Mrs. Cowan's western position. "But God Hisself don't have to raise no boy geniuses at a moment's notice. Pass me one of those green mints, Vivian." She stretched her free hand toward Mrs. Jenkins. "The white ones give me the morning sickness."

"They come in the same box, Eloise. Green and white. In the same damn box." Mrs. Jenkins, whose mints and home provided this evening's entertainment for the club, shut her cards with a click, laid them carefully facedown on the table, then folded her arms like hemp cord and stared at Mrs. Eastman. She looked ready to pounce in panther fashion across the table, to defend her territory with a beast's wit. Mrs. Eastman had on her patient expression, the one she recommended for children with colic.

"I only meant to point out that I *read* somewheres that they put more dye in the white mints than they do in the green, that's all. They start out gray and add twice't the dye to turn them white. Scientific fact. Twenty schoolchildren alone have died in Detroit, Michigan, from a pound of white mints. Now think about *that*."

"All I know," said Mrs. Jenkins, rising clumsily from her chair, "is we've had these same mints for fifteen years and I never heard a word till now. I'm going to put whip cream on my Jell-O if you'll excuse me."

"I didn't read it till last week," Mrs. Eastman called over her shoulder, then she lowered her voice until only the whole room could hear: "Don't either of you tell a dead man, but she's on par*tic*ular edge tonight strictly because her boy was found pig drunk, with a hair ribbon in his mouth, underneath the 11-E overpass. No clothes on him anywhere."

"O," said old Mrs. Cowan. "He was the finest acolyte our church ever had."

"No more he ain't," Mrs. Eastman said happily. "Comes of no discipline."

"Now, now," Mrs. Talley said, watching herself thumb through Mrs. Jenkins's cards. "You ain't exactly the one, Eloise" —here she paused to exchange one of her cards with one in the other pile—"you ain't exactly the one to pass judgment on a drunk, now are you?"

"Well, Mrs. Ida *Mae* Talley." Mrs. Eastman sneered on the "Mae." "Are you sinuating that my husband is a drunk?"

"That's for you to know, Eloise," she said, "and me to hear over coffee."

The truth of the matter was that, although Mr. Eastman sat in his law office with the door shut to clients and associates alike and drank corn whiskey from a Dixie cup, reading obscure poetry and even more obscure philosophy from dusty, dead-looking bindings, he was not a drunk. He was merely partial to alcohol, had told Mrs. Eastman more than once that he and whiskey were blood-related, on better terms with one another than anyone living or dead he'd ever known. Mrs. Eastman believed him through a rare faculty of reflexive apathy, a sixth sense she applied to all situations beyond her ken and control. Once, when Mr. Eastman brought home a litter of eight mongrel dogs, payment for services rendered from one of his poverty clients (who were the only ones he seemed to have, crowded into his office anteroom with chickens and moonshine and quart jars full of pennies clutched under their arms, the room always a three-ring circus to the point that each newly hired legal secretary had but to walk in the door before she quit and walked back out), Mrs. Eastman, in a reflex as immediate as a sneeze, stepped on the dogs' tails, ate the dogs' fur in her potatoes and greens, got nipped on the calves in the middle of dogfights, and she never knew the difference. The dogs existed only as the vaguest of doubts in her mind, much as the person and behavior of Mr.

Eastman, and eventually, one by one, the dogs skulked emphatically from the premises and trotted off westward, as if in search of something that either would caress them passionately or kick them viciously. Leave bad enough alone, Mrs. Eastman always said, as well as, Never look a gifted horse in the mouth.

"Leave bad enough alone *I* always say," Mrs. Eastman told Mrs. Talley. "If I had a boy thirty year old and still at home, I wouldn't make no sinuations on nobody else."

"The best, O! O!" said old Mrs. Cowan, almost luringly. "The best acolyte we ever had."

Both women stared at her.

"Attention ladies!" Mrs. Jenkins called from the kitchen door. She held a tray of eight green Jell-O molds, each topped with pear-shaped smidgens of whipped cream. "Laura June here wants to say goodnight," she said. "Say goodnight, Laura June." Laura June, who was under the tray in her mother's hands, just stood and looked stupidly at the seven crooked smiles fastened maternally on the faces of the women's club. Under her arm showed the hind legs and tail of a tabby cat, and she wore a pink nightgown, hiked up at the waist from the furious squirms of the cat. Because her thumb was plunged up to the knuckle into her mouth, Laura June had difficulty saying goodnight, so she just stood and stared, stupidly, at all the smiles.

"That there is what I call a real teddy bear," Mrs. Talley said sweetly. "What's that there teddy bear's name, honey?"

Laura June turned her head in the direction of Mrs. Talley, squinting her eyes, and the cat, as though synchronized puppet-like to her movements, turned its head around and squinted at the women with two uneven green eyes that matched the color of the Jell-O. One of its eyes had an ugly yellow pustule on the rim, making the whole eye look like an open wound in the act of rankling. Laura June unplugged her mouth long enough to say "Name's Darryl Lee Roy," then she quickly plugged the thumb back, as if any second something more important might fall out into the open.

"Why isn't that just the cutest thing!" Mrs. Eastman cried and clapped her hands in the air over the card table. "Come over here, honey, Mama Eastman has a secret for you." Laura June stayed put; the cat blinked its eyes and only one of them opened again. It appeared to be winking suggestively at Mrs. Eastman. "I have a little boy coming to my house that has the very same name," she said. "Little Darryl."

"Time for Laura June to go to bed," said Mrs. Jenkins. "Go to bed, Laura June." Laura June turned obediently toward a door across the room and stalked stiff-legged across the wooden slats with the cat's head bouncing behind her like a gibbous growth. At the door she stopped, facing the room, and caught Mrs. Eastman's eye. There was an expression of malignancy on her face. She dropped the thumb and the hand wandered with a will of its own to the side of her face where it started to scratch a cheek. It might have been a large, pink spider dropped incredibly there to spin a cobweb.

"It's a lie!" she shouted abruptly and the cat meowed and then both were gone into the dark recesses of the house.

II

The mountains spliced at the southernmost tip of the city limits, then diverged northward to form the east and west boundaries of Hawklenville where Mr. Bertram Eastman lived. An ambitious person could climb to the top of that southern splice—named Devil's Nose by the first Methodist settlers—could sit on one of the numerous granite slabs found there, and he would notice that the town appears to be a discolored blemish in the middle of a dark green arrowhead. If that person were ambitious indeed, he would climb a tree and see the land beyond the mountains, land welling out for miles, green with tobacco, brown with freshly tilled soil, and still farther, the cusp of something huge and dusky-blue. But he would see no people. Though these mountains were the town's sole measure of eminent height, a stranger well-versed in the world would point out that they were only foot-hills, mere knurls in the great body of the Appalachians. Still, from their summits, one could see no people. They are *that* high, Mr. Eastman often said, but quietly and mostly to himself, they are high enough.

From his small back porch, or from what might have been a porch had he chosen to call it one, preferring the word *veranda* because it "sounded like a sigh," Mr. Eastman was watching the last tendrils of light skid away over the top of the moutains. Mr. Eastman, a man not balding but bald, sat in a plastic lawn chair and sipped corn whiskey from a Dixie cup. His shoulders cocked slightly forward and his head tilted slightly backward, giving him the appearance (as the more flexible gossips of the town were quick to mimic) of neither coming nor going. At the moment, though, he was poised over a precipice, at the edge of something, and somehow the boy, Little Darryl, was the nub to which his mind clung. Tomorrow he would come and tomorrow something—he didn't know what—something would happen, for tomorrow Little Darryl would come.

Beads of sweat, tiny as dewdrops, eased from the crown of his head and slid unhindered down the back of his neck. So quickly did they fall, and so brazenly, they could have been the tears of a brokenhearted old woman too tired for pretense. Night had fallen and the mountains crouched against the sky, darker even than the night.

Experience had taught Mr. Eastman that the mountains themselves were deceptive, mute purveyors of nothing but bulk. To the tourist, as he had been when he first brought his wife to the town, they were beautiful, rumpled across the horizon like an immense and living snake. He recalled an incident from those earlier days. They had been walking down Main Street, he and his newly-wed wife, he arm in arm with a woman who was so strik-ing and so lovely, all the more so because of her height and his lack of it, that he thought he might be crushed under the weight of his own pride. They had walked in silence for many minutes, nodding sociably at the passersby, when he noticed the mountains around them, as though for the first time.

"They are like a great undulating serpent, Eloise," he told her, and he was trying to profess his love for her and for their new home. Her eyes almost the color of ripe raspberries, she looked first at the moutains, then down at him, and she stared into his face with an expression that may have been utter tenderness. At last she fluttered her eyelashes and, looking vaguely toward the mountains, said: "Do tell." The mountains were no longer beautiful to Mr. Eastman, hadn't been perhaps from the incident on: and neither was his wife. No longer did he see the mountains surge upward as living things, no longer was the town, nor the county of Hawklen, a place where north and south and west and east converged into only one thing: the place to be. He had been deceived.

This boy, this Little Darryl, would be his salvation.

"Yoo-hoo!" came his wife's voice through the entranceway, through the hallway, through the kitchen and onto the back veranda where he started, like a frightened sparrow, in the lawn chair. "I'm home!"

Mr. Eastman bent down and set his Dixie cup on the floor, then he placed his hands, one grottoed in the bowl of the other, into his lap. Patiently, keenly, like a man for whom time was as yet unborn, he waited to be found out by his wife. An excess of amplified noise, her greeting was meant for the house and not for him, but in a short time she would work her way through every room until she found him out. She was tenacious in that way, could find anything lost, stolen, or converted, except the truth. She had a gift of activity at its most inessential whereabouts, a kind of feverish sprinting in place that left her wrungout and triumphant and as blind as a newt. Mr. Eastman believed he was safe from her, his wife of thirty years, because, when you got right down to it, she didn't know shit from apple butter; and without distinctions the rage to live was merely a delirious murmur. Despite the sounds of a bull ox, Mrs. Eastman, he felt, was a murmurer.

"*There* you are," Mrs. Eastman said and poked her head between the screen door and the door frame. It hung there in space like a giant full moon whose face had a coarse, sketchy expression. The least cloud would obscure any resemblance to humanity it may have had. Or so it seemed to Mr. Eastman who sat quietly with his hands in his lap.

"Here I am," Mr. Eastman said.

Here and there across the backyard a group of crickets screeched to one another in duets, in off-beat duets, in those insistent and eerie cries of utterly invisible creatures involved in communication. *Cheezit*! they said. *Cheezit*!

"Listen to those bugs," Mrs. Eastman said and stepped onto the veranda. She let the screen door slam shut behind her, its springs squealing, and the crickets paused for a measure, then started back up again. With her hands fastened securely onto her hips, elbows akimbo, she peered out into the backyard in order to pin down the source of the sound coming from everywhere and nowhere. "I declare they sound like they're in painful love. Bugs do fall in love and set up house together just like anybody. It's nature is what it is." Mr. Eastman said nothing and sat tight, as if he were just hanging in a closet without any insides; he wanted to pat his wife kindly on the cheek or else smack her very hard in the middle of her face. But he did nothing at all, could have been dead except for the heart pounding madly between the places he breathed.

"Buddy Ruth Quarles run off this morning with that retarded taxicab driver. Took almost everything they owned. In case you're interested." She slapped and killed a periwinkle green insect, then continued on in a cheerful tone. A dollop of hair ticked coquettishly onto her forehead. "Took the TV, took the radio, took the silverware. Took the sofa and the phonograph. Took ever light bulb in the house. Didn't take that half-grown boy of hers. Last anybody saw of Mr. Quarles, he took off down 11-E with a butcher knife, wearing a pair of socks and green pants. He had to borrow the butcher knife. Mr. Eastman, are you listening to me?"

"No, Mrs. Eastman," he said. "I am not."

"Ida Mae said she hadn't known the taxicab driver but three weeks, and him so simple to begin with. They did it with a U-Haul hitched to the taxicab."

"Mrs. Eastman," said Mr. Eastman.

"Can't figure out, though, what she *sees* in him. He had that wart in the corner of his eye. Puckered and bobbed ever time he opened his mouth. I can't figure it. And him so simple too."

Mr. Eastman reached for his Dixie cup, squinting out into the night settled over his yard. It appeared to him to be the inside of a huge windowless box set on its side out in the middle of nowhere. The stars, pricking out relentlessly, didn't fit into his picture.

"I foretold it long ago. Time and again I said, If he don't kill her first, he won't never know where she'll be or what she's doing there. I foretold it twice in the past two years. If she's not six feet under, I said, no telling where she is. There you have it."

"Perhaps she's happy, Mrs. Eastman."

"Well *I like that*!" Mrs. Eastman cried and stomped three paces to the edge of the veranda, then stomped the three paces back. She was furious, looking at him as she might at some bear who still hibernated in the chafe of summer, and her hair bristled like burs along the top of her head. "Happy, Mr. Eastman, is what those bugs have. Any *nor*mal human being might know that already. Any *nor*mal human being might know that happy is a word the government made up. What will our son think? I'll tell you what he'll think, he'll think his daddy's shoes are too little to grow into, that's what. You'll be a stigmatism to him all the days of his life!"

Again, Mr. Eastman sat tight. Thought and action in his wife, usually by tongue but sometimes otherwise, were almost simultaneous in her, rather like thunder and lightning, and Mr. Eastman was forever surprised by the coincidence. For him there was by necessity a gap between the two, first deep thought and much later decisive action. And it was true: it had taken him thirty years to secure a son.

"Do you hear me, Bertram Eastman?" she asked. Stomping up and back, her hair at loose ends, her shadow stomping crabbed and backward behind her through the light from the house, she made Mr. Eastman want to shout; want to scream out madly; made him want to take the box of his backyard and the night and his wife and fling the whole of them over that impenetrable black scar of the mountains. Instead he said absolutely nothing and, too, the silence within him grew absolute.

"Do you *hear* me?"

"I hear you very well, Mrs. Eastman."

"Our son is a responsibility. He's a responsibility for bad and for worse, for sickness and disease, forever and forever, till the dead do us part. He's responsibility is what this boy's made of."

"I know what little boys are made of," he said, raising himself to leave. So soaked with sweat was the back of his collar that it crept toward his collarbone and felt like a cold hand at his throat. Out in the yard the crickets seemed to have gone mad in the interim of their conversation. *Cheezit! cheezit! cheezit!* they sang. Cheee-*zit!* If his wife said anything, he couldn't hear her for the crickets.

III

Little Darryl's people, the Melungeons, came from Goins Hollow, a cul-de-sac at the base of Devil's Nose from whence there was only one exit: a deep green bottleneck steeped in poison ivy and ridden with underbrush and so utterly hidden that the inhabitants themselves were known to leave and never return, set suddenly adrift in the outside world. Brown-eyed and maize-colored, they wedlocked themselves, cheated on themselves, co-alesced with abandon, and produced either geniuses or idiots. They had no in-betweens. They loved each other or they killed each other, and still they endured in Goins Hollow; their endur-ance preceded the first Methodist settlers by many hand-counted years. On a vivid autumn day the smoke of their fires, beckoning upward like unformed fingers, was clearly visible from the town of Hawklenville, but not one soul in Hawklenville ever looked at it.

The Melungeon blood, although not their experience, was fecund as a loam in the body of Little Darryl, the orphan, and by the age of five he knew the appetites of a very old man. He knew when to lie outright and when to tell a lie honestly, when to cheat and when to win fairly. He knew when to be given and when to steal someone blind. He even knew when to attack a problem face-forward, and when to beat a noble retreat into the next county. He was thirteen years old, of a conspicuous un-known origin, and he had lived in nine separate orphanages, one of which burned down mysteriously.

"They got the papers that's stuck to me," Little Darryl told the orphan boys who sat roosting on the next cot, "and there ain't nothing but for me to go with them. They got the papers."

"You could burn them papers," suggested the littlest boy, writhing himself in embarrassment so that the row of boys tilted sideways like a wave washing through. Each little boy had a scar of some kind on some part of his body, and each boy loved Little Darryl with a passion that drew blood. He had seen to that.

"You would, would you," said Little Darryl and leaned over and flipped the littlest boy's nose until he bellowed out. "They got the machines that can resurrect a million a me. You burn one paper and they make ten more. You burn ten papers and they fill a library with them. You burn down a library and they fill the whole shittin' world with paper. They got you up one side and down the other."

"You could run away from here," a boy with a cauliflower ear said, "could run to Kingdom Come from here."

The littlest boy sniffed and said: "That's what I meant back then."

"I already done that once't," Little Darryl said. "They come at me with three cop cars and six guns. They had the papers that's stuck to me. The highest mountain and the lowest hole, they got you if they got them papers that they think is you."

"*I* don't have no papers on *me*," said the boy with a cauliflower ear. He let out a yell and thumped his chest to prove himself. All the little boys fell to scuffling, then they cheered and the cot skittered a few inches along the floor.

"It's because you ain't never done nothing worth the proving of it," Little Darryl said and smacked the boy on his cauliflower ear. They all settled down after that.

"These here people I ain't never seen nor seen their house might think they know what my paper says, but they don't know me. I reckon I got the upper hand under them, I reckon I know who I am." Little Darryl puffed himself up with air, standing slack-kneed on the bed with his shoes on. "I seen worse predicaments." The little boys stared up at him with the expressions of crows strung on a telephone wire. They flapped their arms and stared. "I seen the worser and the worst and they's nothing I seen that could make me forget myself in it. Pain's nothing to the forgetting yourself from it. I know who I am."

"Darryl!" cried the social worker. "Get your shoes off that bed and on the floor." She had on a pink polyester pantsuit that clung to her legs and gave the appearance of a second skin shedding off from the waist down.

"Boooo," said all the little boys, punching each other.

"It's my bed," Little Darryl said. "I'll stand on my own bed with anything on."

"You go home today and you know it. Effective at seven o'clock A.M. it wasn't your bed any more."

"I'll stand on anybody's bed with anything on."

"Let's go," the social worker said grimly. With her free arm cocked in a triangle just above her waist, she held open the door and looked as if the least movement would make her pants disappear. The little boys waited expectantly, booing softly.

"I seen worse than you look on Monday morning," said Little Darryl and got down off the bed. The little boys cheered, scuffled, grew into a wad of arms and legs on top of the cot. At the door Little Darryl looked back into the dormitory room, then he spat viciously on the floor.

"I seen even worser," he said, but the little boys, scuffling, didn't look up again.

IV

"Excessively bright! Excessively bright!" Mrs. Eastman sang aloud, scattering motes of dust helter-skelter with her mud-colored featherduster. The dust settled down again just inches ahead of Mrs. Eastman's movement across the table. "O my boy, O yes *my* boy, O he is ex—*press*—ive—ly—bright!"

Up at cock's crow that morning (the cock one of Mr. Eastman's poverty payments), Mrs. Eastman rampaged through the dawn inside her house with a vengeance and a joy. She had attacked her floors and her ceilings, her walls, her knickknacks. She'd made, then unmade, then made again her beds. She did the same with Little Darryl. First he was a lawyer, then he was a president, then he was a brain surgeon. Nothing suited. She couldn't get over it, she was electrified. And when the doorbell rang she thought she'd liked to have had a heart murmur. With the hand that held the duster pressed against her chest, she prayed to God and sneezed violently. Dust floated everywhere like tiny messengers. A feeling came to her, at the base of her spine, and it said, Practice makes perfect! Pretty is as pretty does! These were the exact sentiments she had expressed, intuitively, to the women's club off and on for thirty years: real mothering would be her forte. She sneezed once more and felt powerful.

By the second ring from the doorbell Mrs. Eastman was prepared, so much so that when she opened the door she had on her wisdom expression, the one she recommended for children with homesickness. On her porch stood a pair of pink polyester pants and Little Darryl, who wore an oversized Prince Albert coat, collar turned up, and a brown fedora hat, brim turned down. His eyes peeped out from under his hat as though from inside a tank turret. Mrs. Eastman said the first thing to come to her mind.

"I didn't know he was such a colored child," she said and smiled maternally. The eyes inside the hat seemed to look through Mrs. Eastman and onto the entranceway carpet. "I could've mistook you for a pickaninny, little boy," she said sweetly.

"They's two people said that to me before and lived," said Little Darryl.

"I'll be running right along," the social worker told Mrs. Eastman, "if you'll just sign these documents. I already stopped by your husband's office."

"The outside of it looked more like one of them goddamn saloons to me," Little Darryl snarled, spitting through his teeth at a fly on the porch. "Smell't of it, too."

"We don't curse in this home, Darryl. We are gentlemen and ladies in this home. Gentlemen and ladies don't curse or spit."

He looked at her, his eyes slightly askew.

"Sign here," said the social worker, and Mrs. Eastman did.

"You might think that's me right there," Little Darryl said through his teeth. Mrs. Eastman could have sworn it came from the paper itself. "But I know where I stand."

"Why of course you do!" Mrs. Eastman cried. "You're on the doorstep of your very own home!" She gave Little Darryl a hug, agitated by the goodness welling inside her like a carbonation, and he stood stiffly as a hanged man.

"From now on you touch me by permission," he said out of a corner of his mouth.

When they looked up the social worker was long gone.

"Food," said Mrs. Eastman. "You must be hungry, little boys are always hungry. They are hungry until they reach the age of twenty and then they are modern afterward."

"I've eat but I could do it again if it was a roast beef with string beans."

Without another word Mrs. Eastman clucked and herded Little Darryl into the kitchen of her house. On his way he picked up two china cats, pilfering them into the pocket of his Prince Albert. A look of sublime pleasure, which Mrs. Eastman mistook for good adjustment, showed above the coat collar. He sidled up to a kitchen window, gazed sullenly onto the backyard with a hooded pucker around his eyes.

"Gentlemen don't wear hats on in their homes," said Mrs. Eastman. Her hands gripped and sliced on the roast as if performing an emergency operation on a still-live body.

"Lady," said Little Darryl, his eyes directed toward the backyard. "I don't like you. I don't like your house, I don't like your husband. The onliest thing to keep me from the murder of you is if'n you pretend you don't see hear smell feel nor taste me. Do you understand me in that head a hair?"

"But I'm your mother." Mrs. Eastman paused, an expression of some awful recognition shrouding her nose and eyes and mouth. "Pretty is as pretty does," she said.

"You're nuts," he said, "and my mother was a thought my daddy thought for about three seconds. Serve me that roast beef with ketchup on it." He sat down at the table, pulling out a jackknife; the silver spoon and knife already on a place mat, he put in his pocket. He left the fork where it was.

"God loves all the little children," Mrs. Eastman said and her voice sounded very far away. "Black and white, smart and stupid."

"Serve it with ketchup and some mayo on the side, lady."

In a rapid, choppy movement Little Darryl flipped open the jack-knife and let the blade hang, for an instant, in the air like an unkept promise. "That God of yourn loves because they got the papers on Him a million years ago. You don't a bit more know who He is than you think you know who I am. I know worser."

"You!" screeched Mrs. Eastman. "You're a mistake!" Her hair and nerves were all unstrung. "I'm not your mother, you won't be a lawyer, you won't be." She couldn't think, and immediately, in a reflexive action, she shifted gears into the vaguest of doubts. Outside the rooster crooned an offbeat love song. "I'm going to call my husband," said Mrs. Eastman, dispassionately.

"Serve me the roast beef first," Little Darryl said, and Mrs. Eastman did, filling a plate with greasy slices that hunkered on top of each other in an orgy of flesh. "I ain't afraid of nobody that'd marry you."

While Mrs. Eastman was gone Little Darryl ate the roast beef and when he finished he roamed around, pocketing certain valuables. Inside the refrigerator he found a hamhock. He put it inside the coat, down near the waistline. Inside a drawer he found the silverware, and he put it all, including a soup ladle, into the front left pocket of the Prince Albert. It bulged outward like a cancerous tumor. He put the remains of the roast beef and a bottle of ketchup into the front right pocket. By the time Mrs. Eastman got back, there was very little left in her kitchen.

"He's on his way home," Mrs Eastman told him, as if the matter were settled at last.

"Whoopee," said Little Darryl. He clinked when he spoke. "You're going to have to go upstairs." Briefly, but certainly, he flashed the jackknife in front of Mrs. Eastman. It caused her to remember a story she'd heard quite a time ago. "You're going to have to show me where your jewry is up there. I'll take my chances with them papers this time."

"You're just a little boy," Mrs. Eastman said. "Just a little children."

"They's bigger than me that's less. Upstairs, lady."

Mrs. Eastman breathed heavily up the stairs, and she felt her heart make little leaps, as though it might creep onto her tongue and expose something. Each crack in the wood of the floor struck her as the place to be, each piece of dust looked like the safest of sizes, and she studied them with the vigilance of a scientist. In the bedroom she had a horrible thought.

"You wouldn't hurt a lady would you?" she asked, but Little Darryl was already rooting through her dressing table. "You wouldn't hurt a lady *would you*?" she asked, a little louder. She got up on her bed and held tightly as a tick to the wood of the headboard. "*Would you?*"

Little Darryl turned around, his hands full of rings and bracelets and necklaces that dangled like liquids through his fingers. Along the lines of his face there slithered a configuration of sheer hatred.

"Lady," he said, almost tenderly, "I wouldn't touch a hair a your head for anything anywhere," and then he disappeared out of the bedroom.

"Rape!" Mrs. Eastman cried, but her heart wasn't in it.

When Mr. Eastman came home all he could hear were his wife's screams, and all he could see was a brown figure in the distance, the plumes of a rooster sticking out like an exhaust under its arms, and all he could think would be forever silent.

RON TANNER

A Model Family

MOTHER BOUGHT US a submarine kit to build as a family project while our father is gone. It has 2,034 plastic pieces, 17 decals, and ten feet of thread-like wire. It is a big model, the parts scattered all over our living room rug, and it comes with twenty-seven pages of instructions written in five different languages. We got the kit weeks ago but haven't had time to start it because there are so many other things to work on around the house.

Father is on the nuclear submarine *Zipperfish* somewhere near Scotland. He left six months ago. He and mother argued about the trip, but he went anyway. He told me and Chip he was going on a secret mission. It sounds a little too adventuresome for my father, who is rather thin and studious, and I would not believe it if my mother didn't have a picture to prove it. Father sent her a snapshot of him and the crew of the *Zipperfish*. Everyone is smiling with their arms around each other and everybody has a "flat-top" haircut, the weirdest looking thing. My little brother Chip says they look like spacemen and now he tells his friends that our father is on a secret mission somewhere near the moon.

Father is a civilian, an electrical engineer, actually. Our basement is crowded with his old radios, television tubes, testing equipment (black boxes with glowing screens and eery lights), and trays and trays of tiny parts, many of them colorful and oddly shaped like hard candy. When people ask what he does I tell them he fixes household appliances, which is no lie. He used to fix all our electrical stuff. Mother has a box in the kitchen closet where she keeps the broken appliances for his return. She bought a do-it-yourself handyman's book, which she reads little by little each day, but she hasn't tried to fix anything since she blew the fuses while working on the blender. The house was dark for hours and we wandered around the living room crunching model pieces underfoot, waiting for Mr. Kiminski, a retired handyman who lives down the street.

Mr. Kiminski wants to take me and Chip hunting, but we don't want to go because he scares us. He looks like one of those sickly Santas we see in front of Saint Mary's Halfway House every year. He has piggish eyes and a short white beard stained brown and yellow. He looks like maybe he knows Chip and I used to pee on his prize geraniums.

After he fixed our fusebox, Mother invited him to dinner. He got upset when he heard that Chip wanted to be a witch for Halloween.

"Witches are girls," he said.

"Witches are monsters," said Chip, dropping a pat of butter into his steamy mashed potatoes.

"You want a dress, then," said the old man.

"Is that what you want, Chip, a dress?" Mother asked.

"I want to be a witch," he said, "with an ugly green face and horrible thoughts." He tore the center out of his bread and squeezed it into a doughy ball.

"These boys need a strong hand," said Mr. Kiminski.

Chip asked if that meant we were going to get spanked.

"You're going hunting," said Kiminski. "You'll learn to live like men."

"They're young, Mr. Kiminski." Mother smiled at us.

"Young pansies if you're not careful." He leaned toward us. "You boys ever shoot a deer?"

Chip began to blubber, whining about *Bambi*, a movie he'd seen recently. Tears dripped all over his plate.

"Mr. Kiminski!" Mother's face was red. "These are not your boys to browbeat."

"They need help."

Mother told him to leave. He said she was a frustrated woman who needed a little looking after. She grabbed a greasy spatula and told him to leave now or regret the consequences. He pinched my cheek and promised to take me and Chip hunting real soon. After he left, Chip and Mother cried for a long time. I was feeling pretty sad myself so I walked down to Kiminski's house and poured turpentine all over his flowers.

Mother says Chip and I are losing our discipline, so she makes Chip take art lessons and she makes me go to speech therapy. I stutter a lot and it nearly drives her crazy, it takes me so long to answer her questions. At school I'm in speech class while the rest of the kids are in study hall, where most of the note passing occurs. I miss out on vital developments in our sixth grade social life and it really hurts my image.

On Wednesday afternoons I take Chip on the train to the city for his art lessons. I wait for him in the park where I try to pick up girls. I'm not that interested in girls, really, but it seems like the thing to do, so I want to be good at it. I've tried several approaches but found I get the best response if I wave my arms and moan like a deaf-mute. Still, the pretty girls avoid me. They go for those hot-shot roller skaters who race around at startling speeds, pirouetting left and right and wheeling backward with their briefcase-sized radios attached to either side of their heads. They have no regard for personal safety. That's why the girls love them.

My mother offered to buy me some roller skates so I'd be more socially acceptable, but I'm real scared of spinning around on tiny wheels like that. My father was a fine ice skater when he was young, she tells me, and someday, if I practice, I can wear his skates, which are in the attic—battered black leather things with rusted runners.

Mother met Father while ice-skating. It was a long time ago, when he was in the Navy. She says he looked exotic wearing his uniform.

"I was a stupid eighteen-year-old," she says. "Just out of high school, a piccolo player in the marching band. My parents were glad to see me go. They had ten kids. It was all they could do just to keep track of us, much less teach us anything important like how to cook. But your father was patient. He got what he wanted."

"Ice skates?" I ask.

"A pretty wife," she says.

I stutter. "You were pretty?"

"I was a prize," she says. "I got plenty of attention. I used to enter beauty contests."

"Chip and I give you plenty of attention."

"Sometimes too much," she says.

"I guess we spoil you," I say.

Chip pretends our father has been gone for years instead of months, and sometimes he imagines him as a hero from television. One week Father is Superman and the next week he is the Hulk. Chip is six, old enough to know better, and Mother gets angry when she hears him describing father as "a big green guy with size fifty biceps and teeth as big as piano keys."

She grabs Chip's collar and says, "Your father is six-feet-tall, his hair is black, his eyes are brown, his teeth are *normal* because he brushes them three times a day, he is clean-shaven, has a large nose like your brother, and for better or worse he is the man half-responsible for you two clowns and I do not want to hear him described in any peculiar fashion. Understand?"

Chip nods yes, then continues watching TV, which is about all he does besides his art lessons. His art teacher wants him to be a landscape painter. She says he has great line control. Chip paints pages and pages of lines for her. Mother claims it takes discipline to paint so many straight lines. I say it's a sign of stupidity.

What Chip lacks in sophistication he makes up for in charm. He has that wholesome kind of freckled face you see on cereal commercials. Women love him. Just now, for instance, an old lady gave him a quarter for picking up her gloves from the floor of the train station. Chip was down there pretending he was a turtle. I have to watch over him all the time, he's so childish. His sneakers are wet from the snow because he forgot to wear his galoshes and his nose is dripping all over the place. I make him sit down finally and we take turns drawing pictures on the foggy train window.

"Last night I dreamed we built a snowman," he says. "And when it melted it turned into Dad."

"Fascinating," I say.

"Maybe we ought to try it," he says.

"Maybe you ought to grow up," I tell him.

"It might work. That kind of thing happens all the time on TV."

"Dad's not like any of your TV heroes. Why should you want to see him?"

"He took us to the amusement park once."

"Twice," I say. "But you were too young to remember."

"I remember everything," says Chip. He's wiping his nose on his coat sleeve. "Even the time we went to Africa."

"That was the zoo."

"We were nearly eaten by headhunters, but Dad fought them off."

"It was the zoo. A little monkey grabbed your pants leg and Dad slapped the monkey's wrist."

"You make up such stories," he says.

"You're lucky to have me around, buddy."

"I'm honored," he says. "I'm truly honored." He turns to the window and draws a goofy face, then writes my name under it.

The city station is large and old like a museum, and hundreds of people are rushing back and forth, everyone with a destination. Their voices echo around the dome of the lobby. Chip and I stop at a newsstand to buy a week's supply of bubble gum. Mother lets us chew only the sugarless kind, so we have to sneak in the normal stuff. Chip makes a point of cramming as many pieces as possible into his mouth. It takes him a long time to chew them down into a manageable wad.

I'm reading my gum wrapper comic when I hear my father's voice suddenly, giving someone directions not far behind me. His voice isn't loud but it's a different color from the rest and it reaches me clearly above the others. I see his shoulders from the back and I know it's him because he walks like no other man. I shout for him to stop but he doesn't hear. I pull Chip with me and run after him. Chip yells complaints because he doesn't know what's happening. I shout for Father, who is lost in the crowd and people turn from all sides to stare at me like I'm crazy. In my mind I'm watching the whole thing on a movie screen, I feel so far away.

We run outside in time to see Father enter a taxi. He glances back but does not see us. I stand there for the longest time watching the cab disappear in traffic.

Chip shakes himself from my grip. "You posing for a statue?"

"That was Dad. He was just here and he didn't see us, like we were ghosts or something."

Chip thinks I'm pulling his leg. He blows a bubble.

"You just saw him drive away, Chip!"

"I saw you lose your marbles."

"Okay, he was different. He had a mustache and longer hair, but he was Dad. You can't mistake a thing like that."

"Father is on a spaceship exploring the galaxy." Chip makes rocket noises.

I push him away. "You don't care. You just make jokes."

"Sure I care," he says. "I'm missing my art lesson."

"Maybe this is part of his secret mission."

"You want a pretzel?" Chip buys a hot pretzel from a vendor and tears it in half. "These things make great nose warmers." He sticks his small nose into the steamy dough of a pretzel half.

"I almost blew his cover. I almost gave him away."

"Dad will be back soon enough. Don't worry."

"Blow your nose," I tell him. "It's dripping all over."

"It's so cold I can't tell," he says. "Do I have icicles?"

"We can't let Mother know."

"She doesn't mind if my nose drips a little."

"About Dad. We can't let her know about Dad in disguise."

"It was a good disguise," says Chip. "It sure had me fooled."

We arrive home just as it starts raining. Mother is cleaning up after her bridge party. The house is foggy with cigarette smoke, and the candy dishes are half-filled with chocolate-covered raisins and nuts which Chip and I eat as fast as possible before Mother tries to put them away. Chip starts to tell her how I went crazy at the train station this afternoon, but I tackle him and push him under the couch to keep him quiet. He kicks and yells.

"What's with you boys?" she says.

"Chip's been making up stories all day," I tell her.

"Let me out," he says.

"Enough of this nonsense," says Mother. "What kind of TV dinner do you two want?" She holds up four frozen choices.

"Spaghetti," says Chip from under the couch.

I choose chicken.

Chip places the foil-wrapped trays in the oven and sets the temperature. "I'm a good cook," he says.

I tell him he's a cooked goose if he opens his mouth again.

Mother suggests we start on the submarine model tonight. She says she will give us a big prize if we finish it before Father comes home. Since we don't know when that will be, we will have to work fast. The model pieces are scattered like the remains of an explosion. We rake them into a big pile and Mother reads the instructions by the light of the TV set. She says the finished model will be in two halves showing each side of the sub's interior with working parts and a crew of tiny plastic men. Chip glues the tiny men into a clump so they will not get lost. Mother makes him unglue them. I work on the torpedo room. Chip starts on the periscope but he loses interest when the cowboys on TV have a shootout. Mother works on the engine room but soon she falls asleep with her head on the book of instructions and a tube of glue in her hands. Chip and I cover her with a throw rug, then we search the house for more candy she might have hidden for future bridge games. We find none.

All night it rains and hails, clattering on the roof, and this morning everything is glazed with ice—ice on telephone lines, ice on doghouses, ice on bushes and trees, ice on every snowy lawn.

"There are skaters in the street!" says Chip, bounding down the stairs.

"What does it mean?" I ask.

"Breakfast," says Mother from the kitchen.

Chip slings his ice skates over the back of his chair. "Everything is covered with rock candy." He runs to the bay window in the living room. "This is a special day like in my dreams."

"No school today." I spoon brown sugar over my oatmeal.

"Plenty of time to shovel the driveway," says Mother.

"It's Dad!" says Chip. "It's Dad coming home!"

Mother drops her spoon and hurries to the window. "Where?"

I step between them, leaning on the windowsill. "Some guy skating up the street. It could be anybody, he's so far away."

"He skates just like Dad," says Chip.

"Yes, he does." Mother is squinting. "Sort of."

"Now we can all go skating together."

Mother leans closer to the window. She stands very still, her lips parted slightly as if she's trying to remember something from long ago. "We don't know for sure," she says finally.

"It's him," says Chip. "He's back." He dances around like a leprechaun.

"He would've called," Mother tells us.

"The telephone lines are down," I say.

"Maybe he didn't have a dime," says Chip.

"Where's the telescope," she says. "Get the telescope."

Chip runs into the den and returns with a small, colorfully painted telescope. "From my pirate's chest," he says.

Mother holds the telescope to her right eye and twists the focus ring. The skater is wearing a navy blue overcoat and bell-bottom trousers and a red scarf, which flutters from his neck. He leans from side to side as he pushes forward, skating nearer.

"Is he carrying presents?"

"Does he have a mustache?" I ask her.

"Or a flat-top haircut?"

"Should we wave?"

"He has a beard," says Mother.

"He's been away a long time," says Chip.

"He looks unhappy." Mother refocuses.

"It's dark and lonely in those little submarines."

"Oh my god, it's Mr. Kiminski."

"Mr. Kiminski!"

"Old man Kiminski skating this way." She drops the telescope and it hits Chip's left foot. "How can I be so stupid, listening to you kids?" She returns to the kitchen.

Chip squints through the telescope. "Jeesh," he says. "It's Mr. Kiminski."

"You boys finish your breakfast."

Chip tosses the telescope onto the couch. "I've lost my appetite."

"You've lost your discipline," she says. "You're high strung and overimaginative and I don't know what I'm going to do with you."

"Sell me at the flea market."

"Get in here and eat your oatmeal." She is angry and Chip obeys.

I stand at the window and watch Mr. Kiminski skate to our house. He takes his time because he knows we are not going anywhere. Perhaps he has known all along that our father has been in the city and never on a submarine, that he's been growing a mustache and longer hair and leading a different life for reasons I can only imagine.

Kiminski puffs great clouds of fog as he struggles up our drive, which is too steep for skating. He loses speed and slips finally, falling into the snowy yard. After many minutes of maneuvering, he regains his balance. He's panting, his beard frosted around his mouth. He takes another step, wobbling on his runners, then he falls again, swiping the air this way and that, he's so angry. I wonder why he takes the time to come here where he knows he's not welcomed. He shuffles on his hands and knees like a seal and clambers at last onto the front steps. The bell rings but none of us moves for the door. We will sit at the breakfast table and pretend Father is here to answer it.

BRET LOTT

This Plumber

I LIKED THIS PLUMBER. He had come to the front door and knocked solidly three times, then three times more before I could answer. I liked that, liked the sound six square knocks made through the apartment. I was there alone. I had things to sort out.

I opened the door, and the plumber stuck out his hand. "Lonny Thompson," he said. "Landlord sent me up. You've got a leak somewhere in your bathroom."

"Rick," I said. We shook hands. He knew how to shake hands; grasped my hand just past the knuckles, then squeezed hard and shook. I judged he was about fifty, fifty-five years old.

He said, "Glad to meet you. Now where's this damned leak?"

He led me to the bathroom, as if he'd been here plenty of times, though I'd never seen him around the building before. We walked through the front room into the kitchen, then into the bathroom, the plumber turning his head, looking everything over. There wasn't much left in the apartment; my wife had taken most everything. Only the sofabed and the black-and-white

73

portable were left in the living room, one of those small rented refrigerators in the kitchen. Even the hamper in the bathroom was gone. "Moving in?" he asked once we were in the bathroom. He didn't look at me.

I said, "Well, not really." I didn't want to go into it.

He set the toolbox on the toilet lid. "Oh," he said, and started unbuttoning the gray down vest he wore over a red and black plaid wool shirt. He took off the vest, then the shirt, and dropped them both on the floor. Under the wool shirt he wore a gray work shirt, the same color as his pants, *Lonny* stitched in red thread above the shirt pocket. He had on old-fashioned plastic-framed glasses, the kind of frames that started out thick across the top and thinned down to wire along the bottom edge of the lenses. He went right to business, got down on his hands and knees and opened the cabinet beneath the sink.

I said, "Cold outside?"

"Where have you been?" he said, his head under the sink. "Thirty-five degrees and dropping. Supposed to get the first snow tonight. Believe it? Snow already."

I said, "I guess I haven't been paying much attention." I squatted down next to him to see if I could tell what he was doing, if I could learn something.

"Bet you haven't been paying attention to any leaks then, neither." He laughed. "Your landlord called me this morning. Five feet square of ceiling in the apartment below came right down on the breakfast table." He pulled his head out from under the sink and looked at me. "How'd you like that for breakfast?" We both laughed. He went back under.

I said, "I know. He called me and told me the whole thing. That's a funny story." I stood up slowly, pushing on my knees, then picked up his shirt and vest from off the floor. They both smelled of cigarettes, years of cigarettes burning down to the filter, I imagined, while he drained sinktraps and tightened pipes; and they smelled of burnt wood. I imagined this plumber standing around a campfire at dawn, a rifle crooked in his arms. I folded the shirt and vest and put them on the toilet tank.

I went to the bedroom and looked out the window. There had been a good blow several days before. Most every leaf had been stripped off the trees, and I saw things I hadn't been able to see in the summer, things like the Ford dealership sign on the main street in town, the charcoal-colored hills, chimneys. The sky was an even ash-gray all the way across. He was right about the snow coming.

All these things looked strange under that gray sky, but what seemed most strange was that the grass down in the yard was still green. That green next to all those bare gray trees and the gray sky and the hills looked odd.

I went back into the bathroom, and I don't think he even knew I left. I said, "Do you know what the problem is? Do you know what's wrong?" I sat on the edge of the tub.

"Tell you the truth, I don't." He pulled out from under the sink, closed the cabinet, and sat Indian style on the floor. "All those pipes look fine. No loose fittings, no watermarks, no nothing. But you better believe there's a leak somewhere." He motioned toward me. "I want to look at the tub next."

I got up quickly and pulled back the curtain.

The plumber kneeled against the tub and ran his fingers along the edge where the walls and the tub met. "This caulking along here can go," he said, "and then every damn time you're standing in the shower, water'll seep down through these joints and collect beneath the tub. I seen that happen before." He came to a small crack on the lip of the tub, stopped and examined it a moment, then went on. "I seen it happen once where all the water collected underneath the floor beneath the tub. This was a bathroom on the first floor of a house, and they didn't have their basement heated. Know what happened?" He grinned up at me. "All this water's been collecting, and then a big freeze

came along and the water froze, broke right through the bottom
of the tub, put a half-inch crack three feet long right down the
center. I seen that."

I said, "No," and crossed my arms.

He finished checking the seal around the tub. "Your caulking's
not shot, that's for sure. Not the greatest, but not shot to hell."
He then started feeling the floor along the tub, pressing down
every few inches with the palm of his hand. "Pull your curtain
closed," he said.

I leaned over him and pulled it along the rod, stepping over
him still kneeling and feeling the floor. I said, "What do you
think?"

"You do keep the bottom of the shower curtain inside the
tub when you shower, don't you?" he said.

I said, "Of course," and laughed.

"You'd be surprised," he said without looking up.

He checked either end of the tub where the curtain touched
the walls. "You know sometimes water sprays out of these edges.
Sometimes people don't get these curtains completely closed." He
flipped the ends of the curtain back and forth to see where they
fell. "Do you have a glass?" he asked, very matter-of-fact, as
though the question were the next logical thing to say. "And fill
it with water," he added. He was still flipping the curtain back
and forth.

I got the red plastic cup from the toothbrush holder and
filled it. I handed it to him, expecting him to drink it.

"Sometimes along the floor, water can seep in, too," he said.
"This is a good test." He then poured the cup of water on the
floor along the edge of the tub. "How about another?" he asked.
I filled it again, and he emptied it on the floor. "If it seeps down
and disappears, why then we've found our leak."

I squatted down next to him, and we both watched the water
there on the floor.

But the water did nothing, only sat in a puddle along the entire edge of the tub. We watched that water for a good three minutes, but nothing happened. "Well," the plumber finally said, "that's not your problem either. I was afraid of this." He stood and dusted off his hands, though I was sure they weren't dirty. "We better mop this up." He waved at the floor.

I got the last clean towel from the closet and dropped it on the water, pushed it along the tub with my foot.

He said, "I'll bet it's your toilet. If it's your toilet, we've got troubles. Your landlord's got troubles."

I dropped the wet towel in the tub.

He took his tool chest from the toilet lid, sat it on the floor, then lifted the lid and flushed the toilet. "Toilets I hate," he said. "That's why I always wait until last for them. Some plumbers don't mind them, some love them. Me, I hate them. Too much water swirling up around everywhere." He stood over the bowl, looking at it as though it would say something to him. After a moment he closed the lid, and saw his folded shirt and vest on the tank. I picked them up, felt to make sure the radiator was cold, then set the shirt and vest there.

"Thanks, buddy," he said.

He set the tank lid on the toilet seat, then flushed the toilet again and played with the bulb, flicking it up and down. He reached his hand down into the rising water and opened and closed the round hatch at the bottom. The inside walls of the tank were all brown and rusted, making the outside of the tank look that much whiter. He put the lid back on, then got back down on his hands and knees and started feeling the floor around the base of the toilet, just as he had along the tub, pressing the palm of his hand down every few inches to test it.

I assumed he was going to ask for another cup of water, so I filled the red plastic cup. I stood with the cup of water and said, "You need some water?"

He had already worked halfway around the toilet, his head back under the tank. He stopped feeling the floor. "Christ, is that all you do?" he said over his shoulder. "Ask questions?" He forced a laugh, but I knew he meant what he said. He went back to testing the floor. "There's enough water in this damn toilet already. If there's a leak, I'll find it with the water that's already here, thank you."

I dumped the water into the sink. "Sorry," I said. I stepped over him and started out the door.

"Hey," he said. I turned around. From where I stood I could see his face under the toilet tank. He was smiling, and said, "Hey, it's these damn toilets I hate. Sorry."

"That's okay," I said. I squatted and watched while he tinkered with a knob on a pipe leading from the tank to the floor.

A few minutes later he was finished. He got up and again dusted off his hands. I stood up with him.

He said, "I'll be damned if I can find what's your problem. I can't find no leak anywhere, so it must be somewhere down in the floor, down below here. I've seen some strange things before, some strange plumbing problems, so nothing I find'll be a surprise." He flushed the toilet again. "You can never tell what's going on when it comes to plumbing," he said, staring at the bowl. "Maybe there's a leak in the roof and when it rains the water pours down between these walls and collects in the ceiling of that apartment below. I've seen that happen before, too. I've seen the ceiling of a first floor apartment fall in because there was a leak in the roof three floors up." He looked at me, then at his shirt and vest on the radiator. "But I'll be damned if I can find a leak here in this bathroom."

He reached for his shirt, but I picked it up first, unfolded it and handed it to him. He sort of smiled as he put it on and buttoned it up. Then I handed him the vest.

He said, "So did you say you were moving in or moving out?"

I put my hands in my pockets. I figured I would have to

say it to someone some time, and I liked this plumber. "Neither, actually," I said. "I guess my wife was the one who moved out." I waited for some reaction. I waited for him to say something.

But he only finished buttoning up the vest, then picked up his toolbox and led me out of the bathroom, through the kitchen and back into the front room. He glanced around the room again.

"One thing's for sure, though," he said.

I said, "Oh?"

"Yeah," he said, "your landlord's going to have to spring for a new toilet some time soon. That one in there's about shot." He stood at the door, his hand on the knob. "I'd say that one in there's at least fifteen years old, and it's not a very good one. He's going to have to get a new one, and I don't envy him having to pay for it."

"How much do they cost?" I said. I wanted to listen to this plumber talk about things he knew.

"Really depends," he said. He seemed to enjoy talking about it, and took his hand off the knob. "You can buy a good one for, oh, about a hundred-fifty, hundred-seventy-five. Last you a good twenty years. But then, on the other hand, you could buy a cheap one, seventy-five to a hundred, have it last fifteen years, and have to flush it three times just to make sure everything goes down." He pushed an imaginary lever on an imaginary toilet several times to show me what he meant.

He turned and opened the door, and I could smell the cigarettes and burnt wood. I didn't want this plumber to leave. I wanted him to stay and tell me more about plumbing, more stories. I said, "I guess you know a lot. About plumbing, I mean."

"Thirty years," he said, and pointed to his head. He smiled. "Thirty years." He walked out into the hall, turned and said, "I'll be seeing you whenever that landlord of yours decides to spring for that toilet. So long."

I said, "See you." I started to close the door, then stepped out into the hall.

"Lonny," I said. "Hey, Lonny."

He was already a few steps down the stairs, but stopped and turned around. He looked surprised. He stared at me a few seconds, then put his hand on the back of his neck.

"Jesus, buddy. Jesus, Rick," he said. He seemed to look past me. "Don't ask me," he said. "Don't ask me a goddamn thing about anything other than plumbing. I'm just the plumber."

I stood there a moment. He looked away. I said, "You hunt, right?"

"Yeah, I hunt," he said. He was quiet a moment, then said, "I'll call you some time when we go hunting. When we go deer hunting. You can go with us. I know where you live." He waved and disappeared down the stairs.

"All right," I called down. "I'll be here."

Back in the apartment I could still smell his shirt and vest. I looked out the window at the odd green against the gray, and smelled the cigarettes and burnt wood. I knew he would call me. I just wondered when.

DAVID LEAVITT

Aliens

A YEAR AGO TODAY I wouldn't have dreamed I'd be where I am now: in the recreation room on the third floor of the State Hospital, watching, with my daughter, ten men who sit in a circle in the center of the room. They look almost normal from a distance—khaki pants, lumberjack shirts, white socks—but I've learned to detect the tics, the nervous disorders. The men are members of a poetry writing workshop. It is my husband Alden's turn to read. He takes a few seconds to find his cane, to hoist himself out of his chair. As he stands, his posture is hunched and awkward. The surface of his crushed left eye has clouded to marble. There is a pale pink scar under his pale yellow hair.

The woman who leads the workshop, on a volunteer basis, rubs her forehead as she listens, and fingers one of her elephant-shaped earrings. Alden's voice is a hoarse roar, only recently reconstructed.

"Goddamned God," he reads. "I'm mad as hell I can't walk or talk."

. . .

It is spring, and my youngest child, my eleven-year-old, Nina, has convinced herself that she is an alien.

Mrs. Tompkins, her teacher, called me in yesterday morning to tell me. "Nina's constructed a whole history," she whispered, removing her glasses and leaning toward me across her desk, as if someone might be listening from above. "She never pays attention in class, just sits and draws. Strange landscapes, star-charts, the interiors of spaceships. I finally asked some of the other children what was going on. They told me that Nina says she's waiting to be taken away by her real parents. She says she's a surveyor, implanted here, but that soon a ship's going to come and retrieve her."

I looked around the classroom; the walls were papered with crayon drawings of cars and rabbits, the world seen by children. Nina's are remote, fine landscapes done with Magic Markers. No purple suns with faces. No abrupt, sinister self-portraits. In the course of a year Nina suffered a violent and quick puberty, sprouted breasts larger than mine, grew tufts of hair under her arms. The little girls who were her friends shunned her. Most afternoons now she stands in the corner of the playground, her hair held back by barrettes, her forehead gleaming. Recently, Mrs. Tompkins tells me, a few girls with glasses and large vocabularies have taken to clustering around Nina at recess. They sit in the broken bark beneath the slide and listen to Nina as one might listen to a prophet. Her small eyes, exaggerated by her own glasses, must seem to them expressive of martyred beauty.

"Perhaps you should send her to a psychiatrist," Mrs. Tompkins suggested. She is a good teacher, better than most of her colleagues. "This could turn into a serious problem," she said.

"I'll consider it," I answered, but I was lying. I don't have the money. And besides, I know psychiatry; it takes things away. I don't think I could bear to see what would be left of Nina once she'd been purged of this fantasy.

Today Nina sits in the corner of the recreation room. She is quiet, but I know her eyes are taking account of everything. The woman with the elephant-shaped earrings is talking to one of the patients about poetry *qua* poetry.

"You know," I say to her afterward, "it's amazing that a man like Alden can write poems. He was a computer programmer. All our married life he never read a book."

"His work has real power," the teacher says. "It reminds me of Michelangelo's *Bound Slaves*. Its artistry is heightened by its rawness."

She hands me a sheet of mimeographed paper—some examples of the group's work. "We all need a vehicle for self-expression," she says.

Later, sitting on the sun porch with Alden, I read through the poems. They are full of expletives and filthy remarks—the kind of remarks my brother used to make when he was hot for some girl at school. I am embarrassed. Nina, curled in an unused wheelchair, is reading "The Chronicles of Narnia" for the seventeenth time. We should go home soon, but I'm wary of the new car. I don't trust its brakes. When I bought it, I tested the seat belts over and over again.

"Dinner?" Alden asks. Each simple word, I remember, is a labor for him. We must be patient.

"Soon," I say.

"Dinner. It's all—" He struggles to find the word; his brow is red, and the one seeing eye stares at the opposite wall.

"Crap," he says. He keeps looking at the wall. His eyes are expressionless. Once again, he breathes.

Nearby, someone's screaming, but we're used to that.

A year ago today. The day was normal. I took my son, Charles, to the dentist. I bought a leg of lamb to freeze. There was a sale on paper towels. Early in the evening, on our way to a restaurant, Alden drove the car through a fence, and over an embankment. I remember, will always remember, the way his body fell almost gracefully through the windshield, how the glass shattered around him in a thousand glittering pieces. Earlier, during the argument, he had said that seat belts do more harm than good, and I had buckled myself in as an act of vengeance. This is the only reason I'm around to talk about it.

I suffered a ruptured spleen in the accident, and twenty-two broken bones. Alden lost half his vision, much of his mobility, and the English language. After a week in intensive care they took him to his hospital and left me to mine. In the course of the six months, three weeks, and five days I spent there, eight women passed in and out of the bed across from me. The first was a tiny, elderly lady who spoke in hushed tones and kept the curtain drawn between us. Sometimes children were snuck in to visit her; they would stick their heads around the curtain rod and gaze at me, until a hand pulled them back and a voice loudly whispered, "Sorry!" I was heavily sedated; everything seemed to be there one minute, gone the next. After the old woman left, another took her place. Somewhere in the course of those months a Texan mother arrived who was undergoing chemotherapy, who spent her days putting on make-up, over and over again, until, by dusk, her face was the color of bruises.

My hospital. What can you say about a place to which you become addicted? That you hate it, yet at the same time, that you need it. For weeks after my release I begged to be readmitted. I would wake crying, helplessly, in the night, convinced that the world had stopped, and I had been left behind, the only survivor. I'd call the ward I had lived on. "You'll be all right, dear," the nurses told me. "You don't have to come back, and besides, we've kicked you out." I wanted cups of Jell-O. I wanted there to be a light in the hall at night. I wanted to be told that six months hadn't gone by, that it had all been, as it seemed, a single, endless moment.

To compensate, I started to spend as much time as I could at Alden's hospital. The head nurse suggested that if I was going to be there all day, I might as well do something productive. They badly needed volunteers on the sixth floor, the floor of the severely retarded, the unrecoverable ones. I agreed to go in the afternoons, imagining story corner with cute three-year-olds and seventy-year-olds. The woman I worked with most closely had been pregnant three times in the course of a year. Her partner was a pale-skinned young man who drooled constantly and could not keep his head up. Of course she had abortions. None of the administrators was willing to solicit funds for birth control because that would have meant admitting there was a need for birth control. We couldn't keep the couple from copulating. They hid in the bushes and in the broom closet. They were obsessive about their lovemaking, and went to great lengths to find each other. When we locked them in separate rooms, they pawed the doors and screamed.

The final pregnancy was the worst because the woman insisted that she wanted to keep the baby, and legally she had every right. Nora, my supervisor—a crusty, ancient nurse—had no sympathy, insisted that the woman didn't even know what being pregnant meant. In the third month, sure enough, the woman started to scream and wouldn't be calmed. Something was moving inside her, something she was afraid would try to kill her. The lover was no help. Just as easily as he'd begun with her, he'd forgotten her, and taken up with a Down's syndrome dwarf who got transferred from Sonoma.

The woman agreed to the third abortion. Because it was so late in the pregnancy, the procedure was painful and complicated. Nora shook her head and said, "What's the world coming to?" Then she returned to her work.

I admire women who shake their heads and say, "What's the world coming to?" Because of them, I hope, it will always stop just short of getting there.

Lately, in my own little ways, I, too, have been keeping the earth in orbit. Today, for instance, I take Alden out to the car and let him sit in the driver's seat, which he enjoys. The hot vinyl burns his thighs. I calm him. I sit in the passenger seat, strapped in, while he slowly turns the wheel. He stares through the windshield at the other cars in the parking lot, imagining, perhaps, an endless landscape unfolding before him as he drives.

Visiting hours end. I take Alden in from the parking lot, kiss him good-bye. He shares a room these days with a young man named Joe, a Vietnam veteran prone to motorcycle accidents. Because of skin-grafting, Joe's face is six or seven different colors —beiges and taupes, mostly—but he can speak, and has recently regained the ability to smile. "Hey, pretty lady," he says as we walk in. "It's good to see a pretty lady around here."

Nina is sitting in the chair by the window, reading. She is sulky as we say good-bye to Alden, sulky as we walk out to the car. I suppose I should expect moodiness—some response to what she's seen this last year. We go to pick up Charles, who is sixteen and spends most of his time in the Olde Computer Shoppe—a scarlet, plum-shaped building that serves as a reminder of what the fifties thought the future would look like. Charles is a computer prodigy, a certified genius, nothing special in our circuit-fed community. He has some sort of deal going with the owner of the Computer Shoppe, which he doesn't like to talk about. It involves that magical stuff called software. He uses the Shoppe's terminal and in exchange gives the owner a cut of his profits, which are bounteous. Checks arrive for him every day—from Puerto Rico, from Texas, from New York. He puts the money in a private bank account. He says that in a year he will have enough saved to put himself through college—a fact I can't help but appreciate.

The other day I asked him to please explain in English what it is that he does. He was sitting in my kitchen with Stuart Beckman, a fat boy with the kind of wispy mustache that indicates a willful refusal to begin shaving. Stuart is the dungeon master in the elaborate medieval war games Charles's friends conduct on Tuesday nights. Charles is Galadrian, a lowly elfin-warrior with minimal experience points. "Well," Charles said, "let's just say it's a step toward the great computer age when we won't need dungeon masters. A machine will create for us a whole world into which we can be transported. We'll live inside the machine—for a day, a year, our whole lives—and we'll live the adventures the machine creates for us. We're at the forefront of a major breakthrough—artificial imagination. The possibilities, needless to say, are endless."

"You've invented that?" I asked, suddenly swelling with Mother Goddess pride.

"The project is embryonic, of course," Charles said. "But we're getting there. Give it fifty years. Who knows?"

Charles is angry as we drive home. He sifts furiously through an enormous roll of green print-out paper. As it unravels, the paper flies in Nina's hair, but she is oblivious to it. Her face is pressed against the window so hard that her nose and lips have flattened out.

I consider starting up a conversation, but as we pull into the driveway I, too, feel the need for silence. Our house is dark and unwelcoming tonight, as if it is suspicious of us. As soon as we are in the door, Charles disappears into his room, and the world of his mind. Nina sits at the kitchen table with me until she has finished her book. It is the last in the Narnia series, and as she closes it, her face takes on the disappointed look of someone who was hoping something would never end. Last month she entered the local library's Read-a-Thon. Neighbors agreed to give several dollars to UNICEF for every book she read, not realizing that she would read fifty-nine.

It is hard for me to look at her. She is sullen, and she is not pretty. My mother used to say it's one thing to look ugly, another to act it. Still, it must be difficult to be betrayed by your own body. The cells divide, the hormones explode; Nina had no control over the timing, much less the effects. The first time she menstruated she cried not out of fear but because she was worried she had contracted that disease that causes children to age prematurely. We'd seen pictures of them—wizened, hoary four-year-olds, their skin loose and wrinkled, their teeth already rotten. I assured her that she had no such disease, that she was merely being precocious, as usual. In a few years, I told her, her friends would catch up.

She stands awkwardly now, as if she wants to maintain a distance even from herself. Ugliness really is a betrayal. Suddenly she can trust nothing on earth; her body is no longer a part of her, but her enemy.

"Daddy was glad to see you today, Nina," I say.

"Good."

"Can I get you anything?"

She still does not look at me. "No," she says. "Nothing."

Later in the evening, my mother calls to tell me about her new cordless electric telephone. "I can walk all around the house with it," she says. "Now, for instance, I'm in the kitchen, but I'm on my way to the bathroom." Mother believes in Christmas newsletters, and the forces of fate. Tonight she is telling me about Mr. Garvey, a local politician and neighbor who was recently arrested. No one knows the details of the scandal; Mother heard somewhere that the boys involved were young, younger than Charles. "His wife just goes on, does her gardening as if nothing happened," she tells me. "Of course, we don't say anything. What could we say? She knows we avoid mentioning it. Her house is as clean as ever. I even saw *him* the other day. He was wearing a sable sweater just like your father's. He told me he was relaxing for the first time in his life, playing golf, gardening. She looks ill, if you ask me. When I was your age I would have wondered how a woman could survive something like that, but now it doesn't surprise me to see her make do. Still, it's shocking. He always seemed like such a family man."

"She must have known," I say. "It's probably been a secret between them for years."

"I don't call secrets any basis for a marriage," Mother says. "Not in her case. Not in yours, either."

Lately she's been convinced that there's some awful secret

between Alden and me. I told her that we'd had a fight the night of the accident, but I didn't tell her why. Not because the truth was too monumentally terrible. The subject of our fight was trivial. Embarrassingly trivial. We were going out to dinner. I wanted to go to a Chinese place. Alden wanted to try an Italian health food restaurant that a friend of his at work had told him about. Our family has always fought a tremendous amount about restaurants. Several times, when the four of us were piled in the car, Alden would pull off the road. "I will not drive with this chaos," he'd say. The debates over where to eat usually ended in tears, and abrupt returns home. The children ran screaming to their rooms. We ended up eating tunafish.

Mother is convinced I'm having an affair. "Alden's still a man," she says to me. "With a man's needs."

We have been talking so long that the earpiece of the phone is sticking to my ear. "Mother," I say, "please don't worry. I'm hardly in shape for it."

She doesn't laugh. "I look at Mrs. Garvey, and I'm moved," she says. "Such strength of character. You should take it as a lesson. Before I hang up, I want to tell you about something I read, if you don't mind."

My mother loves to offer information, and has raised me in the tradition. We constantly repeat movie plots, offer authoritative statistics from television news specials. "What did you read, Mother?" I ask.

"There is a man who is studying the Holocaust," she says. "He makes a graph. One axis is fulfillment/despair, and the other is success/failure. That means that there are four groups of people—those who are fulfilled by success, whom we can understand, and those who are despairing even though they're successful, like so many people we know, and those who are despairing because they're failures. Then there's the fourth group—the people who are fulfilled by failure, who don't need hope to live. Do you know who those people are?"

"Who?" I ask.

"Those people," my mother says, "are the ones who survived."

There is a long, intentional silence.

"I thought you should know," she says, "that I am now standing outside, on the back porch. I can go as far as seven hundred feet from the house."

Recently I've been thinking often about something terrible I did when I was a child—something which neither I nor Mother has ever really gotten over. I did it when I was six years old. One day at school my older sister, Mary Elise, asked me to tell Mother that she was going to a friend's house for the afternoon to play with some new Barbie dolls. I was mad at Mother that day, and jealous of Mary Elise. When I got home, Mother was feeding the cat, and without even saying hello (she was mad at me for some reason, too) she ordered me to take out the garbage. I was filled with rage, both at her and my sister, whom I was convinced she favored. And then I came up with an awful idea. "Mother," I said, "I have something to tell you." She turned around. Her distracted face suddenly focused on me. I realized I had no choice but to finish what I'd started. "Mary Elise died today," I said. "She fell off the jungle gym and split her head open."

At first she just looked at me, her mouth open. Then her eyes—I remember this distinctly—went in two different directions. For a brief moment, the tenuousness of everything—the house, my life, the universe—became known to me, and I had a glimpse of how easily the fragile network could be exploded.

Mother started shaking me. She was making noises but she couldn't speak. The minute I said the dreaded words I started to cry; I couldn't find a voice to tell her the truth. She kept shaking me. Finally I managed to gasp, "I'm lying, I'm lying. It's not true." She stopped shaking me, and hoisted me up into the air. I closed my eyes and held my breath, imagining she might hurl me down against the floor. "You monster," she whispered. "You little bastard," she whispered between clenched teeth. Her face was twisted, her eyes glistening. She hugged me very fiercely and then she threw me onto her lap and started to spank me. "You monster, you monster," she screamed between sobs. "Never scare me like that again, never scare me like that again."

By the time Mary Elise got home, we were composed. Mother had made me swear I'd never tell her what had happened, and I never have. We had an understanding, from then on, or perhaps we had a secret. It has bound us together, so that now we are much closer to each other than either of us is to Mary Elise, who married a lawyer and moved to Hawaii.

The reason I cannot forget this episode is because I have seen, for the second time, how easily apocalypse can happen. That look in Alden's eyes, the moment before the accident, was a look I'd seen before.

"I hear you're from another planet," I say to Nina after we finish dinner.

She doesn't blink. "I assumed you'd find out sooner or later," she says. "But, Mother, can you understand that I didn't want to hurt you?"

I was expecting confessions and tears.. Nina's sincerity surprises me. "Nina," I say, trying to affect maternal authority, "tell me what's going on."

Nina smiles. "In the Fourth Millennium," she says, "when it was least expected, the Brolian force attacked the city of Landruz, on the planet Abdur. Chaos broke loose all over. The star-worms escaped from the zoo. It soon became obvious that the community would not survive the attack. Izmul, the father of generations, raced to his space-cruiser. It was the only one in the city. Hordes crowded to get on board, to escape the catastrophe and the star-worms, but only a few hundred managed. Others clung to the outside of the ship as it took off and were blown across the planet by its engines. The space-cruiser broke through the atmosphere just as the bomb hit. A hundred people were cast out into space. The survivors made it to a small planet, Dandril, and settled there. These are my origins."

She speaks like an oracle, not like anything I might have given birth to. "Nina," I say, "*I* am your origin."

She shakes her head. "I am a surveyor. It was decided that I should be born in earthly form so that I could observe your planet and gather knowledge for the rebuilding of our world. I was generated in your womb while you slept. You can't remember the conception."

"I remember the exact night," I say. "Daddy and I were in San Luis Obispo for a convention."

Nina laughs. "It happened in your sleep," she says. "An invisible ray. You never felt it."

What can I say to this? I sit back and try to pierce through her with a stare. She isn't even looking at me. Her eyes are focused on a spot of green caught in the night outside the window.

"I've been receiving telepathic communications," Nina says. "My people will be coming any time to take me, finally, to where I belong. You've been good to this earthly shell, Mother. For that, I thank you. But you must understand and give me up. My people are shaping a new civilization on Dandril. I must go and help them."

"I understand," I say.

She looks at me quizzically. "It's good, Mother," Nina says. "Good that you've come around." She reaches toward me, and kisses my cheek. I am tempted to grab her the way a mother is supposed to grab a child—by the shoulders, by the scruff of the neck; tempted to bend her to my will, to spank her, to hug her.

But I do nothing. With the look of one who has just been informed of her own salvation, the earthly shell I call Nina walks out the screen door, to sit on the porch and wait for her origins.

. . .

Mother calls me again in the morning. "I'm in the garden," she says, "looking at the sweetpeas. Now I'm heading due west, toward where those azaleas are planted."

She is preparing the Christmas newsletter, wants information from my branch of the family. "Mother," I say, "it's March. Christmas is months away." She is unmoved. Lately, this business of recording has taken on tremendous importance in her life; more and more requires to be saved.

"I wonder what the Garveys will write this year," she says. "You know, I just wonder what there is to say about something like that. Oh my. There he is now, Mr. Garvey, talking to the paper boy. Yes, when I think of it, there have been signs all along. I'm waving to him now. He's waving back. Remember, don't you, what a great interest he took in the Shepards' son, getting him scholarships and all? What if they decided to put it all down in the newsletter? It would be embarrassing to read."

As we talk, I watch Nina, sitting in the dripping spring garden, rereading *The Lion, the Witch and the Wardrobe*. Every now and then she looks up at the sky, just to check, then returns to her book. She seems at peace.

"What should I say about your family this year?" Mother asks. I wish I knew what to tell her. Certainly nothing that could be typed onto purple paper, garnished with little pencil drawings of holly and wreaths. And yet, when I read them over, those old newsletters have a terrible, swift power, each so innocent of the celebrations and catastrophes that the next year's letter will record. Where will we be a year from today? What will have happened then? Perhaps Mother won't be around to record these events; perhaps I won't be around to read about them.

"You can talk about Charles," I say. "Talk about how he's inventing an artificial imagination."

"I must be at least seven hundred feet from the house now," Mother says. "Can you hear me?"

Her voice is crackly with static, but still audible.

"I'm going to keep walking," Mother says. "I'm going to keep walking until I'm out of range."

That night in San Luis Obispo, Alden—can you remember it? Charles was already so self-sufficient then, happily asleep in the little room off ours. We planned that night to have a child, and I remember feeling sure that it would happen. Perhaps it was the glistening blackness outside the hotel room window, or the light rain, or the heat. Perhaps it was the kind of night when spaceships land and aliens prowl, fascinated by all we take for granted.

There are some anniversaries that aren't so easy to commemorate. This one, for instance: one year since we almost died. If I could reach you, Alden, in the world behind your eyes, I'd ask you a question: Why did you turn off the road? Was it whim, the sudden temptation of destroying both of us for no reason? Or did you hope the car would bear wings and engines, take off into the atmosphere, and propel you—us—in a split second, out of the world?

I visit you after lunch. Joe doesn't bother to say hello, and though I kiss you on the forehead, you, too, choose not to speak. "Why so glum?" I ask. "Dehydrated egg bits for breakfast again?"

You reach into the drawer next to your bed, and hand me a key. I help you out, into your bathrobe, into the hall. We must be quiet. When no nurses are looking, I hurry us into a small room where sheets and hospital gowns are stored. I turn the key in the lock, switch on the light.

We make a bed of sheets on the floor. We undress; and then, Alden, I begin to make love to you—you, atop me, clumsy and quick as a teenager. I try to slow you down, to coach you in the subtleties of love, the way a mother teaches a child to walk. You have to relearn this language as well, after all.

Lying there, pinned under you, I think that I am grateful for gravity, grateful that a year has passed and the planet has not yet broken loose from its tottering orbit. If nothing else, we hold each other down.

You look me in the eyes and try to speak. Your lips circle the unknown word, your brow reddens and beads with sweat. "What, Alden?" I ask. "What do you want to say? Think a minute." Your lips move aimlessly. A drop of tearwater, purely of its own accord, emerges from the marbled eye, snakes along a crack in your skin.

I stare at the ruined eye. It is milky white, mottled with blue and gray streaks; there is no pupil. Like our daughter, Alden, the eye will have nothing to do with either of us. I want to tell you it looks like the planet Dandril, as I imagine it from time to time—that ugly little planet where even now, as she waits in the garden, Nina's people are coming back to life.

RAND BURKERT

The Stone Inscription of Caleb Pellor

N o t e : The following account is the work of Caleb Pellor, one of the reclusive inhabitants of Pellor County. It is scratched upon the surface of a limestone ridge, ninety-thousand and forty-one railroad ties west of Edsel City, and a day's walk due south of Trago's Gas. The silhouette of Mr. Pellor, burned into the rock, must suffice for a vague portrait of the author. He is tall and skeletal, with a cloud of hair hovering about his head; in his upraised right hand, distinctly shadowed in white on the charred lime, he holds a roller skate key.

I

My grandparents remember the days of abundance, one hundred years ago, when the train brought bundles in the winter, every winter, to supplement our diet of snakes.

Each bundle came with a label.

"This is MACKEREL. You will find it useful to you."

"This is RHUBARB. You will find it useful to you."

Each year only one thing came, in no great quantity, but Grandma and Grandpa never complained. Mackerel or Rhubarb was enough to sustain them for a year until the next bundle came. Their minds, not their stomachs, wanted food; snakes abounded in Pellor County, even throughout the winter, but Grandma and Grandpa craved new words with a perennial hunger: VENISON, WHEAT, CORN.

They met on the tail end of the year of SHIRTS. The delicacy had proven inedible, but useful nonetheless, as the label had promised. Still, autumn had come, and the word was stale.

Grandpa had a big white sheet tied between four cacti. He lay on his back in the shade, watching flies buzzing in the rippling heat. Grandma came running after a rattlesnake, jumped long-limbed over a rock, and Grandpa sat up. She had on one of the long-tailed white shirts from the train, and nothing else.

"Hey good-looking."

She stopped up short, and the snake tried hiding in Grandpa's shade. Courteously, Grandpa grabbed it by the scaly throat and squeezed, and the poison came out in opalescent drops on his thumb.

"I caught him for you good."

She knew just looking at him he was the rich man. For one thing, he had his sheet. All of the other Pellors slept under the biggest saguaro they could find. The width of a cactus shadow was normally sufficient to accommodate most Pellors, who had adapted to rolling clockwise in their sleep during the day, to evade the creeping sun.

Grandpa's sheet had blown out of the east in a windstorm. He'd seen it coming at him, swooping like a vulture out of the whirling sand and dust, had grabbed it with the quick wrist of a hunter. The sheet curled and lashed, but he wrestled back, and when the windstorm died he had himself a house, the envy of all Pellor County.

He said to Grandma, "You can come in here if you like, and eat your snake."

"I know you Mr. Wesley Pellor," she said, "you're a rake and you fancy yourself one and I wouldn't share the shade of a plain cactus with you, let alone your fancy house, luxury though it is and tempting too—"

Grandpa flayed the snake.

"That's my snake," she said.

"I know it is." He knocked a spark into a pile of splinters from a railroad tie, and blew.

"You're cooking my snake."

"That's right." The splinters blazed. He looked over at Grandma; she was sitting on a rock, flushed red and angry.

"You know," he said, not even expecting to say it, "I'd give you more SHIRTS than we've been given."

"Don't say that."

"It's true."

Shirts were considered the best thing in Pellor County at that time. But the words caught in my Grandpa's throat when he tried to say them again. He felt a sickly pressure in his lungs, and prayed that the train would come soon with a new bundle, a better word.

"I would give you more—"

Sunsets? That was an old trick: red fading to lavender on the horizon and the old line bartered for trust, "I would give you a whole lot of sunsets." He didn't have the heart, for that.

She sat still on her rock, staring at her bare toes.

"Give me my snake," she said.

He held out the white fibers of rattlesnake flesh steaming on a flat gray stone. She walked away wagging her head, confused, tugging her white tails down around her knees.

"Shirt," Grandpa muttered. He lay back and let his feet singe a little in the fire.

Lucky man, his train came the next day. October noon,

and all of the Pellors except Grandpa baked in the ineluctable sun, when someone shouted from the ridge, "It's here!"

The children raced first, to snatch their morsel of danger, laying their heads on the track and counting each others' courage, then scattering in joy and fright when the train drew near.

An arm extended from the red caboose—whether fleshly or angelic no one could tell—and dropped a bundle on the tracks while the train sped on, whistling and clanging to regale us with its rare voice.

These are *CIGARS*. They will be useful to you.

Eager hands ripped the bag and Cigars poured out across the tracks. My Grandpa took the bag and the label, and his share of the Cigars. When he laid eyes on Grandma, he offered her everything. He could hardly breathe for the pleasure of repeating the phrase: "I would give you more CIGARS than we have been given, more CIGARS than we have been given I would give."

The moon that night: a whiter circle on the pale white sheet. Flowers opened on the four green corners of the house: sly saguaro, or shy. Grandma, unaccustomed to Grandpa's grand way of life, rolled a half-circle in her sleep.

She woke with the sun in her eyes and her footsoles straight in line with his, and took it as a good sign—if she had spent the whole night sleeping, she would have completed the whole circle, and awakened at his side.

II

Colonel Fletcher Pellor came from the east with a bible, a compass, and a canteen. The Afwatapankoy Indian region was an olive-shaded square on his map called "The Cavity of Pestilence." He hoped only to survive.

Now we are all half Pellor, half Afwatapankoy Indian. Our religion is a felicitous wedding of two doomed strains. We place our faith in both Christ and snakes, in both what we want to be, and what we want to eat.

"Be like Christ. Be grateful for snakes."

My mother was a religious woman in her spare time, the first preacher of the era of planes, when the bundles began to fall from the sky.

As children we would play our game of dare whenever we heard the roaring engines come. We'd spread out on the sand, all across the county, and when the roar became loud we'd cringe. Only one person died this way, my brother Ned.

These are APRICOTS. You will find them useful to you.

Father pulled the heavy bag from off of Ned, who looked the same as he always did, except still.

Mother cried a long time, soaking Ned in the brine of her eyes. Everyone waited frozen at a respectful distance, in a circle. Father patted her hair with his big hands. "He had as quick a wrist as the best," he said, "a sheet-grabbing wrist like your father's, Hannah, a wrist like the best."

No one even opened the bundle until my mother stood straight again, with a half-smile, and said, "Be like Christ. Be grateful for the gifts of the air. Be grateful for these APRICOTS," and looking over her shoulder at the quavering, hot sand she added, "Be grateful for snakes."

That night we buried Ned between the four cacti where Grandpa had kept his house before his sheet had crumbled into crisp brown dust in the sun. Walking away from the grave, Father said, "I would give—" and Mother snapped, "I know."

The unspoken word ached inside my father, and about this time he became a mystic, prone to dancing alone on the ridgetop and talking in his sleep, to God. He had an idea he would go to the place where the bundles were made, and carry back the words of the next thousand years.

One day he called everybody to the railroad track; he was grieved to see that Mother hadn't come, but the other Pellors listened intently to his revelation.

"Now let's say where I'm standing on this particular railroad tie is the here and now."

He jumped once and the tie rocked a little, to make itself known.

"Here you say to your honey, you'd give her more APRICOTS than you have been given. It's the sweetest thing you know how to say. Girls, you say the same and everything's fine, because you both know what you mean, namely, you want to give each other sustenance. And I don't mean just food, right?"

Now he put one toe on the next railroad tie west.

"Let's just imagine that this here tie is another year, and all of these ties going thisaway are the years of the past. Then if you go far enough like I'm doing now, not too far, you'll be standing on the year where Colonel Fletcher married our Great Mother. And what did she say?"

I raised my hand but he didn't call on me; someone else got to answer, my best friend Roy whose father owned Colonel Fletcher's bible.

"She said, 'I'd give you more snakes than we have been given,' and she gave him a snake."

"Good! Now you can see we've all got to be grateful for snakes. And the lucky thing is, we've got a whole lot more to be grateful for."

"The gifts of the air," I yelled.

"That's right," he said, striding east again, toward the future, taking more than one year at a stride, "all of the very useful gifts down through Apricots."

He stopped on the wrong tie, and Roy let him know it. "You're standing in the future!" he screamed.

Father looked up slyly. "I know," he said.

"I know the future."

We all gasped. Mother made a lot of racket out behind him, scaring up a snake.

"Now I've given this a lot of thought, and I've decided it wouldn't be right to tell you what lies ahead down this here track since God has chosen to reveal everything to us in his own way, and I'd be interfering wrongly in the way progress is supposed to progress. But I want you all to know that the future is going to be sweet, just as Apricots is sweeter than Snakes, just as Snakes is sweeter than whatever the hell came before."

We all cheered.

"And there's one more thing. I want all of you people, when there's trouble between you, to come to me, if the year's word has gone stale. Then and if that's the case I might reveal the future, because there's no sense any of us being sad when there's so many sweet words to be said down this way." He turned reverently to the east, and knelt at the portal of our future happiness. Not so far away Mother hacked savagely at her snake, shouting "Yah! Yah! Yah!"

That night I saw the silhouettes of Mother and Father on the ridgetop, and because of the echo I could hear Father murmuring urgently, "I would give you more GALADRIARHANAS than we will be given."

Poor Mother! She couldn't thrill to a future she couldn't see, and her voice floated down wan and slivered, like the moon: "I don't know what that is."

"It's a sphere like the sun, golden iridescent green like a beetle's back; it sings when you blow on it, and it's taste is unimaginably good, believe me Hannah, it is."

But October brought no Galadriarhanas.

These are MUNG BEANS. You will find them useful to you.

Father cracked a Mung Bean between his teeth and grimaced; it was the birth of disappointment, but also of idealism.

"They should of brought Galadriarhanas," he mumbled,

"but it stands to reason they didn't. Galadriarhanas are just too good for this earth. So they sent the next best thing, and these Mung Beans are just the merest symbol of the Galadriarhanas that exist in heaven, and much to be grateful for because they're the best we can have."

So my parents concurred, in a manner of speaking, and they both said, "Be like Christ, a Child of God. Be grateful for these MUNG BEANS. And be grateful for snakes, and all of the gifts of the air."

It was a year of groans in the night; they echoed off the ridge, from cacti where the neighbors lived, and meteors hissed like anger in the sky.

Roy's father, Mr. Randolph Pellor, came to my father for help. It troubled him that Lucille Pellor, his wife, seemed to regard him as the backbone or discarded molt of a rattler, something to sidestep with nostrils curled.

"The problem is, we're all damn sick and tired of saying Mung Beans, a word we all sniggered at and despised, frankly, from the very first day—"

"Well the fact of the matter is," said my father, leaning toward him and whispering confidentially, "those Mung Beans are only the earthly representations of heaven's own Galadriarhanas."

The news was all over Pellor County the next day, and above the constant hum of locusts and flies I could hear another, more tuneful: "I would give you more GALADRIARHANAS than we have been given; more GALADRIARHANAS than we have been given I would give."

III

Next October brought a victory for Mother, for realism and the old, simple faith, when that year's heavy bundle fell with a loud metallic rattle and clunk.

These are ROLLER SKATES. You will find them useful to you.

Father said, "These in no way resemble their heavenly counterparts the Altalenas, but they are extraordinary all the same and much to be grateful for."

But what were they? We nibbled; they weren't for eating. We spun the wheels on our palms, and listened. Then Roy sat down and pulled them on over his feet. When he stood up, the wheels dug into the sand.

"They're for walking," he said, "when there's a high wind."

I saw myself sharing the dignity of the saguaro, standing tall and defiant with dust and locusts flying past me and my hair flapping in the gale: my feet firmly rooted to the sand and soil. In my mind I lifted one foot high, and plugged it down upwind, not to let the storm gain ground. The beautiful gift of Roller Skates! Mother said, "Be like Christ; be grateful for these ROLLER SKATES," and we were.

It was the happiest year. We had festive gatherings, cactus-jumping competitions and snake-flaying relays. In the summer, Father got everybody together by the railroad, so we could all learn our history and see how it progressed from good to better.

Grandpa got to talk about Cigars. He kept losing his balance and gaining it on the wrong tie, and someone would yell, "That's Shirts you're standing on," or "That's Ham!"

"Though I may not," he said, "my life stands firmly on Cigars." He winked at Grandma, and we all clapped. "Ochre like a sheet fried in the sun. Two tips, one fat, one thin. Makes you cough, happy. Dried runt offshoot of a cactus, maybe, without the needles. You light one end on fire, the fat one. Glows orange, black ash, smoke. Aroma like—like something burning. I can't hardly remember now. Warms you up. That's a Cigar."

Lucille Pellor got to do Ham.

"Comes strung, a big soft rock. Inside there's meat: salt pink sky with cirrus clouds of fat. That's Ham."

Father handled the thorny problem of Mung Beans tactfully, without offending God or men: "Radiant Galadriarhanas in the plain green pauper's weeds of earthly incarnation. Taste like dirt, earth's answer to water vapor. Mung Beans."

But there our history ended, for the present. Our satisfaction spoke itself in the soft whirr of Roller Skate wheels and the gratitude of my Mother's prayer. Then Roy's father read what he could from Colonel Fletcher's bible, a little brown pill of paper that shed flakes whenever he'd turn a page; Grandpa said he'd smoke that bible if he had half a chance.

"The wilderness and the dry land shall be glad, the desert shall rejoice and blossom; like the crocus it shall blossom abundantly, and rejoice with joy and singing."

IV

One night a tremor shook the ground, and drove the snakes from hiding, with the year's crisp, translucent skin beginning to crack away, and their unclosing eyes blinded by blue milk: self-blinded, not to know their own bareness. Blind snakes scurrying in fear from the omnipresent football, as if the earth itself was a hungry man, and the tremor, a spasm of hot pursuit. Where could they go? Under a rock the earth shook; under all other rocks it shook as well. The snakes beat a harrowing zig and zag on crackling bellies until, inspired by terror, they sought the only refuge left to them, and stood on end.

Little, balanced poles with turquoise eyes upraised, importuning the moon: We are blind, receive us. How did it feel, I wondered, to be betrayed by the warm, placid earth? I thought of the saguaro with its arms flung high, of my father dancing and jumping on the ridgetop, scraping silver flakes from heaven, the words to come.

This is CHEESE. You will find it useful to you.

There were yellow chunks with crevices full of nacreous ooze, orange piles sloppy with purple and green mold, and a few clean, smooth slices that tasted metallic, like railroad spikes. When we first opened the bag, unfamiliar insects clambered down from the Cheese to try their legs on desert soil.

Father said, "This Cheese has not been made disgusting for no purpose, but to make us look to its more glorious counterpart in heaven, Hariasannaroo."

Mother said, "Be like Christ. Be grateful for snakes. Be grateful for this CHEESE. And most of all, remember the Roller Skates."

We all trudged heavily home, ashamed of our ingratitude, but consoling each other with nostalgia, as Mother had proposed.

"But Roller Skates, now!"

"Ah, Roller Skates!"

Only my father stayed behind in the hot sun, kneeling beside the rancid bundle, picking through the pile of orange-yellow slag and nibbling, to feed his memory for history lessons to come. He was still there at sunset, and when Mother brought him food he said, "No, Hannah, this Cheese is good." But that night we saw his contorted outline on the ridgetop, and heard him retching; and he may have decided then that only heavenly food would ever feed his yearning, because when we climbed up the bluff the next morning, we found him dead.

I missed his voice. I listened for it until I had nightmares of hearing: shouts and whistles, screeches and long oscillating wails, clatters and slams, but never my father's voice, never again his sweet assurance that our lives rolled inexorably, happily, east. Then the noise of my nightmare ruptured a blue haze, and I saw things, as well: a canyon of flat gray walls, smoother than the ridge, and a line of multicolored beetles rolling, and a railroad track arched in a smoky sky. Father, smiling or grimacing, floated gracefully along the track on Roller Skates, and I listened for his voice.

That was the inspiration for my civic project. We pried up railroad ties in the western end of Pellor County and laid them in between the gaps of other ties to make a smooth run, and I put on my Roller Skates to rejuvenate the word: ROLLER SKATE. When I got through, the word had all the shine of the first day.

"I would give you more ROLLER SKATES than we have been given."

I would give you the power to command a cooling wind: to make the world rush toward you as I will, and embrace you: to discover the smooth flight of birds and transfix me with your grace, the fluid motion of your limbs.

V

This is DUNG. You will find it useful to you.

Mother had a stone-gray look on her face, and she said, "Be like Christ, a Child of God. Be grateful for this DUNG. Be grateful for snakes. Remember the Roller Skates."

We needed Father to glorify the word. We stared at the mound of Dung that had burst from the bag, and were silent.

By April, the mound sprouted yellow crocuses and grasses I had never seen; by August the moisture of the Dung had been consumed, and the little hill shriveled to a brown measle in the sand. It might have been a grave for our gratitude, if we hadn't had Roller Skates to buck our spirits and give us hope, as we glided west between the steel rails, that October would prove my father right again.

This is DUNG. You will find it useful to you.

Another little hill sent up its unfamiliar shoots and crocuses. We all hoped, my Mother hoped, that they would live,
but they died: curled up brown by July.

We haven't bothered to count the years. Step among the
saguaros at night when it is cool, and count the tuberculous
lumps in the sand and soil.

VI

I was there when Colonel Fletcher's bible gave up the ghost
for good.

Roy had the little thing cupped in his hand. There were
only a few words left on each page, but he had all the rest
memorized.

The book said, "Your rounded—"

"Thighs are like jewels," said Roy, and I added lustily,
"the work of a master hand!"

I was only sixteen and he was nineteen, and he was reading for all the good reasons and I was reading for lust.

"Your two," said the book.

"Breasts!" I said, and Roy scowled, and continued: "are
like two fawns, twins of a gazelle."

A windstorm hit us then, came over the ridge before we
could hide. Roy said, "It's your fault," and we both crouched
by a rock, Roy shielding the bible between clenched hands.
Still, the wind swept in between his fine, bony fingers, and the
bible buzzed against his palms like a locust, flustered and
inceased. Roy thought fast, and tried to slip the little bible into
his mouth. It was a good idea, but the wind beat him, blew the
words of God into a place even safer; they slammed against
his epiglottis with the force of damnation and he might have
choked, if he hadn't swallowed.

Roy was the most moral fellow I knew. He didn't blame
me to his father, and he told the truth.

"Father," he said, "I cannot tell a lie. I swallowed that bible in the windstorm."

"It's all right, son. You done all right."

Roy had a desperate need for that bible the next year, when he met Flora Pellor and said, "I would give you more bibles than we were given," and she said, "What's that?"

He sat her down on the ridge for a week, and recited the entire bible by memory. I brought up food every day, but he never ate much of it, and after a while he ceased to notice whether Flora was listening or not. She slept at night and he didn't.

Flora heard the Creation and the Fall and then she snoozed; she woke up for the Flood but fell asleep before the Covenant. When she woke up again the Children of Israel were slaves of the Pharaoh, and it disturbed her that the Lord hardened Pharaoh's heart, so that he would not let the Children of Israel go out of his land. Then she fell asleep.

The dark circles under Roy's eyes rippled out until his entire face was gray. But his eyes remained bright blue, and he spoke clearly; I often sat at the bottom of the ridge and listened to the drone of his words and Flora's gentle snore. She was wide awake when God let Satan afflict Job with boils, and then she must have fallen asleep; she later told me it was a damn shame Job had been nailed by a sack of Dung and hadn't received a better burial. Then she woke up again and again, horrified to hear that Jesus had been crucified, again.

"Stop," she said, "I've heard enough!"

But Roy kept on to the end: scalding bowls of pestilence and then "The grace of our Lord Jesus Christ be with you all. Amen."

"That is the bible," he said. "I would give you more of them than exist in the world."

"No thank you!" she said.

"Will you marry me?"

"You're a pessimist and a bore."

Oh Mother!—I thought, still sitting at the base of the ridge, "Shield me from what Roy is feeling now!" Roy had swallowed his bible; but the scattered, shattered pieces of my Roller Skates had been swallowed by the sand.

Roy became a hermit, and painted the gifts of the air on the walls of his cave, with blue fluid from the eyes of molting snakes. "I paint them and they're gone," he said. "The color is fugitive."

"I'm going to become a hermit too!" I said.

"Find your own cave."

VII

One hand on my shoulder, gray hair brushing my face, eyes peering down in the violet dawn, my mother:

"I worry about you Caleb."

"Why?"

"You've been whimpering in the night."

"I have?"

"Yes."

"So have you!"

Mother and I broke into peals of laughter, seared the October morning so that the sun spilled out on the track and made the steel rails gleam.

That day a bundle fell, and we ambled toward the spot where it had landed, in no great hurry to find out what it was.

"Dung again," I said.

"Be grateful," she muttered—her abbreviated grace. "Oh Caleb," she said, hugging me tightly, "I would give you anything there was, anything that might be. But that won't help you Caleb, I know. A time *will* come; and you'll have to say whatever words you can."

She stopped herself and walked on in silence a little, swinging my hand in hers.

Then she let go.

"I won't fear for you," she said.

In the spring, I chased a rattler to the base of a tall saguaro where a girl sat grinning in the sun. She grabbed the snake by the throat and squeezed; it gagged.

"I caught him for you," she said, and she began to flay my snake. "That's my snake," I said.

"I know it is."

"I'll do that myself, thank you."

She kept working, and paid me no mind. Her arms were strong, her eyes brightly laughing. "Will you give me that?" I asked.

"No."

I lunged, and she ran away along the railroad track. What a runner she was! I fought to catch up with her, and for a moment I imagined we were skating.

VIII

"I would give you more ROLLER SKATES than we have been given."

"What are they?"

I rutted in the soil for fragments of leather, hollow wheels stuffed with dust and the metal frame skeletons of Roller Skates, and I sat like an idiot running fingers through the pile of junk in my lap, as if that would conjure what I needed, the gift as it had been given from the air. My fingers were bleeding, and my eyes were bloodshot from scrabbling in the dark, and Mother said, "Say what you can, Caleb, and don't be driving me and yourself insane."

So I went and sat with Emma under the tall saguaro, meaning to be cheerful but behaving like a stone. I stuttered, "I would give," and stopped.

"Yes?"

"I would give you more DUNG than we have been given."

She smiled, and gently touched my arm. I felt sick, thinking of my father retching on the ridgetop. But then the nausea passed, and we were happy.

Now there have been no more tremors of the earth; I have not seen the snakes standing on end again, and we are hoping, can only hope, for something better from the sky.

I have heard the roaring of engines, and now the children have scurried out to lie, squinting, on their backs, hoping for something better from the sky.

ROBIN HEMLEY

Riding the Whip

THE NIGHT BEFORE my sister died, a friend of my parents, Natalie Ganzer, took me and her niece to a carnival. I couldn't stand Natalie, but I fell in love with the niece, a girl about fifteen, named Rita. On the ferris wheel Rita grabbed my hand. On any other ride I would have thought she was only frightened and wanted security. But this ferris wheel was so tame and small. There was nothing to be afraid of at fifty feet.

When we got down and the man let us out of the basket, I kept hold of Rita's hand, and she didn't seem to mind.

"Oh, I'm so glad you children are enjoying the evening," said Natalie. "It's so festive. There's nothing like a carnival, is there?"

Normally, I would have minded being called a child, but not tonight. Things were improving. There was nothing to worry about, my mother had told me over the phone earlier that evening. Yes, Julie had done a stupid thing, but only to get attention.

Still, there was something wrong, something that bugged me about that night, where I was, the carnival and its sounds. I was having too much fun and I knew I shouldn't be. Already, I had won a stuffed animal from one of the booths and given it to Rita. And usually I got nauseated on rides, but tonight they just made me laugh. Red neon swirled around on the rides and barkers yelled at us on the fairway. Popguns blew holes in targets, and there were so many people screaming and laughing that I could hardly take it in. I just stood there feeling everyone else's fun moving through me, and I could hardly hear what Rita and Natalie were asking me. "Come on, Jay," shouted Rita. My hand was being tugged. "Let's ride The Whip." The whip. That didn't make any sense to me. A whip wasn't something you rode. It was something to hurt you, something from movies that came down hard on prisoners' backs and left them scarred.

"You can't ride a whip," I shouted to her over the noise.

She laughed and said, "Why not? Don't be scared. You won't get sick. I promise."

"Aren't you having fun, Jay?" Natalie asked. "Your parents want you to have fun, and I'm sure that's what Julie wants too."

I didn't answer, though I was having fun. Things seemed brighter and louder than a moment before. I could even hear a girl on the ferris wheel say to someone, "You're cute, did you know that?" One carny in his booth stood out like a detail in a giant painting. He held a bunch of strings in his hand. The strings led to some stuffed animals. "Everyone's a winner," he said.

The carnival was just a painting, a bunch of petals in a bowl, which made me think of Julie. She was an artist and painted still lifes mostly, but she didn't think she was any good. My parents had discouraged her, but I bought a large painting of hers once with some paper money I cut from a notebook. A week before the carnival, she came into my room and slashed the painting to bits. "She's not herself," my mother told me. "You know she loves you."

Now we stood at the gates of The Whip. Rita gave her stuffed animal to Natalie, who stood there holding it by the paw as though it were a new ward of hers. The man strapped us into our seat and Rita said to me, "You're so quiet. Aren't you having fun?"

"Sure," I said. "Doesn't it look like it?"

"Your sister's crazy, isn't she?" asked Rita. "I mean, doing what she did."

I knew I shouldn't answer her, that I should step out of the ride and go home.

"She just sees things differently," I said.

"What do you mean?" Rita asked. She was looking at me strangely, as though maybe I saw things differently too. I didn't want to see differently. I didn't want to become like my sister.

"Sure she's crazy," I said. "I don't even care what happens to her."

Then the ride started up and we laughed and screamed. We moved like we weren't people anymore, but changed into electrical currents charging from different sources.

In the middle of the ride something grazed my head. There was a metal bar hanging loose along one of the corners, and each time we whipped around it, the bar touched me. It barely hit me, but going so fast it felt like I was being knocked with a sandbag. It didn't hit anyone else, just me, and I tried several times to get out of the way, but I was strapped in, and there was no way to avoid it.

At the end of the ride I was totally punch-drunk and I could barely speak. Rita, who mistook my expression for one of pleasure, led me over to Natalie.

"That was fun," said Rita. "Let's go on The Cat and Mouse now."

My vision was blurry and my legs were wobbling a bit. "I want to go on The Whip again," I said.

Natalie and Rita looked at each other. Natalie reached out toward my head, and I pulled back from her touch. "You're *bleeding*, Jay," she said. Her hand stayed in mid-air, and she looked at me as though she were someone in a gallery trying to get a better perspective on a curious painting.

I broke away from them into the crowd and made my way back to The Whip. After paying the man I found the same seat. I knew which one it was because it was more beat up than the rest, with several gashes in its cushion, as though someone had taken a long knife and scarred it that way on purpose.

MICHELLE CARTER

Teacher

CARTER IS SAYING that his sister Linda called today. Linda lives in Exwife's apartment complex and calls Carter every time Exwife flosses her teeth.

I can feel the bartender's eyes on me from across the room. I remembered to chalk and pencil my birth date before we left but it scares the hell out of me to have to hand over a faked license, especially to bartenders as tough-looking as this one. She must be in her sixties and she's got her hair in these two icy gray-blonde braids that hang down almost to her elbows.

"Judy's battery goes dead yesterday," Carter says, "late afternoon. Around dinnertime this triple-A truck pulls in and the guy goes up the stairs looking for Judy's apartment."

I'm glad it's sort of dark. We've never been in this bar before, but one of Carter's guitar students said it had a great jukebox so we had to check it out. There's a lot of weird stuff on the walls, stuff that must have been real racy years ago. Fat women doing exercises naked. Nixon naked, hitchhiking. But there's a nice rosy glow from the neon beer displays behind the bar and all around the room. There's a flickering Budweiser sign and an Olympia one with a glowing green forest and a golden river through it. But most of them are for beers I've never heard of before.

Carter starts cracking peanuts that he pulls one by one from the bag that's ripped open and lying between us. He pulls them apart, lets the nuts drop onto one pile, throws the shells into another.

Carter just turned thirty-five. He's acting funny these days, but he'll get around it. I remember last semester when I walked into senior writing class at Gill High and first saw him, standing up there. I said to myself right away: that's got to be the prettiest beard I ever saw. And then second, after listening to him talk for a minute and then play a few songs to get us acquainted, songs that sounded like magic: this is a man who could change a life.

"This morning Linda decides to go for a run," he says. "She goes downstairs. Eight A.M. The tow truck's still there."

A man about the bartender's age walks in carrying a big square TV box. A woman trails close behind wearing the same kind of heavy coat that he's got on, the same close-cropped hair, greasy, like they comb it with buttered toast or something. The bartender nods to them, scoops ice into two glasses, and sets them on one end of the bar. The old couple sits down by the glasses and the bartender fills them almost full with scotch, adds a spritz of soda.

"*Eight* A.M.," Carter says, slow and even. "A tow truck, rig and all, out there all night for all the world to see."

He's looking down at his drink now, saying almost to it more than to me, "Tow-truck drivers. Jesus Christ."

I ask Carter if I can eat one of his peanuts if he's just going to leave them lay. He doesn't answer so I help myself.

"Your Cheatin' Heart" comes on the jukebox. It seems real pathetic to me.

Carter wrote a song for Exwife once, just a couple months ago when I first started taking guitar lessons from him. It's called, "You Rub Me the Wrong Way Baby (But That's Better Than No Rubbin' at All)." He taught me how to play it, open D tuning, flat pick style. That was right around the time my brother Joe got picked up for dealing, and I know how hard it's been for my mother since Dad left, but I can't make up for Joe. I can't be good for two kids. And I know it's mean of me, but all I could say to her when I left was, "Forget it, Ma. Maybe you blew it, but I've got a man of my own to think about now."

You'll cry and cry, the whole night through, your cheatin' heart will tell on you. That line always makes me picture a little heart with its hands on its hips, screaming, hey out there, wait'll I tell you what she did *this* time. I giggle and then feel silly, because we just killed a pitcher and I don't want Carter to think I can't hold my beer.

The bartender is back to glaring at me. Her hair's drawn so tight around her face it's like those braids have stretched her smile into pure anger, wide and flat. It's like I've done her some wrong just by sitting here.

"She don't want me here," I say. It takes Carter a minute to register.

"Quit talking like some old blues picker," he finally says. "You know your grammar—what'd you get on that SAT test?" He's shaking a peanut shell at me. "Seven something, wasn't it? High seven-hundreds? You didn't used to talk like that."

I turn and stare hard at the bartender but she won't look away.

"Did you hear what I said to you?" I ask Carter.

"I heard you. Say it right. Doesn't, not don't."

"She doesn't want me here," I say.

"That's better," he says. "That's right."

Carter gets up to bring us another round. I tell him, scotch and soda, and he looks at me and looks at my beer mug, then shrugs.

The old couple at the end of the bar have still got their coats on. They've got a TV set up right in front of them, right in front of their drinks. The box sits empty on the floor by the man's feet.

I can see Carter talking quiet to the bartender now. I wonder if he's making excuses for me. I don't want to stare, but her eyes are still on me, I can feel it.

Carter sets our drinks down and I see that he's given up on beer too. His drink looks just like mine only fatter, and when I ask him why he says it's a double.

"I need it," he says.

I guess he really does, he's been acting so quirky. A couple weeks ago he packs off to this so-called seminar. Three days in Big Sur. Totally on the up-and-up, he tells me. It's run by the Workshops for the Eighties Foundation and it's called, "Music-Teach as Life-Style." And can you believe he pulls into the carport (after having holed up with this Joni Mitchell type from Eureka all weekend, missing almost all of those twenty-buck-an-hour classes), and I run out to meet the car and see this bumper-sticker, with each letter a different color and a rainbow arching over the words. It says, "Music is Entropy Spelled Backward." I look at it and I look at Carter and I say, Carter, entropy spelled backward is yportne, which was not exactly what I'd imagined my first words to him would be after our first separation.

Scotch doesn't taste like I thought it would. It tastes the way nail-polish remover smells.

"So Linda runs for twenty minutes or so, and she comes around the block of her apartment just in time to see Judy hop into the passenger seat of that rig, and him, the tire monkey, close the door, climb in the other side, and drive them both away out to tire-monkey heaven."

Somehow Carter's scotch is two-thirds gone. That was fast, I say, and when he doesn't answer I think he must not know what I mean, so I nod at the glass but he doesn't look up to see. He takes his notebook and pen from his back pocket and starts jotting something in it, business as usual, he's lost in a new lyric. I'm starting to get used to that now, though at first it hurt me sometimes. We'd be lying around maybe, or cuddling, and I'd be feeling happy and involved in the moment, maybe I'd be talking about how great things are going, and out of nowhere he'd break away and dive for the notebook he kept by the bed. It didn't bother me much until I started peeking once in a while and realized that nothing he wrote ever had a single thing to do with me.

It happened once when we were making love, I swear to God.

"I've been thinking, Carter," I say. "Have you ever thought of taking up running?"

Without raising his head he rolls his eyes way back to see me, which is sort of scary looking.

"I mean, you're always talking about how old you feel, like you're a hundred years old, for Chrissakes. Linda's about your age, and you were just saying about how she runs."

I wait but he doesn't answer. He's sending shivers up my spine.

"Stop looking at me like that," I say. "It's creepy."

He looks back down at his drink.

"Answer me," I say. "I hate it when you don't answer me."

"Linda's different," he says, and I can tell he thinks that's the end of it.

"Different how?" I say.

"She's married, for one thing. Just two years now."

"So what?"

"So she's a wife now, that's what. She's a young married woman in a young married apartment on a young married street on a young married planet."

He drains his glass—scotch, water, ice, all of it.

"And you, you're so different? What about you makes you so goddamn old?"

He stands up and looks down at me. He's not a tall man, but he seems high up right now.

"She's just starting a life," he says. "Babies. New toasters.

Plans for vacations two years from now. I," he stops for a second, "am a thirty-five-year-old up-and-coming kid-out-of-nowhere musician with a lot of promise. I have fit this description for," he closes his eyes, counts, "twenty years now. Giving lessons and teaching high school. Just for the time being."

He blows his nose on a cocktail napkin on his way to the bar.

An old black man in a checkered jacket is yelling from the far end of the counter at the couple with heavy coats. I think he wants them to turn the TV around so he can see, but they don't look up. There's a commercial on.

Carter's talking to the bartender again and making her laugh, which really gets me. For me he's moody, quiet, on the verge of depression half the time, but give him a sicko ax-murderer crazy-lady bartender and he's a regular Steve Martin. I get a big kick out of watching him though, when he isn't aware of it—it's like being some kind of Peeping Tom except that I just want to watch him walk around. Like when he's talking to people like this, or teaching, or playing in clubs. But there are other times too, when we're at home and it's dark except for a little glow from a streetlamp. When he turns out the light and it gets dark like that, I can open my eyes and watch him making love to me. I can trace the outlines of his shoulders, his neck, the soft hair that curls around his ears, and look into his eyes with the force of everything I feel. And he doesn't have to know.

"There's a story I've been wanting to tell you," he says when he gets back from the bar. "Because I'm your teacher," he adds, and laughs.

Both our glasses are half-empty when he sets them on the table. He's gotten us both doubles this time.

"I got to sipping on your drink too when I was talking to Emily over there," he says. He sits down hard, not quite in the center of the chair.

I start to say, what's this story about, but he shushes me and holds his palm out flat like Diana Ross singing "Stop in the Name of Love" on an old Ed Sullivan film clip. I'm sitting there and waiting and he's not moving or even looking at me, so after a minute I just turn away because it's making me sort of sad.

The beer signs are looking really pretty, glowing red and green and gold.

Budweiser.

Moosehead Ale.

Lone. Flash. Star. Flash.

I can't get it out of my head now. *Stop in the name of love, before you break my heart, think it oh-oh-ver.*

"That's Blind Lemon Jefferson," Carter says. "Only decent thing on this machine, though they've got some white kid singing it."

Carter sings along with the jukebox, "Nobody knows the way I feel this morning. Nobody knows the way I feel this morning."

"You want to know the first time I ever heard that one," he says. "I was just a kid, not much older than you, sitting in this bar somewhere in Wyoming." He tilts his head back. "Was it Wyoming, I don't know. But this song was playing on the box, only sung by somebody real, you know. That was some great bar, all these crusty old codgers matching shots, mostly not saying a word. And all along the walls was this long series of portraits some guy had done, had been doing for years, of all the regulars there—railroad men, Indians, bums, and the like. These pictures were pretty sketchy, just black line drawings shaded in with something. But somehow every picture told you everything you ever could have needed to know about any one of those guys."

He starts cracking peanuts again, one after another, into two piles.

"When any of those guys dies," he says, "their picture gets a gold star. In the bottom corner, on the glass."

He tosses a nut into his mouth for the first time.

"Is that it?" I ask.

"That's all there needs to be," he says without looking at me.

"I mean is that the story you wanted to tell me?"

He glances up at me now, a look with nothing behind it. "No," he says.

Goddamn, that old woman has got her eye on me again. I let my hair loose from behind my ears—somebody told me that makes you look older. There's a movie on the TV now, somebody in a wide-brim hat driving a Packard around. That couple's still just the way they were before, except now there are eight or ten empty glasses lined up on the man's side and in between the two of them. The black man has gone. The bartender stares at me.

Carter drains his glass and I can hear him crunching ice. Then he's back up at the bar and just look at that old prune lighten up. It's like somebody pulled some strings somewhere and raised her face about an inch. Her eyes seem to sparkle. She almost looks pretty.

Think it oh-oh-ver, haven't I been good to you, think it over, haven't I been sweet to you?

Carter leans heavy on the bar now, both forearms flat on the counter. He whispers something. She rests her fingertips on his wrist when she laughs.

I used to look at people acting like this and wonder, are they sleeping together, how long have they been lovers, what stage of the game are they in. But at some point I figured out that I always pick the wrong people. Because all around the world, the people who are lovers are the ones at opposite corners of rooms from each other, at parties, at offices. Their eyes are always turned away, their attention put to something else, anything but each other.

It seems like no one has come or gone in a long time. Everything feels still, closed in, and tomb-like, like there are no doors or windows. The air is smoky, hot and thick, nothing moves. A new song is playing but I can't hear what it is, it's on just loud enough to be some kind of noise.

The bartender pushes through the swinging gate and walks up next to Carter. They just stand at first, facing each other, then Carter puts out his hand and she takes it. She rests her other hand on his shoulder and he slides an arm around her waist. The woman moves Carter in time to the music. She does the steps and he's following, slow and sleepy. I remember how she seemed frail before, but now her body seems sturdy, powerful. Her eyes are flashing. She's the strongest thing in the world.

Carter sets another scotch in front of me. The ice cubes look soft around their edges.

For some reason that I don't know, I feel like I want to cry.

"Carter," I say.

He's got his notebook out again. He's laid it right on top of the peanuts and shells and he's writing something. I don't know how much time has passed. The bartender's locking the doors.

"Carter."

He nods. I lean over and see he's just drawing pictures— faces, half-moons, clusters of little stars.

"What was that story you were going to tell me?"

The bartender's key ring jingles as she circles behind us to the back door. The jukebox is off and I can hear her humming.

Carter puts down his pen and wraps his hand around his scotch. The tabletop is crowded now, there's beer mugs, a pitcher, a couple different sizes of cocktail glasses. I can tell his hand is squeezing hard, but the glass is wider than his grip and the fingers don't meet.

He raises his drink and holds it in the air. I lift mine to join it.

"To us," he says, and clinks my glass.

"To you," I say, and then, "to Teacher."

I want to try and empty my scotch though it's more than half-full. I feel the coolness crawling down the inside of everything, changing to warm as it slides and then back to cool again. I slam down the glass drained, and wait for Carter to congratulate me. But there's a funny look in his eyes, wet and hollow but scared somehow. I guess it's whatever look that is people get in their eyes when they're drinking.

JESSE LEE KERCHEVAL

Underground Women

La photographie

I AM TAKING a photograph of a Lavomatic near the Gare du Nord in Paris. It will be a color photograph and so shows the walls sharp yellow, the machines the shiny white that means clean. The front of the Lavomatic is plate glass. Glass that lets out into the night the bright fluorescent light of the laundry. Glass that reflects a red hint of an ambulance beacon. Glass that lets the photographer catch this scene, this knot of official people grouped casually around a dark wrinkled shape on the floor. Catch at an angle of extreme foreshortening the stubby, already almost blue legs, the one outflung hand holding one black sock.

It will be the photograph of a dead woman.

Le Grand Hôtel

It is on the evening of my first day in Paris that I take the photograph of the dead woman in the Lavomatic and then check into Le Grand Hôtel de l'Univers Nord. At first I am tempted to find the name humorous—do the East, West, and South quarters of the universe keep seperate grand hotels?—but decide against it. I do not know enough French to have any sense of humor in it at all.

Madame Desnos crie

And it is the photograph of the Lavomatic or rather my memory of the dead woman in it that wakes me up so early at Le Grand Hôtel. I catch Madame Desnos the propriétaire, in her leopard-spotted robe, still breaking the baguettes for the guests' breakfasts

"Mademoiselle . . . ," she says, waving me to a seat at the counter. "His ankles," she remarks pleasantly, cracking off a six-inch hunk of bread. I think it is something colloquial and smile. "His knees," she adds, breaking off another piece, which I helpfully arrange in its basket. "My husband has sent me a postcard," Madame Desnos pauses to choose another loaf, "so he is not dead, and worse still, he says he misses me." She starts on a new loaf. "His spine." I drop a basket and when I bend to pick it up I see Madame Desnos's legs beneath her spotted robe. Like the woman in the Lavomatic Madame Desnos's legs are protected only by hose fallen in wrinkled waves around her ankles, though hers are pink with only a foreshadowing of heavy blue veins. I begin to cry. Madame Desnos cries too, taking the scarf from her hair to wipe our tears. Her hair is the faded red of a very old dachshund.

"No, no, it's not so bad. I've paid off the loan he took out on the place the last time he came back." She pokes me in the navel with the last loaf of bread. "Smile," she says. "The mails are slow and people die every day." She breaks the bread in two. "His neck."

Le Grand Hôtel encore

After breakfast I become the desk clerk at Le Grand Hôtel. Perhaps in France people who want jobs as desk clerks always get up early and help with breakfast.

"Remember," says Madame Desnos, "this arrondissement may be filled with hotels run by Algerians for Algerians, Vietnamese for Vietnamese, and Moroccans for Moroccans, but Le Grand Hôtel de l'Univers Nord is a French hotel," she waves a fine thin hand at the lobby, "that just happens to be filled with Algerians, Vietnamese, and Moroccans."

Monsieur Peret

I am polishing the big brass room keys the guests leave each morning when they go out to work or to look for work when a small man with very large false teeth appears suddenly at the door and rushes to kiss Madame Desnos on the cheek.

"Ah, Monsieur Peret," she says without looking up.

"Ah, ah, ah . . ." Monsieur Peret moans, "business is so bad, Madame, I have come to beg you to encourage your new clerk to mention the closeness of my excellent facilities to your guests." Monsieur Peret slides down the counter torward me and takes one end of the key I am polishing in his very tiny very clean hand. "Surely, Madame, you have already told your new clerk how much more reasonable my coin laundry is than that place over on the Rue de Ste. Marie, and how it is my standard and well-honored policy to offer one free wash with every three validated referrals? Surely, Madame, I need not mention these things myself." Monsieur Peret draws the key across the counter with my hand still attached. "Au revoir," he says, pecking me lightly with his dentures.

La photographie encore

I tell Madame Desnos about the photograph I took the night before of a dead woman in Monsieur Peret's Lavomatic and she makes me go with her at once to the developer's.

"It does not suprise me that a dead woman should bring Monsieur Peret's business trouble," says Madame Desnos as we wait for Monsieur Blanc, the developer, to bring out the prints. "Monsieur Peret was not good to his wife," she says, "and such things do not always go unpunished. He worked her so hard in that Lavomatic that to get some rest she went to a doctor and let him remove a part. Ah, but once the doctors start on someone they can never have done with them, and so they kept at poor Madame Peret until there was nothing left at all."

Monsieur Blanc brings out the dripping prints but Madame Desnos refuses to look at them until he leaves the room. She takes my hand and I look again at the round dead shape of the woman in the Lavomatic.

"It's the way the customers are all just doing their wash, not even looking at her, that makes me want to cry," I tell Madame Desnos.

"Ah, but the only way a woman can make a mark on this world," says Madame Desnos, "is with her body, surely not even a dead one should be allowed to go to waste. At least by dying in the Lavomatic she made a friend on the other side in Madame Peret." Madame Desnos puts the woman in the Lavomatic into a brown envelope for safekeeping. "Let us go see Monsieur Peret and let his complaining cheer us up."

Monsieur Peret encore

"Oh, she was not even a regular customer," Monsieur Peret complains before we are even inside the plate glass wall of the Lavomatic. "And these people," he looks over his shoulder at the Moroccans and Algerians who are passing by outside in their dirty clothes, then waves a tiny clean hand at the empty laundry, "They are so superstitious. This picture on the wall," he takes Madame Desnos's sleeve and draws her to a small copy of a woodcut that is hardly noticeable on the bright yellow wall. "It has been here for years—my poor wife picked it out the last time she was ever here—suddenly after this incident, over which I had no control, they complain about this picture. Just to cause me grief. There is nothing as irrational as a woman who has dirty laundry and wants an excuse not to do her wash." Monsieur Peret shakes his head. I move closer to examine the woodcut. It depicts five virgin martyrs being flayed.

Madame Desnos touches a long thin finger to one of the martyers. "Perhaps if you feel you must replace this thoughtful gift of your wife's—would it not fit in somewhere in your own rooms?—the mademoiselle here could be of some service to you. I have just discovered she is a most accomplished photographer and plan to have some postal cards of the hotel made up expressly to utilize her talents."

"Well," Monsieur Peret looks from the flayed virgins to me, "perhaps a nice shot of myself, in a very white shirt, standing poised and attentive in front of the Lavomatic."

"Ah, well . . . perhaps the matter requires some thought," Madame Desnos says, "but I am certian if I talk to the mademoiselle we could all get what we deserve."

"Indeed," says Monsieur Peret.

Madame Desnos takes my arm as we leave. "We must think of something appropriate," she says to me.

Au cinéma

"Only every tenth movie shown in France can be made in America," Madame Desnos tells me as I am handing out the room keys to the returning guests. "And only every tenth song played on the radio. But," she says, "there are ways and there are ways; if a song is sung in French it is a French song—no matter if it is "The Yellow Rose of Texas." So tonight we shall go to the movies and what we will see will be American movies so old they have become French by default."

After the last guest is in she tells the Algerians playing cards in the lobby where she will be in case the hotel catches fire or her husband returns and we leave for the cinema.

"This theater has been running the same American serials since I was a young bride," Madame Desnos tells me as we hurry to find our seats before the house lights go down. "I don't come often but slowly I am getting to see the beginning, middle, and end of them all."

We find our seats just in time. The lights go out. The titles come up on the screen *The Queen of the Underground Women*. It stars Gene Autry as a radio station operator; under his Melody Ranch lives a kingdom of underground Amazons. After the titles the Queen of the Underground Women stands facing the camera and declares:

"Our lives are serene. Our minds are superior. Our achievements are greater than theirs. We must capture Gene Autry."

Madame Desnos pulls my arm and we get up and leave. Outside she shakes her head. "They are making a terrible mistake," she says.

Père Lachaise

After the keys are turned in the next morning Madame Desnos announces we are going to make a small pilgrimage—"A pilgrimage is a trip that is its own reward," she says—to Père Lachaise, one of Paris's great cemeteries. On the way to the Métro she stops near the station and buys a stalk of hollyhocks. "For Madame Peret," she explains.

"Is Madame Peret buried at Père Lachaise then?" I ask.

"No," says Madame Desnos, "there was so little left of her that Monsieur Peret let the doctors have that too, but it is a good place to be buried and a good place to visit the dead. We'll put the flowers on someone else's tomb and if it is important perhaps they will tell Madame Peret we called."

In the Métro on the way to Père Lachaise we sit in seats marked reserved in descending order for disabled veterans, the civil blind, civil amputees, pregnant women, and women with childern in arms.

Madame Desnos shrugs. "So we are pregnant," she says, "that at least they don't make you carry papers to prove."

We walk from the Métro stop through the gate of the cemetary and then on over the crumbling hills of mausoleums, each family vault the size of an elevator, each with its shards of stained glass and leaf-clogged altar. There are cats everywhere, asleep under brown wreaths, fat and indifferent to the rain.

"Do you know," Madame Desnos asks, "that in Germany they only bury you for just a while—say until your husband remarries or your children move away. Then up you come, tombstone and all, and another German goes in your place. Busy people, the Germans."

We pass the tombs of Molière and La Fontaine, who are probably not really buried there, and the monument to the love of Héloïse and Abelard, who most certianly are not, and then the grave of Colette, who is but hidden under her husband's name, and walk on until we reach the columbarium with its tiered drawers of ashes.

"I am sure this is where Madame Peret would have chosen. She was a frugal woman and there really wasn't much of her left." Madame Desnos runs one thin finger down a line of drawers. Names, dates, beloved this and thats—then she stops, her fingertip poised on a drawer with a black-and-white photograph of a young woman, a flapper, wearing only lipstick and long jet beads, a graceful hand poised beneath her chin and jet, jet eyes. No names, no dates.

Madame Desnos puts the hollyhocks in the flapper's dry urn.

Madame Desnos crie encore

On the way back to Le Grand Hôtel we stop to shop at Printemps. Madame Desnos instructs me to buy a black bra.

"You American girls are not safe on the streets," she says to me and to the saleswoman in Lingerie. "Looking innocent is no protection." I remember Madame Peret's flayed virgins and think perhaps Madame Desnos has a point.

We stop at a café for coffee and brandy to ward off the rain and then because of this must also stop across the street at an art nouveau underground toilette.

"Madame Desnos!" the attendant cries out when she comes down off the ladder where she has been fixing one of the tanks.

"Marie-Louise!" Madame Desnos squeals back, "I thought you were still in the Place St. Germaine."

"No, no I have been here for almost a month—a promotion."

"Indeed," says Madame Desnos, waving her long fine hand at the stained-glass lilies set in the stall doors, hand-painted lily tiles, the murals of lily-languid young women.

I walk over and examine a beveled glass case behind the

attendant's station. It is filled with little mementos of a sort nieces bring back to their favorite aunt. There is a stuffed baby alligator from Florida next to a set of Eiffel tower salt and pepper shakers.

"Those were Madame Galfont's," Marie-Louise says, coming up behind me. "She was here for many years, since before the war, and had many regular clients."

"Madame Galfont has . . . ," asks Madame Desnos with another wave of her hand, "passed on?"

"No, well, I usually say that she retired. It is a painful point." Marie-Louise shakes her head. "Did you see the signs on your way down the stairs?" She points up at some black and yellow government posters. "This new government—now they have boarded up pissoirs so the men too must pay a franc for a stall. Madame Galfont met a man in this way, and so she left . . . ." Marie-Louise spreads her short arms in an encompassing gesture, ". . . this. I trained under Madame Galfont, to me it was as if she had abdicated." Marie-Louise shakes her head. Madame Desnos shakes her head. "So there was a meeting of all the attendants all the women, and they voted that I should come here and now I must be the one to show the new women how things have always been done, but I am no Madame Galfont." Marie-Louise takes a small Polaroid snapshot out of the beveled case. Madame Galfont smiles out of it, perhaps at some satisfied client, some tourist amazed at this splendid museum toilette. I look closer. I recognize Madame Galfont from another photograph, though in that one she is not smiling. I show Marie-Louise the woman in the Lavomatic. She cries. Madame Desnos cries. I cry.

Marie-Louise touches the printed image of Madame Galfont's outstreached hand. "A man's sock," she says and shakes her head one last time.

Marie-Louise takes the final picture of Madame Galfont and places it in the beveled case near the smiling Galfont, propping it up behind a pencil case from the Swiss Alps. The box cuts off the bottom of the picture—suddenly there is only the Lavomatic. White-coated officials view it with pride as busy customers concentrate on their wash. Madame Galfont is removed from the photograph as abruptly, as thoroughly, as she was from the Lavomatic itself, and yet . . . she is there. Gene Autry walking the hollow soil of his Melody Ranch, hurried Parisians whose footsteps I can hear on the sidewalk above—who cannot feel the presence of the Queen of the Underground Women? I turn to Madame Desnos.

"I have something for Monsieur Peret," I say.

La photographie encore une fois

I go back to Monsieur Blanc with the negative of the death of Madame Galfont.

"Cropped and blown up?" he asks.

"And framed," I say, "as large as possible and framed."

"Ah, well, for a friend of Monsieur Peret's I think it can be arranged."

Monsieur Peret pour la dernière fois

Monsieur Peret straightens the framed photograph on the nail from which he has already exiled Madame Peret's virgin martyrs. "I am overcome," he says, still unable to decide once and for all that the picture is hanging level—he feels a certian unease about it. "Madame Desnos is too generous, too kind—a gift such as this . . . ." Monsieur Peret stands lost in admiration for this magic mirror-copy of his Lavomatic and does not even notice two women behind him become nervous, take their laundry still damp from the dryers and leave.

Madame Desnos ne crie pas

When I return to Le Grand Hôtel I find a telegram lying open on the counter.

COMING HOME, BABY. STOP.

It is not signed but I am sure Monsieur Desnos felt there would be no confusion. I go upstairs to pack. When I come back down with my bags Madame Desnos's are standing in the hall.

"One moment!" she calls from behind the counter in the lobby. I watch as she takes each long brass room key and drops it into her net shopping bag. We pick up our bags and she locks the door of Le Grand Hôtel de l'Univers Nord behind us and puts that key too in her bag. We check our luggage at the Gare du Nord and then walk slowly toward the Seine.

"I have been in Paris a long time, but I was born in Troyes," says Madame Desnos as we draw even with Notre Dame de Paris, Our Lady of Paris. "Troyes too has a cathedral, and in it the columns grow into trees and the arched vaults are draped with grapevines. I think in Troyes they have done kinder things with their stone," she waves her fine hand at Notre Dame's great east front, "than in Paris. In Troyes there are even carved escargot feeding among the marble vines."

We cross to the middle of the bridge from the Ile de Cité and stand looking back at the city.

"And in Troyes there is a woman who sits every day in the market and sells vegetables that the other vendors have thrown down on the floor as too old or too rotten, yet from this woman even the mayor must wait in line each day and pay for the privilege of her weighing him out old parsnips." Madame Desnos unties her bag and reaches out the keys, "I think you would have to live in Troyes a long time to find out why this is so."

"Perhaps there are places where it is better for a woman to live."

Madame Desnos holds one of the brass keys between her long fine fingers and lets it drop into the Seine. I watch as one-by-one they fall, golden beads on a rosary, raising a tiny glinting splash apice.

"Perhaps," Madame Desnos says, "perhaps."

DAVID UPDIKE

Summer

IT WAS THE FIRST WEEK in August, the time when summer briefly pauses, shifting between its beginning and its end: the light had not yet begun to change, the leaves were still full and green on the trees, the nights were still warm. From the woods and fields came the hiss of crickets; the line of distant mountains was still dulled by the edge of summer haze, the echo of fireworks was replaced by the rumble of thunder and the hollow premonition of school, too far off to imagine though dimly, dully felt. His senses were consumed by the joy of their own fulfillment: the satisfying swat of a tennis ball, the dappled damp and light of the dirt road after rain, the alternating sensations of sand, mossy stone, and pine needles under bare feet. His days were spent in the adolescent pursuit of childhood pleasures: tennis, a haphazard round of golf, a variant of baseball adapted to the local geography: two pine trees as foul poles, a broomstick as the bat, the apex of the small, secluded house the dividing line between home runs and outs. On rainy days they swatted bottle tops across the living room floor, and at night vented budding cerebral energy with games of chess thoughtfully played over glasses of iced tea. After dinner they would paddle the canoe to the middle of the lake, and drift beneath the vast, blue-black dome of sky, looking at the stars and speaking softly in tones which, with the waning summer, became increasingly philosophical: the sky's blue vastness, the distance and magnitude of stars, an endless succession of numbers, gave way to a rising sensation of infinity, eternity, an imagined universe with no bounds. But the sound of the paddle hitting against the side of the canoe, the faint shadow of surrounding mountains, the cry of a nocturnal bird brought them back to the happy, cloistered finity of their world, and they paddled slowly home and went to bed.

Homer woke to the slant and shadow of a summer morning, dressed in their shared cabin, and went into the house where Mrs. Thyme sat alone, looking out across the flat blue stillness of the lake. She poured him a cup of coffee and they quietly talked, and it was then that his happiness seemed most tangible. In this summer month with the Thymes, freed from the complications of his own family, he had released himself to them and, as interim member—friend, brother, surrogate son—he lived in a blessed realm between two worlds.

From the cool darkness of the porch, smelling faintly of moldy books and kerosene and the tobacco of burning pipes, he sat looking through the screen to the lake, shimmering beneath the heat of a summer afternoon: a dog lay sleeping in the sun, a bird hopped along a swaying branch, sunlight came in through the trees and collapsed on the sandy soil beside a patch of moss, or mimicked the shade and cadence of stones as they stepped to the edge of a lake where small waves lapped a damp rock and washed onto a sandy shore. An inverted boat lay decaying under a tree, a drooping American flag hung from its gnarled pole, a haphazard dock started out across the cove toward distant islands through which the white triangle of a sail silently moved.

The yellowed pages of the book from which he occasionally read swam before him: ". . . Holmes clapped the hat upon his head. It came right over the forehead and settled on the bridge of his nose. 'It is a question of cubic capacity' said he . . ." Homer looked up. The texture of the smooth, unbroken air was cleanly divided by the sound of a slamming door, echoing up into the woods around him. Through the screen he watched Fred's sister Sandra as she came ambling down the path, stepping lightly between the stones in her bare feet. She held a towel in one hand, a book in the other, and wore a pair of pale blue shorts— faded relics of another era. At the end of the dock she stopped, raised her hands above her head, stretching, and then sat down. She rolled over onto her stomach and, using the book as a pillow, fell asleep.

Homer was amused by the fact, that although she did this every day, she didn't get any tanner. When she first came in her face was faintly flushed, and there was a pinkish line around the snowy band where her bathing suit strap had been, but the back of her legs remained an endearing, pale white, the color of eggshells, and her back acquired only the softest, brownish blur. Sometimes she kept her shoes on, other times a shirt, or sweater, or just collapsed onto the seat of the boat, her pale eyelids turned upward toward the pale sun; and as silently as she arrived, she would leave, walking back through the stones with the same, casual sway of indifference. He would watch her, hear the distant door slam, the shower running in the far corner of the house. Other times he would just look up and she would be gone.

On the tennis court she was strangely indifferent to his heroics. When the crucial moment arrived—Homer serving in the final game of the final set—the match would pause while she left, walking across the court, stopping to call the dog, swaying out through the gate. Homer watched her as she went down the path, and, impetus suddenly lost, he double faulted, stroked a routine backhand over the back fence, and the match was over.

When he arrived back at the house she asked him who won, but didn't seem to hear his answer. "I wish I could go sailing," she said, looking distractly out over the lake.

At night, when he went out to the cottage where he and Fred slept, he could see her through the window as she lay on her bed, reading, her arm folded beneath her head like a leaf. Her nightgown, pulled and buttoned to her chin, pierced him with a regret that had no source or resolution, and its imagined texture floated in the air above him as he lay in bed at night, suspended in the surrounding darkness, the scent of pine, the hypnotic cadence of his best friend's breathing.

Was it that he had known her all his life, and as such had grown up in the shadow of her subtle beauty? Was it the condensed world of the lake, the silent reverence of surrounding woods, mountains, which heightened his sense of her and brought the warm glow of her presence into soft, amorous focus? She had the hair of a baby, the freckles of a child, and the sway of motherhood. Like his love, her beauty rose up in the world which spawned and nurtured it, and found in the family the medium in which it thrived, and in Homer distilled to a pure distant longing for something he had never had.

One day they climbed a mountain, and as the components of family and friends strung out along the path on their laborious upward hike, he found himself tromping along through the woods with her with nobody else in sight. Now and then they would stop by a stream, or sit on a stump, or stone, and he would speak to her, and then they would set off again, he following her. But in the end this day exhausted him, following her pale legs and tripping sneakers over the ruts and stones and a thousand roots, all the while trying to suppress a wordless, inarticulate passion, and the last mile or so he left her, sprinting down the path in a reckless, solitary release, howling into the woods around him. He was lying on the grass, staring up into the patterns of drifting clouds when she came ambling down. "Wher'd you go? I thought I'd lost you," she said, and sat heavily down in the seat of the car. On the ride home, his elbow hopelessly held in the warm crook of her arm, he resolved to release his love, give it up, on the grounds that it was too disruptive to his otherwise placid life. But in the days to follow he discovered that his resolution had done little to change her, and her life went on its oblivious, happy course without him.

His friendship with Fred, meanwhile, continued on its course of athletic and boyhood fulfillment. Alcohol seeped into their diet, and an occasional cigarette, and at night they would drive into town, buy two enormous cans of Australian beer and sit at a small cove by the lake, talking. One night on the ride home Fred accelerated over a small bridge, and as the family station wagon left the ground their heads floated up to the ceiling, touched, and then came crashing down as the car landed and Fred wrestled the car back onto course. Other times they would take the motorboat out onto the lake and make sudden racing turns around buoys, sending a plume of water into the air and everything in the boat crashing to one side. But always with these adventures Homer felt a pang of absence, and was always re-lived when they headed back toward the familiar cove, and home.

As August ran its merciless succession of beautiful days, Sandra drifted in and out of his presence in rising oscillations of sorrow and desire. She worked at a bowling alley on the other side of the lake, and in the evening Homer and Fred would drive the boat over, bowl a couple of strings, and wait for her to get off work. Homer sat at the counter and watched her serve up sloshing cups of coffee, secretly loathing the leering gazes of whiskered truck drivers, and loving her oblivious, vacant stare in answer, hip cocked, hand on counter, gazing up into the neon air above their heads. When she was finished, they would pile into the boat and skim through darkness the four or five miles home, and it was then, bundled beneath sweaters and blankets, the white hem of her waitressing dress showing through the darkness, their hair swept in the wind and their voices swallowed by the engine's slow, steady growl, that he felt most powerless to her attraction. As the boat rounded corners he would close his eyes and release himself to gravity, his body's warmth swaying into hers, guising his attraction in the thin veil of centrifugal force. Now and then he would lean into the floating strands of her hair and speak into her fragrance, watching her smile swell in the pale half-light of the moon, the umber glow of the boat's rear light, her laughter spilling backward over the swirling "V" of wake.

Into the humid days of August a sudden rain fell, leaving the sky a hard, unbroken blue and the nights clear and cool. In the morning when he woke, leaving Fred a heap of sighing covers in his bed, he stepped out into the first rays of sunlight that came through the branches of the trees and sensed, in the cool vapor that rose from damp pine needles, the piercing cry of a blue jay, that something had changed. That night as they ate dinner—hamburgers and squash and corn-on-the-cob— everyone wore sweaters, and as the sun set behind the undulating line of distant mountains—burnt, like a filament of summer into his blinking eyes—it was with an autumnal tint, a reddish glow. Several days later the tree at the end of the point bloomed with a sprig of russet leaves, one or two of which occasionally fell, and their lives became filled with an unspoken urgency. Life of summer went on in the silent knowledge that, with the slow, inexorable seepage of an hourglass, it was turning into fall. Another mountain was climbed, annual tennis matches were arranged and played. Homer and Fred became unofficial champions of the lake by trouncing the elder Dewitt boys, unbeaten in several years. "Youth, youth," glum Billy Dewitt kept saying over iced tea afterward, in jest, though Homer could tell he was hiding some greater sense of loss.

And the moment, the conjunction of circumstance that, through the steady exertion of will, minor adjustments of time and place, he had often tried to induce, never happened. She received his veiled attentions with a kind of amused curiosity, as if smiling back on innocence. One night they had been the last ones up, and there was a fleeting, shuddering moment before he stepped through the woods to his cabin and she went to her bed that he recognized, in a distant sort of way, as the moment of truth. But to touch her, or kiss her, seemed suddenly incongruous, absurd, contrary to something he could not put his finger on. He looked down at the floor and softly said goodnight. The screen door shut quietly behind him and he went out into the darkness and made his way through the unseen sticks and stones, and it was only then, tripping drunkenly on a fallen branch, that he realized he had never been able to imagine the moment he distantly longed for.

The Preacher gave a familiar sermon about another summer having run its course, the harvest of friendship reaped, and a concluding prayer that, "God willing, we will all meet again in June." That afternoon Homer and Fred went sailing, and as they swept past a neighboring cove Homer saw in its sullen shadows a girl sitting alone in a canoe, and in an eternal, melancholy signal of parting, she waved to them as they passed. And there was something in the way that she raised her arm which, when added to the distant impression of her fullness, beauty, youth, filled him with longing as their boat moved inexorably past, slapping the waves, and she disappeared behind a crop of trees.

The night before they were to leave they were all sitting in the living room after dinner—Mrs. Thyme sewing, Fred folded up with the morning paper, Homer reading on the other end of the couch where Sandra was lying—when the dog leapt up and things shifted in such a way that Sandra's bare foot was lightly touching Homer's back. Mrs. Thyme came over with a roll of newspaper, hit the dog on the head and he leapt off. But to Homer's surprise Sandra's foot remained, and he felt, in the faint sensation of exerted pressure, the passive emanation of its warmth, a distant signal of acquiescence. And as the family scene continued as before it was with the accompanying drama of Homer's hand, shielded from the family by a haphazard wall of pillows, migrating over the couch to where, in a moment of breathless abandon, settled softly on the cool hollow of her arch. She laughed at something her mother had said, her toe twitched, but her foot remained. It was only then, in the presence of the family, that he realized she was his accomplice, and that, though this was as far as it would ever go, his love had been returned.

LORRIE MOORE

Amahl and the Night Visitors: A Guide to the Tenor of Love

11/30. Understand that your cat is a whore and can't help you. She takes on love with the whiskery adjustments of a gold-digger. She is a gorgeous nomad, an unfriend. Recall how just last month when you got her from Bob downstairs, after Bob had become suddenly allergic, she leaped into your lap and purred, guttural as a German chanteuse, familiar and furry as a mold. And Bob, visibly heartbroken, still in the room, sneezing and giving instructions, hoping for one last cat nuzzle, descended to his hands and knees and jiggled his fingers in the shag. The cat only blinked. For you, however, she smiled, gave a fish-breath peep, and settled.

"Oh, well," said Bob, getting up off the floor. "Now I'm just a thing of her kittenish past."

That's the way with Bob. He'll say to the cat, "You be a good girl now, honey," and then just shrug, go back downstairs to his apartment, play jagged, creepy jazz, drink wine, stare out at the wintry scalp of the mountain.

.   .   .

12/1. Moss Watson, the man you truly love like no other, is singing December 23 in the Owonta Opera production of *Amahl and the Night Visitors.* He's playing Kaspar, the partially deaf Wise Man. Wisdom, says Moss, arrives in all forms. And you think, Yes, sometimes as a king and sometimes as a hesitant phone call that says the king'll be late at rehearsal don't wait up, and then when you call back to tell him to be careful not to let the cat out when he comes home, you discover there's been no rehearsal there at all.

At three o'clock in the morning you hear his car in the driveway, the thud of the front door. When he comes into the bedroom, you see his huge height framed for a minute in the doorway, his hair lit bright as curry. When he stoops to take off his shoes, it is as if some small piece of his back has given way, allowing him this one slow bend. He is quiet. When he gets into bed he kisses one of your shoulders, then pulls the covers up to his chin. He knows you're awake. "I'm tired," he announces softly, to ward you off when you roll toward him. Say: "You didn't let the cat out, did you?"

He says no, but he probably should have. "You're turning into a cat mom. Cats, Trudy, are the worst sort of surrogates."

Tell him you've always wanted to run off and join the surrogates.

Tell him you love him.

Tell him you know he didn't have rehearsal tonight.

"We decided to hold rehearsal at the Montessori school, what are you now, *my* mother?"

In the dark, discern the fine hook of his nose. Smooth the hair off his forehead. Say: "I love you Moss are you having an affair with a sheep?" You saw a movie once where a man was having an affair with a sheep, and acted, with his girlfriend, the way Moss now acts with you: exhausted.

Moss's eyes close. "I'm a king, not a shepherd, remember? You're acting like my ex-wife."

His ex-wife is now an anchorwoman in Missouri.

"Are you having a regular affair? Like with a person?"

"Trudy," he sighs, turns away from you, taking more than his share of blanket. "You've got to stop this." Know you are being silly. Any second now he will turn and press against you, reassure you with kisses, tell you oh how much he loves you. "How on earth, Trudy," is what he finally says, "would I ever have the time for an affair?"

12/2. Your cat is growing, eats huge and sloppy as a racehorse. Bob named her Stardust Sweetheart, a bit much even for Bob, so you and Moss think up other names for her: Pudge, Pudge-muffin, Pooch, Poopster, Secretariat, Stephanie, Emily. Call her all of them. "She has to learn how to deal with confusion," says Moss. "And we've gotta start letting her outside."

Say: "No. She's still too little. Something could happen." Pick her up and away from Moss. Bring her into the bathroom with you. Hold her up to the mirror. Say: "Whossat? Whossat pretty kitty?" Wonder if you could turn into Bob.

12/3. Sometimes Moss has to rehearse in the living room. King Kaspar has a large black jewelry box about which he must sing to the young, enthralled Amahl. He must open drawers and haul out beads, licorice, magic stones. The drawers, however, keep jamming when they're not supposed to. Moss finally tears off his fake beard and screams, "I can't do this shit! I can't sing about money and gewgaws. I'm the tenor of love!" Last year they'd done *La Bohème* and Moss had been Rodolfo.

This is the sort of thing he needs you for: to help him with his box. Kneel down beside him. Show him how one of the drawers is off its runner. Show him how to pull it out just so far. He smiles and thanks you in his berserk King Kaspar voice: "Oh, thank you, thank you, thank you!" He begins his aria again: " 'This is my box. This is my box. I never travel without my box.' "

All singing is, says Moss, is sculpted howling.

Say, "Bye." Wheel the TV into the kitchen. Watch Mac-Neil-Lehrer. Worry about Congress.

Listen to the goose-call of trains, all night, trundling by your house.

12/4. Sometimes the phone rings, but then the caller hangs up.

12/5. Your cat now sticks her paws right in the water dish while she drinks, then steps out from her short wade and licks them, washes her face with them, repeatedly, over the ears and down, like an itch. Take to observing her. On her feet the gray and pink configurations of pads and fur look like tiny baboon faces. She sees you watching, freezes, blinks at you, then busies herself again, her face in her belly, one leg up at a time, an intent ballerina in a hairy body stocking. And yet she's growing so quickly, she's clumsy. She'll walk along and suddenly her hip will fly out of whack and she'll stop and look at it, not comprehending. Or her feet will stumble, or it's difficult for her to move her new bulk along the edges of furniture, her body pushing itself out into the world before she's really ready. It puts a dent in her confidence. She looks at you inquiringly: *What is happening to me?* She rubs against your ankles and bleats. You pick her up, tuck her under your chin, your teeth clenched in love, your voice cooey, gooey with maternity, you say things like, "How's my little dirt-nose, my little fuzz-face, my little honey-head?"

"Jesus, Trudy," Moss yells from the next room. "Listen to how you talk to that cat."

12/6. Though the Christmas shopping season is under way, the store you work at downtown, Owonta Flair, is not doing well. "The malls," groans Morgan, your boss. "Every Christmas the malls! We're doomed. These candy cane slippers. What am I gonna do with these?"

Tell her to put one slipper from each pair in the window along with a mammoth sign that says, MATES INSIDE. "People only see the sign. Thom McAn did it once. They got hordes."

"You're depressed," says Morgan.

12/7. You and Moss invite the principals, except Amahl, over to dinner one night before a rehearsal. You also invite Bob. Three kings, Amahl's unwed mother, you, and Bob: this way four people can tell cranky anecdotes about the production, and two people can listen.

"This really is a trashy opera," says Sonia, who plays Amahl's mother. "Sentimental as all get-out." Sonia is everything you've always wanted to be: smart, Jewish, friendly, full-haired as Easter basket grass. She speaks with a mouthful of your spinach pie. She says she likes it. When she has swallowed, a piece of spinach remains behind, wrapped like a gap around one of her front teeth. Other than that she is very beautiful. Nobody says anything about the spinach on her tooth.

Two rooms away the cat is playing with a marble in the empty bathtub. This is one of her favorite games. She bats the marble and it speeds around the porcelain like a stock car. The noise is rattley, continuous.

"What is that weird noise?" asks Sonia.

"It's the beast," says Moss. "We should put her outside, Trudy." He pours Sonia more wine, and she murmurs, "Thanks."

Jump up. Say: "I'll go take the marble away."

Behind you you can hear Bob: "She used to be mine. Her name is Stardust Sweetheart. I got allergic."

Melchior shouts after you: "Aw, leave the cat alone, Trudy. Let her have some fun." But you go into the bathroom and take the marble away anyhow. Your cat looks up at you from the tub, her head cocked to one side, sweet and puzzled as a child movie star. Then she turns and bats drips from the faucet. Scratch the scruff of her neck. Close the door when you leave. Put the marble in your pocket.

You can hear Balthazar making jokes about the opera. He calls it *Amyl and the Nitrates*.

"I've always found Menotti insipid," Melchior is saying when you return to the dining room.

"Written for NBC, what can you expect," Sonia says. Soon she is off raving about *La Bohème* and other operas. She uses words like *verismo, messa di voce*, Montserrat Caballe. She smiles. "An opera should be like contraception: about *sex, not* children."

Start clearing the plates. Tell people to keep their forks for dessert. Tell them that no matter what anyone says, you think *Amahl* is a beautiful opera and that the ending, when the mother sends her son off with the kings, always makes you cry. Moss gives you a wink. Get brave. Give your head a toss. Add: "Papage*no*, Papage*na*—to me, *La Bohème*'s just a lot of scarves."

There is some gulping of wine.

Only Bob looks at you and smiles. "Here. I'll help you with the plates," he says.

Moss stands and makes a diversionary announcement: "Sonia, you've got a piece of spinach on your tooth."

"Christ," she says, and her tongue tunnels beneath her lip like an elegant gopher.

12/8. Sometimes still Moss likes to take candlelight showers with you. You usually have ten minutes before the hot water runs out. Soap his back, the wide moguls of his shoulders registering in you like a hunger. Press yourself against him. Whisper: "I really do like *La Bohème*, you know."

"It's okay," Moss says, all forgiveness. He turns and grabs your buttocks.

"It's just that your friends make me nervous. Maybe it's work, Morgan that forty-watt hysteric making me crazy." Actually you like Morgan.

Begin to hum a Dionne Warwick song, then grow self-conscious and stop. Moss doesn't like to sing in the shower. He has his operas, his church jobs, his weddings and bar mitzvahs—in the shower he is strictly off-duty. Say: "I mean, it *could* be Morgan."

Moss raises his head up under the spray, beatific, absent. His hair slicks back, like a baby's or a gangster's, dark with water, shiny as a record album. "Does Bob make you nervous?" he asks.

"Bob? Bob suffers from terminal sweetness. I like Bob."

"So do I. He's a real gem."

Say: "Yeah, he's a real chum."

"I said *gem*," says Moss. "Not *chum*." Things fall quiet. Lately you've been mishearing each other. Last night in bed you said, "Moss, I usually don't like discussing sex, but—" And he said, "I don't like disgusting sex either." And then he fell asleep, his snores scratching in the dark like zombies.

Take turns rinsing. Don't tell him he's hogging the water. Ask finally, "Do you think Bob's gay?"

"Of course he's gay."

"How do you know?"

"Oh, I don't know. He hangs out at Sammy's in the mall."

"Is that a gay bar?"

"Bit of everything." Moss shrugs.

Think: Bit of everything. Just like a mall. "Have you ever been there?" Scrub vigorously between your breasts.

"A few times," says Moss, the water growing cooler.

Say: "Oh." Then turn off the faucet, step out onto the bath mat. Hand Moss a towel. "I guess because I work trying to revive our poor struggling downtown I don't get out to these places much."

"I guess not," says Moss, candle shadows wobbling on the shower curtain.

12/9. Two years ago when Moss first moved in, there was something exciting about getting up in the morning. You would rise, dress, and, knowing your lover was asleep in your bed, drive out into the early morning office and factory traffic, feeling that you possessed all things, Your Man, like a Patsy Cline song, at home beneath your covers, pumping blood through your day like a heart.

Now you have a morbid fascination with news shows. You get up, dress, flick on the TV, sit in front of it with a bowl of cereal in your lap, quietly curse all governments everywhere, get into your car, drive to work, wonder how the sun has the nerve to show its face, wonder why the world seems to be picking up speed, even old ladies pass you on the highway, why you don't have a single erotic fantasy that Moss isn't in, whether there really are such things as vitamins, and how would you rather die cancer or a car accident, the man you love, at home, asleep, like a heavy, heavy heart through your day.

"Goddamn slippers," says Morgan at work.

12/10. The cat now likes to climb into the bathtub and stand under the dripping faucet in order to clean herself. She lets the water bead up on her face, then wipes herself, neatly dislodging the gunk from her eyes.

"Isn't she wonderful?" you ask Moss.

"Yeah. Come here you little scumbucket," he says, slapping the cat on the haunches, as if she were a dog.

"She's not a dog, Moss. She's a cat."

"That's right. She's a cat. Remember that, Trudy."

12/11. The phone again. The ringing and hanging up.

12/12. Moss is still getting in very late. He goes about the business of fondling you, like someone very tired at night having to put out the trash and bolt-lock the door.

He sleeps with his arms folded behind his head, elbows protruding, treacherous as daggers, like the enemy chariot in *Ben-Hur.*

. . .

12/13. Buy a Christmas tree, decorations, a stand, and lug them home to assemble for Moss. Show him your surprise.

"Why are the lights all in a clump in the back?" he asks, closing the front door behind him.

Say: "I know. Aren't they great? Wait till you see me do the tinsel." Place handfuls of silver icicles, matted together like alfalfa sprouts, at the end of all the branches.

"Very cute," says Moss, kissing you, then letting go. Follow him into the bathroom. Ask how rehearsal went. He points to the kitty litter and sings: " 'This is my box. I never travel without my box.' "

Say: "You are not a well man, Moss." Play with his belt loops.

12/14. The white fur around the cat's neck is growing and looks like a stiff Jacobean collar. "A rabato," says Moss, who suddenly seems to know these things. "When are we going to let her go outside?"

"Someday when she's older." The cat has lately taken to the front window the way a hypochondriac takes to a bed. When she's there she's more interested in the cars, the burled fingers of the trees, the occasional squirrel, the train tracks like long fallen ladders, than she is in you. Call her: "Here pootchy-kootchy-honey." Ply her, bribe her with food.

12/15. There are movies in town: one about Brazil, and one about sexual abandonment in upstate New York. "What do you say, Moss. Wanna go to the movies this weekend?"

"I can't," says Moss. "You know how busy I am."

12/16. The evening news is full of death: young marines, young mothers, young children. By comparison you have already lived forever. In a kind of heaven.

.   .   .

12/17. Give your cat a potato and let her dribble it about soccer-style. She's getting more coordinated, conducts little dramas with the potato, pretends to have conquered it, strolls over it, then somersaults back after it again. She's not bombing around, crashing into the sideboards anymore. She's learning moves. She watches the potato by the dresser leg, stalks it, then pounces. When she gets bored she climbs up onto the sill and looks out, tail switching. Other cats have spotted her now, have started coming around at night. Though she will want to go, do not let her out the front door.

12/18. The phone rings. You say hello, and the caller hangs up. Two minutes later it rings again, only this time Moss answers it in the next room, speaks softly, cryptically, not the hearty phone voice of the Moss of yesteryear. When he hangs up, wander in and say, blasé as paste, "So, who was that?"

"Stop," says Moss. "Just stop."

Ask him what's the big deal, it was Sonia wasn't it.

"Stop," says Moss. "You're being my wife. Things are repeating themselves."

Say that nothing repeats itself. Nothing, nothing, nothing. "Sonia, right?"

"Trudy, you've got to stop this. You've been listening to too much *Tosca.* I'm going out to get a hamburger. Do you want anything?"

Say: "I'm the only person in the whole world who really knows you, Moss. And I don't know you at all anymore."

"That's a different opera," he says. "I'm going out to get a hamburger. Do you want anything?"

Do not cry. Stick to monosyllables. Say: "No. Fine. Go."

Say: "Please don't let the cat out."

Say: "You should wear a hat it's cold."

. . .

12/19. Actually what you've been listening to is Dionne War-wick's Golden Hits—musical open heart surgery enough for you. Sometimes you pick up the cat and waltz her around, her purr staticky and intermittent as a walkie-talkie.

On "Do You Know the Way to San Jose," you put her down, do an unfortunate Charleston, while she attacks your stock-inged feet, thinking them large rodents.

Sometimes you knock into the Christmas tree.

Sometimes you collapse into a chair and convince yourself that things are still okay.

When Robert MacNeil talks about mounting inflation, you imagine him checking into a motel room with a life-size, blow-up doll. This is, once in a while, how you amuse yourself.

When Moss gets in at four in the morning, whisper: "There are lots of people in this world, Moss, but you can't be in love with them all."

"I'm not," he says, "in love with the mall."

12/20. The mall stores stay open late this last week before Christmas. Moss is supposed to be there, "in the gazebo next to the Santa gazebo," for an *Amahl and the Night Visitors* promo-tional. Decide to drive up there. Perhaps you can look around in the men's shops for a sweater for Moss, perhaps even one for Bob as well. Last year was a bad Christmas: you and Moss re-turned each other's gifts for cash. You want to do better this year. You want to buy: sweaters.

The mall parking lot, even at 7 p.m., is, as Moss would say, packed as a bag, though you do manage to find a space.

Inside the mall entranceway it smells of stale popcorn, dry heat, and three-day-old hobo urine. A drunk, slumped by the door, smiles and toasts you with nothing.

Say: "Cheers."

. . .

To make your journey down to the gazebos at the other end of
the mall, first duck into all the single-item shops along the way.
Compare prices with the prices at Owonta Flair: things are a
little cheaper here. Buy stuff, mostly for Moss and the cat.

In the pet food store the cashier hands you your bagged
purchase, smiles, and says, "Merry Christmas."

Say: "You, too."

In the men's sweater shop the cashier hands you your
bagged purchase, smiles, and says, "Merry Christmas."

Say: "You, too."

In the belt shop the cashier hands you your bagged purchase, smiles, and says, "Come again."

Say: "You, too." Grow warm. Narrow your eyes to seeds.

In the gazebo next to the Santa gazebo there is only an older
man in gray coveralls stacking some folding chairs.

Say: "Excuse me, wasn't *Amahl and the Night Visitors*
supposed to be here?"

The man stops for a moment. "There's visitors," he says,
pointing out and around, past the gazebo to all the shoppers.
Shoppers in parkas. Shoppers moving slow as winter. Shoppers
who haven't seen a crosswalk or a window in hours.

"I mean the opera promotional."

"The singers?" He looks at his watch. "They packed it in
a while ago."

Say thank you, and wander over to Cinema 1-2-3 to read
the movie posters. It's when you turn to go that you see Moss
and Bob coming out together from the bar by the theater. They
look tired.

Adjust your packages. Walk over. Say: "Hi. I guess I missed
the promo, so I was thinking of going to a movie."

"We ended it early," says Moss. "Sonia wasn't feeling well.
Bob and I just went into Sammy's for a drink."

Look and see the sign that, of course, reads SAMMY'S.

Bob smiles and says, "Hello, Trudy." Because Bob says *hello* and never *hi*, he always manages to sound a little like Mister Rogers.

You can see some of Moss's makeup and glue lines. His fake beard is sticking out from his coat pocket. Smile. Say: "Well, Moss. Here all along I thought it was Sonia, and it's really Bob." Chuck him under the chin. Keep your smile steady. You are the only one smiling. Not even Bob. You have clearly said the wrong thing.

"Fuck off, Trudy," Moss says finally, palming his hair back off his forehead.

Bob squirms in his coat. "I believe I forgot something," he says. "I'll see you both later." And he touches Moss's arm, turns, disappears back inside Sammy's.

"Jesus Christ, Trudy." Moss's voice suddenly booms through the mall. You can see a few stores closing up, men coming out to lower the metal night gates. Santa Claus has gotten down from the gazebo and is eating an egg roll.

Moss turns from you, charges toward the exit, an angry giant with a beard sticking out of his coat pocket. Run after him and grab his sleeve, make him stop. Say: "I'm sorry, Moss. What am I doing? Tell me. What am I doing wrong?" You look up at his face, with the orange and brown lines and the glue patches, and realize: He doesn't understand you've planned your lives together. That you have even planned your deaths together, not really deaths at all but more like a *pas de deux*. Like Gene Kelly and Leslie Caron in *An American in Paris*, only older.

"You just won't let people be," says Moss, each consonant spit like a fish bone.

Say: "People be? I don't understand. Moss, what is happening to us?" You want to help him, rescue him, build houses and magnificent lawns around him.

"To *us?*"

Moss's voice is loud. He puts on his gloves. He tells you you are a child. He needs to get away. For him you have managed to reduce love, like weather, to a map and a girl, and he needs to get away from you, live someplace else for a while, and think.

The bag with the cat food slips and falls. "The opera's in three days, Moss. Where are you going to go?"

"Right now," he says, "I'm going to get a hamburger." And he storms toward the mall doors, pushes against all of them until he finds the one that's open.

Stare and mumble at the theater candy concession. "Good and Plenty. There's no Good and Plenty." Your bangs droop into your vision. You keep hearing "Jingle Bells," over and over.

In the downtown theaters of your childhood, everything was made of carved wood, and in the ladies' rooms there were framed photographs of Elizabeth Taylor and Ava Gardner. The theaters had names: The Rialto, The Paramount. There were ushers and Good and Plenty. Ushers with flashlights and bow ties. That's the difference now. No ushers. Now you have to do everything by yourself.

"Trudy," says a voice behind you. "Would you like to be accompanied to the movies?" The passive voice. It's Bob's. Turn to look at him, but as with the Good and Plenty, you don't really see, everything around you vague and blurry as glop in your eye.

Say: "Sure. Why not."

In Cinema 3, sit in seats close to the aisle. Listen to the Muzak. The air smells like airplane air.

"It's a strange thing about Moss," Bob is saying, looking straight ahead. "He's so busy with the opera, it pushes him up against certain things. He ends up feeling restless and smothered. But, Trudy, Moss is a good man. He really is."

Don't say anything, and then say, finally, "Moss who?"

Stare at the curtain with the rose-tinted lights on it. Try to concentrate on more important matters, things like acid rain.

Bob taps his fingers on the metal arm of the seat. Say:

"Look, Bob. I'm no idiot. I was born in New York City. I lived there until I was four. Come on. Tell me: Who's Moss sleeping with?"

"As far as I know," says Bob, sure and serious as a tested hypothesis, "Moss isn't sleeping with anyone."

Continue staring at the rose lights. Then say in a loud contralto: "He's sleeping with *me*, Bob. That's who he's sleeping with."

When the lights dim and the curtains part, there arrive little cigarette lighters on the screen telling you not to smoke. Then there are coming attractions. Bob leans toward you, says, "These previews are horrible."

Say: "Yeah. Nothing Coming Soon."

There are so many previews you forget what movie you've come to see. When the feature presentation comes on, it takes you by surprise. The images melt together like a headache. The movie seems to be about a woman whose lover, losing interest in her, has begun to do inexplicable things like yell about the cat, and throw scenes in shopping malls.

"What is this movie about?"

"Brazil," whispers Bob.

The audience has begun to laugh at something someone is doing; you are tense with comic exile. Whisper: "Bob, I'm gonna go. Wanna go?"

"Yes, in fact, I do," says Bob.

It's ten-thirty and cold. The mall stores are finally closed. In the parking lot, cars are leaving. Say to Bob: "God, look how many people shop here." The whole world suddenly seems to you like a downtown dying slow.

Spot your car and begin to head toward it. Bob catches your sleeve. "My car's the other way. Listen. Trudy. About Moss: No matter what's going on with him, no matter what he decides he has to do, the man loves you. I know he does."

Gently pull your sleeve away. Take a step sideways toward

your car. Headlights, everywhere headlights and tires crunching. Say: "Bob, you're a sweet person. But you're sentimental as
all get-out." Turn on the nail of your boot and walk.

At home the cat refuses to dance to Dionne Warwick with you.
She sits on the sill of the window, rumbling in her throat, her tail
a pendulum of fluff. Outside, undoubtedly, there are suitors,
begging her not to be so cold-hearted. "Ya got friends out there?"
When you turn off the stereo, she jumps down from the sill and
snakes lovingly about your ankles. Say something you never
thought you'd say. Say: "Wanna go out?" She looks at you, all
hope and supplication, and follows you to the door, carefully
watching your hand as it moves for the knob: she wants you to
let her go, to let her go and be. Begin slowly, turn, pull. The
suction of door and frame gives way, and the cold night in-
sinuates itself like a kind of future. She doesn't leave immediately.
But her whole body is electrified, surveying the yard for eyes and
rustles, and just to the left of the streetlight she suddenly spots
them—four, five, phosphorescent glints—and, without a nudge,
without ever looking back, she scurries out, off the porch, down
after, into some sweet unknown, some somehow known unknown, some new yet very old religion.

12/21. Every adoration is seasonal as Christmas.

Moss stops by to get some things. He's staying with Balthazar for a few days, then after the opera and Christmas and
all, he'll look for an efficiency somewhere.

Nod. "Efficiency. Great. That's what hell is: efficient." You
want to ask him if this is all some silly opera where he's leaving
in order to spare you his tragic, bluish death by consumption.

He says, "It's just something I've got to do." He opens
cupboards in the kitchen, closets in the hallway, pulls down
boxes, cups, boots. He is slow about it, doesn't do it in a mean
way, you are grateful for that.

"What have you been doing tonight?" he asks, not looking, but his voice is urgent as a touch.

"I watched two hours of MacNeil-Lehrer. You can get it on channel seven and then later on channel four."

"Right," says Moss. "I know."

Pause. Then say: "Last night I let the cat out. Finally."

Moss looks at you and smiles.

Smile back and shrug, as if all the world were a comedy you were only just now appreciating. Moss begins to put a hand to your shoulder but then takes it back. "Congratulations, Trudy," he murmurs.

"But she hasn't come back yet. I haven't seen her since last night."

"She'll come back," says Moss. "It's only been a day."

"But it's been a whole day. Maybe I should put in ads."

"It's only been one day. She'll come back. You'll see."

Step away from him. Outside, in front of the streetlight, something like snow is falling. Think back again to MacNeil-Lehrer. Say in a level tone: "You know, there are people who know more about it than we do, who say that there is no circumnavigating a nuclear war, we will certainly have one, it's just a matter of time. And when it happens, it's going to dissolve all our communications systems, melt silicon chips—"

"Trudy, please." He wants you to stop. He knows this edge in your voice, this MacNeil-Lehrer edge. All of the world knotted and failing on your tongue.

"And then if you're off living someplace else, in some efficiency, how will I be able to get in touch with you? There I'll be, Moss, all alone in my pink pom-pom slippers, the entire planet exploding all around, and I won't be able to talk to you, to say—" In fifth grade you learned the first words ever spoken on the telephone: *Mr. Watson, come here, I want you.* And suddenly, as you look at him, at the potatoey fists of his cheeks, at his broom-blonde hair, it hits you as it would a child: Someday, like everybody, this man you truly love like no other is going to die. No matter how much you love him, you cannot save him. No matter how much you love: nothing, no one, lasts.

"Moss, we're not safe."

And though there's no flutter of walls, or heave of the floor, above the frayed-as-panic rug, shoes move, and Moss seems to come unstuck, to float toward you, his features beginning to slide in downward diagonals, some chip in his back dissolving, allowing him to bend. His arms reach out to bring you close to his chest. The buttons of his shirt poke against you, and his chin hooks, locks around your neck. When he is gone, the world will grow dull as Mars.

"It's okay," he whispers, his lips moving against your hair. Things grow fuzzy around the edge like a less than brilliant lie. "It's okay," says Moss.

MONA SIMPSON

Approximations

In MY FAMILY, there were always two people. First, my mother and father. Carol and John.

They danced. Hundreds of evenings at hundreds of parties in their twenties. A thousand times between songs her eyes completely closed when she leaned against him. He looked down at the top of her head; her part gleamed white, under and between the dark hair. He rubbed her back, trying to rouse her, but she became indistinct, blurring against his jacket. He hugged her imperceptibly closer, moving his hand in slower circles on her back, but when he talked it was to someone else over her head. He closed a big hand on her ear.

How do I know this? I don't. But there was a black and white snapshot with my father staring at someone outside the frame. I was looking at the picture when, for some reason, I asked my mother where he was.

I was young, only four years old, and I had no memories of my father. I must have been repeating a question someone else had asked me. My mother was ironing. It was 1960 and all her summer clothes were seersucker and cotton. Her hands stalled over the iron when I asked the question.

"He's gone," she said, not looking at me. The windows were open. A string of hummingbirds moved on the lilac bush outside. "But," she said, gathering her cheeks, "he'll be coming back."

"When?"

For a moment, her mouth wavered, but then her chin snapped back into a straight line and she pushed the iron over the perforated pink and white fabric again.

"I don't know," she said.

So we waited, without mentioning it, for my father. In the meantime, we got used to living alone. Just the two of us.

Other people asked me questions.

"Any news from your Dad?"

"I don't know."

"You must miss him." Other mothers got maternal, pulling me close to their soft, aproned bellies.

For a moment, but only for a moment, I'd let my eyes close. Then I jerked away. "No," I said.

Saturday nights, we went ice-skating. We wore skin-colored tights and matching short dresses made out of stretch fabric. We skated in tight concentrated figures, our necks bent like horses', following the lines of an 8. Then, when the PA system started up, we broke into free skating, wild around the rink. My mother skated up behind me and caught me at the waist.

"This is how you really lose the pounds," she called, slapping her thigh, "skating fast."

I was always behind. Jerry, the pro, did a t-stop to impress my mother, shaving a comet of ice into the air. They skated around together and I had to slow down to wipe the melting water from my face.

When the music stopped, my mother pulled me over to the

barrier, where we ran our skate tips into the soft wood. She pointed up to the rows of empty seats. They were maroon, with the plush worn down in the centers.

"See, when you're older, you can bring a boy you're dating here to see you skate. He can watch and think, hey, she's not just another pretty girl, she can really do something."

She peered into my face with a slanted gaze as if, through a crack, she could see what I'd become.

Taking the skates off, on the bench, was all joy. You could walk without carrying your own weight. Your feet and ankles were pure air. The floors were carpeted with rubber mats, red and black, like a checkerboard. In regular shoes, we walked like saints on clouds. The high domed arena was always cold.

The first time we heard from my father was 1963 in the middle of winter. We got a long distance phone call from Las Vegas and it was him.

"We're going to Disneyland!" my mother said, lifting her eyebrows and covering the mouthpiece with her hand.

Into the phone, she said she'd take me out of school. We'd fly to Las Vegas and then the three of us would drive west to Disneyland. I didn't recognize his voice when my mother held out the receiver.

"Hello, Melinda. This is Daddy."

I shrugged at my mother and wouldn't take the phone. "You'll know him when you see him," she whispered.

We waited three days for our summer linen dresses to be dry-cleaned. "It's going to be *hot*," my mother warned. "Scorching," she added with a smile. It was snowing dry powder when we left Illinois. We only saw white outside the airplane window. Halfway there, we changed in the tiny bathroom, from our winter coats to sleeveless dresses and patent leather thongs. It was still cool in the plane but my mother promised it would be hot on the ground.

It was. The air was swirling with dirt. A woman walked across the airport lobby with a scarf tied around her chest; it trailed behind her, coasting on air.

My mother spotted my father in the crowd, and we all pretended I recognized him too. He looked like an ordinary man. His hair was balding in a small circle. He wore tight black slacks, a brown jacket and black leather, slip-on shoes. His chin stuck out from his face, giving him an eager look.

He had a car parked outside and my mother got into the front seat with him. We passed hotels with bright blue swimming pools and the brown tinge of the sky hung over the water, like a line of dirt on the rim of a sleeve.

My father's apartment was in a pink stucco building. When we walked up with our suitcases, his three roommates were crowded on the porch, leaning on the iron bannister. They wore white V-neck T-shirts and thick dark hair pressed out from under them. I hadn't seen men dressed like that before.

"He told us you had long blonde hair."

"You look like your Dad."

"She's prettier than her Dad."

When my father smiled, the gaps between his teeth made him look unintentionally sad, like a jack-o-lantern. He looked down and I felt he was proud of me. He touched my hair. I loved him blindly, the feeling darkening over everything, but it passed.

My mother stepped up to the porch. "Don't you want to introduce me to your friends, too?"

My father introduced each man separately and each man smiled. Then my father gave me a present: a package of six, different-colored cotton headbands. I held it and didn't tear the cellophane open.

My father worked as a waiter in a hotel restaurant. We had dinner there, eating slowly while he worked, watching him balance dishes on the inside of his arm. He sat down with us while my mother was sipping her coffee. He crossed one leg over the other, smoking luxuriously. My mother leaned closer and whispered in my ear.

"When are we going to Disneyland?" I asked, blankly, saying what she said to say but somehow knowing it was wrong.

My father didn't answer me. He looked at my mother and put out his cigarette. That night in the apartment, they fought. My father's roommates closed the doors to their rooms.

"So, when are we going," my mother asked gamely, crossing one leg over the other on a dinette chair.

His shoulders sloped down. "You were late," he said finally. "You were supposed to be here Monday. When you didn't come, I lost the money I'd saved."

"In three days, how? How could you do that?"

"On the tables."

"You, you can't do this to her," my mother said, her voice gathering like a wave.

They sent me outside to the porch. I heard everything, even their breath, through the screen door. There was a box of matches on the ground and I lit them, one by one, scratching them against the concrete and then dropping them in the dirt when the flames came too close to my fingers. Finally it was quiet. My father came out and opened the screen door and I went in.

They set up the living room couch as a bed for me. They both undressed in my father's bedroom. He pulled off his T-shirt and sat on the bed to untie his shoes. My mother looked back at me, over her shoulder, while she unzipped her dress. Finally, she closed the door.

The next morning my father and I got up before my mother. We went to the hotel coffee shop and sat on stools at the counter. I was afraid to ask for anything; I said I wasn't hungry. My father ordered a soft-boiled egg for himself. His eyes caught on the uniformed waitress, the coffee pot tilting from her hand, a purse on the other end of the counter. The egg came in a white coffee cup. He chopped it with the edge of a spoon, asking me if I'd ever tasted a four-minute egg. I ate a spoonful and I loved it. No other egg was ever so good. I told my father how good it was hoping we could share it. But he slid the whole cup down, the spoon in it, without looking at me and signalled the waitress for another egg.

Walking back to the apartment, he kicked sand into the air. There were no lawns in front of the parked trailers, but the sand was raked and bordered with rows of rocks. My father's black slip-on shoes were scuffed. He was holding my hand but not looking at me.

"So we'll go to Disneyland next trip," he said.

"When?"

Suddenly, I wanted dates and plans and the name of a month, not to see Disneyland but to see him. Taking long steps, trying to match his pace, I wanted to say that I didn't care about Disneyland. I dared myself to talk, after one more, two more, three more steps, all the way to the apartment. But I never said it. All I did was hold his hand tighter and tighter.

"I don't know," he said, letting my hand drop when we came to the steps in front of his apartment.

On the plane home, I was holding the package of headbands in my lap, tracing them through the cellophane. My mother turned away and looked out the window.

"I work," she said finally. "I pay for your school and your books and your skates and your lessons. *And*," she said in a louder whisper, "I pay the rent."

She picked up the package of headbands and then dropped it back on my lap.

"A seventy-nine cent package of headbands."

It wasn't fair and I knew it.

The next year my mother went back to Las Vegas without me. She and Jerry, the ice-skating pro, got married. She came back without any pictures of the wedding and Jerry moved in with us.

She said she didn't want to bother with a big wedding since it was her second marriage. She wore a dress she already had.

My mother and I spent all that summer in the arena, where Jerry ran an ice-skating school. All day long the air conditioners hummed like the inside of a refrigerator. Inside the door of my locker was a picture of Peggy Fleming. Inside my mother's was Sonja Henie. In the main office, there were framed pictures of Jerry during his days with Holiday On Ice and the Ice Capades. In them, he didn't look like himself. He had short bristly hair and a glamorous smile. His dark figure slithered backward, his arms pointing to two corners of the photograph. The lighting was yellow and false. In one of the pictures it was snowing.

We practiced all summer for the big show in August. The theme was the calendar; the chorus changed from December angels to April bunnies and May tulips. I couldn't get the quick turns in time with the older girls, so I was taken out of the chorus and given a role of my own. After the Easter number was over and the skaters in bunny costumes crowded backstage, I skated fast around the rink, blowing kisses. A second later, the Zamboni came out to clear the ice. I stood in back before my turn, terrified to go out too early or too late, with the velvet curtain bunched in my hand.

My mother came up behind me every show and gave me a push, saying "now, go" at the right time. I skated completely by instinct. I couldn't see. My eyes blurred under the strong spotlight. But one night, during the Easter dance, my mother was near the stage exit, laughing with Jerry. She kept trying to bend down to tie her laces and he pulled her up, kissing her. Finally, looking over his shoulder, she saw me and quickly mouthed "go." I went out then but it was too late. I heard the Zamboni growling behind me. I tried to run, forgetting how to skate and fell forward, flat on the ice. My hands burned when I hurried up behind the moving spotlight and I saw that I'd torn my tights. The edges of the hole on my knee were ragged with blood.

I sat down on the ice backstage while the music for my

mother's number started up. I knew it by heart. Jerry led my
mother in an elementary waltz. She glinted along the ice, shifting
her weight from leg to bent leg. Her skates slid out from her
body. She was heavier than she had once been. She swayed,
moving her head to glance off the eyes of the crowd. Under the
slow spotlight, she twirled inside the box of Jerry's arms.

I quit skating after that. When my mother and Jerry went
to the rink I stayed home or went out to play with the other kids
in the neighborhood. The next year I joined the girl scout troop.

Eventually, my mother stopped taking lessons, too. Then
Jerry went to the rink himself every day, like any other man
going to a job.

One Saturday, there was a father/daughter breakfast sponsored
by my girl scout troop. I must have told my mother about it. But
by the time the day came, I'd forgotten and I was all dressed in
my play clothes to go outside. I was out the front door when my
mother caught me.

"Melinda."

"What?"

"Where are you going?"

"The end of the block."

"Don't you remember your girl scout breakfast? You have
to go in and change."

I didn't want to go. I was already on the driveway, strad-
dling my bike.

"I don't feel like going to that. I'd rather play."

My mother was wearing her housecoat, but she came outside anyway, holding it closed with one hand over her chest.

"He took the day off and he's in there now getting dressed.
Now, come on. Go in and put something on."

"No," I said, "I don't want to."

"Won't you do this for me?" she whispered. "He wants to
adopt you."

We stood there a minute and then the screen door opened.

"Let her go, Carol. She doesn't have to go if she doesn't want to go. It's up to her."

Jerry was standing in the doorway, all dressed up. His hair was combed down and wet from just taking a shower. He was wearing a white turtle-neck sweater and a paisley ascot. I felt sorry for him, looking serious and dressed up like that, and I wanted to change my mind and go in but I thought it was too late and I flew off on my bike. None of the other fathers would be wearing ascots anyway, I was thinking.

My father called again when I was ten, to say he wanted to take me to Disneyland. He said he was living in Reno, Nevada, with a new wife. He and my mother bickered a long time on the phone. He wanted to send a plane ticket for me to come alone. My mother said either both of us went or neither. She said she was afraid he would kidnap me. She held out. Finally, they agreed he'd send the money for two tickets.

Around this time, my mother always told me her dreams, which were about things she wanted. A pale blue Lincoln Continental with a cream-colored interior. A swimming pool with night lights and a redwood fence around the yard. A house with a gazebo you couldn't see from the road.

She had already stopped telling Jerry the things she wanted because he tried to get them for her and he made mistakes. He approximated. He bought her the wrong kind of record player for Christmas and he got a dull gold Cadillac, a used car, for her birthday.

Before we went to California, my mother read about something she wanted. A New Sony Portable Color Television. A jewel. She wanted a white one, she was sure it came in white. In the short magazine article she'd clipped out, it said the TVs were available only in Japan until early 1967, next year, but my mother was sure that by the time we went, they would be all over California.

Jerry took us to the airport and he was quiet while we

checked on our luggage. When we got onto the plane, we forgot about him. We made plans to get my father to buy us the New Sony. It was this trip's Disneyland. We'd either win it or lose it depending on how we played.

At the airport in Los Angeles, we met Velma, my father's new wife. She was a good ten years older and rich; her fingers were full of jewelry and she had on a brown fur coat.

This trip there was no struggle. We went straight to Disneyland. We stayed in the Disneyland Hotel. The four of us went through Disneyland like a rake. There was nothing we didn't see. We ate at restaurants. We bought souvenirs.

But knowing the real purpose of our trip made talking to my father complicated. As I watched my mother laugh with him I was never sure if it was a real laugh, for pleasure, or if it was work, to get our TV. My father seemed sad and a little bumbling. With everyone else around, my father and I didn't talk much.

"How's school?" he asked, walking to the Matterhorn.

"Fine," I said, "I like it."

"That's good," he said.

Our conversations were always like that. It was like lighting single matches.

And I was getting nervous. We were leaving in a day and nothing was being done about the New Sony. The last night, Velma suggested that I meet my father downstairs in the lobby before dinner, so the two of us could talk alone. In our room, my mother brushed my hair out in a fan across my back.

I was nervous. I didn't know what to say to my father.

My mother knew. "See if you can get him to buy the TV," she said. "I bet they've got one for sale right nearby."

I said I hadn't seen any in the stores.

"I think I saw one," she said, winking, "a white one."

"What should I do?" I knew I had to learn everything.

"Tell him you're saving up for it. He'll probably just buy it for you." My mother wasn't nervous. "Suck in your cheeks," she said, brushing glitter on my face. She was having fun.

I didn't want to leave the room. But my mother gave me a short push and I went slowly down the stairs. I tried to remember everything she told me. *Chin up. Smile. Brush your hair back. Say you're saving for it. Suck in your cheeks.* It seemed I was on the verge of losing one of two things I badly wanted. With each step it seemed I was choosing.

I saw my father's back first. He was standing by the candy counter. Whenever I saw my father I went through a series of gradual adjustments, like when you step out of the ice rink, in summer, and feel the warm air. I had to focus my vision down from an idea as vague as a color, to him. He was almost bald. The way his chin shot out made him always look eager. He was buying a roll of Lifesavers.

"Would you like anything?" he asked, seeing me and tilting his head to indicate the rows of candy arranged on the counter.

I thought for a wild moment. I could give up the plan, smile and say yes. Yes I want a candy bar. Two candy bars. He'd buy me two of the best candy bars there. I could stand and eat them sloppily, all the while gazing up at my father. If I smiled, he would smile. He would bend down and dab the chocolate from my mouth with a handkerchief moist with his own saliva.

But I didn't say yes, because I knew it would end. I knew I'd remember my father's face, soft on mine, next year when no letters came. I would hate my best memory because it would prove that my father could fake love or that love could end or, worst of all, that love was not powerful enough to change a life, his life.

"No," I said, "I'm saving up my money."

"What?" he said, smiling down at me. He was unravelling the paper from his Lifesavers.

I gulped. "I'm saving my money for a new Sony portable color television," I said.

He scanned the drugstore for a moment. I think we both knew he was relinquishing me to my mother.

"Oh," he said finally, nodding.

.   .   .

We didn't get the Sony. On the way home, neither of us mentioned it. And when the plane landed, we didn't call Jerry. We
took a taxi from the airport. When we got home, my mother
collapsed on the blue-green couch and looked around the room
disapprovingly. The suitcases were scattered on the floor.

"You didn't say one big word the whole time we were
there," she said. "Here, you're clever. You should hear yourself
kidding around with Jerry. You say three syllable words and . . . .
There, you didn't say one smart thing in front of him. Let me
tell you, you sounded dumb."

She imitated a dumb person, stretching her eyes wide open
and puffing air into her cheeks.

She sighed. "Go out and play," she said. "Go out and play
with your friends."

But I just stood there looking at her. She got worse. She
kicked off her shoes. She began throwing pillows from the couch
onto the floor.

"Not one big word. The whole time we were there," she
said.

"And you didn't smile. Here, you're sharp, you're animate.
There you slumped. You looked down. You really just looked
ordinary. Like any other kid around here. Well, it's a good thing
we're back because I can see now this is just where you belong.
With all the mill workers' kids. Well, here we are. Good."

She was still yelling when I walked out the door. Then I
did something I'd never done before. I walked down to the end
of our road and I hitchhiked. I got picked up by a lady who lived
two blocks away. I told her I was going to the arena.

From the lobby I saw Jerry on the ice. I ran downstairs to
my mother's locker and sat alone, lacing up skates. I ran up the
hall on my skate points and I ran onto the ice fast, my arms
straight out to the sides. I went flying toward Jerry.

He was bending over a woman's shoulders, steering her into
a figure eight.

A second later he saw me and I was in his arms, breathing against the wool of his sweater. He put a hand over my ear and told his student something I couldn't understand.

A few seconds later, when I pulled myself away, the student was gone. I stopped crying and then there was nothing to do. We were alone on the ice.

I looked up at Jerry; it was different than with my father. I couldn't bury my face in Jerry's sweater and forget the world. I stood there nervously. Jerry was still Jerry, standing in front of me shyly, a man I didn't know. My father was gone for good and here was Jerry, just another man in the world, who had nothing to do with me.

"Would you like me to teach you to do loops?" he asked quietly.

I couldn't say no because of how he looked, standing there with his hands in his pockets.

I glanced up at the empty stands around us. I was tired. And cold. Jerry started skating in tight, precise loops. I looked down at the lines he was making on the ice.

"I'll try," I said, beginning to follow them.

EHUD HAVAZELET

Natalie Wood's Amazing Eyes

I WILL NOT FORGET what Doug has given me. Not small things. When I clear out time to think about it, I know he has given me a lot.

Doug gave me the movies. I had always enjoyed them, but in a random, unspecific way. I would forget movies I had seen, and be just as willing to be terrified or sentimental the third time as the first. I didn't know names. It was the blonde with the hair over her face, or the one who looked like Spencer Tracy, but not exactly. Doug had books. He knew behind the screen stories. One of the first things Doug showed me was a picture of himself at a table with Martin Scorsese. It is quite a big table and Scorsese is all the way on the other side.

Doug has given me this house to live in. It is a ridiculous house; Doug's boss, Ernie Fike, built it for his bride, Mona. The automatic garage door plays "Amazing Grace" when it opens. There are mirrors over the bed and a ditch in the backyard where Fike was digging a pool. Fike's napkins say things like: "To our wives and sweethearts. May they never meet." He has glasses decorated with women whose clothes disappear when you tilt them. In the bathroom, upstairs, the light switch is a woman's breast. You have to press the nipple to turn on the light. When I told Doug I didn't think I could touch it, he put a Band-Aid over the top.

Fike and Mona lived here six months before she ran off to Las Vegas. Fike told us to move in because the memories were too painful, but I'm sure it was the pictures. They still come, every week or so, each showing Mona with a different man. Sometimes they're having drinks on a veranda or toweling off after a dip in the pool. Most of the time, they're in bed. The men look like young doctors in the soaps, and Mona's eyes are closed and her head back, in every shot. Fike moved after Mona had some of the photos made into postcards. She wrote, "Thinking of you," and signed them, "Mrs. Ernie Fike." Fike swears he heard the postman giggle and two tellers talking about him at the bank. Since he doesn't want them, I keep the pictures now. I look at Mona's clothes and try to see what she and her friends are drinking. I wonder if they're at The Sands or Caesar's Palace. I'm happy for Mona and would miss it if she stopped writing.

Fike says we can stay as long as we like it here. There is talk of a big promotion for Doug in the works and if things keep going well, Fike says, we'll be able to buy this house outright in no time at all.

We love them all, not just the famous or critically acclaimed. We've seen *Stella Dallas* six times, *Laura*, four. We laughed so hard at *The Palm Beach Story*, we made ourselves sick and had to leave. We know whole sections of *The Thin Man* by heart, though none of our friends are interested any longer, and certainly, none are willing to come with us into Manhattan for the Nelson Eddy–Jeanette MacDonald operettas the Thalia puts on as a joke. We've lost friends who've tired of our Spring Byington or Edward Arnold birthday parties, and I've been told point blank that something must be wrong with anyone who gets so much from the movies, unreal and in the dark as they are.

Doug showed me where to look. In the beginning, he was patient, and there was all the time in the world. He loved it, that I'd go back with him a second or third time to the same movie, and when he told me things, I remembered. I remembered Bruce Dern's first appearance, *Wild River*, and Dustin Hoffman's, *The Tiger Makes Out*. We could cry, if we wanted, and afterward we could talk or just be together, quietly. We were in the old place then, on the West Side. We walked for hours and hardly said a word, and the whole city was like a movie.

Doug's job is the break we needed. When I met him, he was carrying a case full of screenplays and talking of impossible things. Now, Fike treats him like a son and tells him there is always room at the top, for those who know how to climb.

When Doug was mentioned for a promotion, he decided to begin working nights. We talked it over, and I brought up our movies. Of course, I would never stand in Doug's way. Still, I was hurt when Doug didn't seem to realize what this would mean. I'm not sure what I would have said if he told me, "No, Caroline, I turned them down. The evenings are ours," but as we picked our way silently through our Salad Nicoise, I heard him say something like that over and over in my head.

Doug encourages me to go to movies alone. He still hangs the schedules over the breakfast table and puts arrows near the ones that shouldn't be missed. At night, if he's not too tired, we talk about the movies I've been to. When I told him I noticed an aborigine wearing Adidas in *Apocalypse Now*, he seemed pleased, so I've been telling him other things, some of them not true. I can't know how he misses the movies, Doug says. He likes to think about me there, and to know I'm happy.

We talk a lot, Doug and I, sometimes over the phone during the day. I tell him about my life. I tell him if we're going to stay in this house, certain changes must be made. I tell him the living room is all wrong, the kitchen too cluttered, not at all right for people of our sort. We talk about things to do in the city, things to draw me out of the house, my options. There's school, I could always finish school, and there's my old job at the clinic; there are any number of things I could do, Doug says. If I get serious, he wants to know. Just tell him and he'll make the time to discuss it.

I haven't told him this.

I've been going to Times Square, to the houses where they show movies all day. Some of these movies are decent, but most are Kung Fu or sex. I'm not going to say I go only to the worthwhile ones, either.

The theaters are wonderful. Huge caverns with balconies and footlights, felt seats, and massive curtains folded like sculpture to the sides of the screen. Many were built for vaudeville, and entering them you feel as if those days were preserved somehow, like when you turn on an old radio and expect to hear Harry James. It never wears off, the shock of coming in from the noise and the glare, the heat, to a cool dark chamber, hundreds of seats, shadows, eyes, cigarette ends. It's a separate world. The air is full of possibilities.

I sit there and watch the movies. Sometimes, they are entertaining, spy movies with Charles Bronson or Clint Eastwood as a lean killer. Other times, I don't pay attention. From the dark around me come noises. There is snoring and whispering and from far off in the balcony, quiet sounds like crying. There are moans and the sound of lips on skin and sometimes, the frank spill of water on the floor. The air carries many smells, and though I stay for hours, I cannot grow accustomed to it. If I look around, there is movement by the walls, figures pass through the exit light's dull red.

I have had encounters in these theaters.

Once a man sat behind me and talked to me for a long

while. I looked ahead but I was not watching the movie. When I didn't answer, he undid his pants and then I heard his breathing change. When he got up to leave, he pushed his hand through my hair and said, "Bitch."

Another time, I heard sirens and voices from the foyer. People dragged themselves to look. On the screen, a naked woman lay on the bed as two young men approached. When the noises grew louder, I went out, too. A man was sitting by the wall, under the movie posters with their frame of flashing lights, and where the top of his head should have been were only blood and white bits of bone. I could not take my eyes off him until a cop began to move us away. When he put a hand on my arm, I started to run. It was Columbus Circle before I could make myself stop.

Maybe I should have been talking to Doug. There are things it's his responsibility to know. I wanted to tell him about the man in pink, but I couldn't.

He was over six feet, dressed completely in pink, from boots to suit to wide-brimmed hat. He stood under the exit sign, black skin luminous, as if it were taking light out of the air. When he sat in the section next to mine, several rows ahead, the screen grew brighter for a moment, and I could see he was looking at me.

He moved into my section, a few rows in front. The climactic fight scene was beginning; bodies careened through the air and a Samurai in a white robe watched from a hillside. The audience started to cheer. He stared directly at me, back almost full to the screen, openly, calmly, and when the Samurai sent a severed head flying, the audience screamed, and he moved into the seat next to mine.

He stared, as if I was across the theater, still. He had a trim mustache and very white eyes and when the reflected light changed, they were all I could see of his face. A scent came from him that I had never smelled before, and I found myself wondering what it could be, his fragrance, watching to see if he would smile.

I sat there until he put a hand out and lifted my skirt. He did not move then, did not come closer or reach farther with his hand. He held the hem of my skirt up as if he would bend toward me, but he didn't. I felt the theater air wind up my thighs and I watched his face in the dark.

Afterward, I stood on the street outside Doug's building. Many windows were blank, but on the fourth floor, I could see the lights in Doug's office. I stood on the street for several minutes debating whether to go up, and then for several more, willing Doug to the library window. I left then, went home and to bed. When Doug returned later, I pretended I was asleep.

From now on, this is all I will remember:

In *The Searchers*, Natalie Wood has been made impure by living with the Indians. John Wayne tracks her down to kill her but just at the end, something, maybe something in her amazing eyes, changes him. He takes her in his arms and says, "Let's go home, Debby."

In *Only Angels Have Wings*, Cary Grant is in love with Thomas Mitchell, but there's nothing he can do about it. When Mitchell is dying, Cary Grant lights a cigarette and puts it between Mitchell's lips, a parting kiss.

In *The Big Heat*, all the women are eliminated. Glenn Ford's wife is blown up and his daughter taken away. Gloria Grahame, in atonement, has her lovely face splashed with boiling coffee. She dies. When Ford returns to the squad room, not a woman left in his world, he says, "Keep that coffee hot, Hugo."

When Doug invites Fike and one of his girls for dinner, I serve them heart. The cookbook describes it as "a homey treat." Slice the heart, across the grain, into quarter-inch pieces. Pour into ovenproof dish of boiling water. Add carrots, celery (with leaves), onion, salt (to taste), green pepper. Cook until tender, one and a half to two hours. Add, if you wish, lemon juice or dry wine. Goes well with rice or potato dumplings.

Doug, Fike, and Rhonda have drinks while I finish cooking. Doug told Fike to bring whatever he liked. He brought a bottle of scotch and a bottle of gin, two kinds of bourbon, light and dark rum, and a melon liqueur that Rhonda says is dreamy over ice cream. All the bottles have been opened, and Fike is showing Doug how to use the ice machine that freezes little plastic nudes into the cubes.

After I serve the food, Rhonda takes a bite and asks what it is. I tell her and she runs from the table. Doug looks down at his plate. I can see his face changing. Fike continues eating and says he knew right away. I go after Rhonda and Doug grabs my arm in the kitchen.

"What are you trying to do?" he says.

"I'm sorry," I say. "Wasn't it good?"

"Ruin your own life, Caroline. Don't try to ruin mine."

Rhonda is all right after she washes her face a few times. Doug has cleared the table and Fike is freshening the drinks. He comes into the kitchen while I make the dessert.

"That wasn't a very nice thing to do to Rhonda," Fike says. "She's sensitive. She cries when dogs get killed on TV."

I add caramel to the sauce. This is the hard part, the cookbook says. It should simmer but must not boil. I bring the wooden spoon around slowly and watch the sauce for signs of trouble. Fike lifts his glass and makes breathing sounds as he drinks.

"I liked it, though," he tells me. "I like all the organs."

The sauce has started to thicken. I reduce the flame and bring the spoon around faster.

"That looks good, too," Fike says. "Let me help you."

Doug comes into the kitchen just as Fike puts a hand on my breast. I see Doug stop for a second, then take a carton of ice cream from the freezer. He returns to the living room where Rhonda has started to sing. Fike pushes my breast in small circular motions.

"Is this helping, Caroline?"

.   .   .

The man in the ticket booth knows me, or says he does when I ask. He tells me the theater is closed for cleaning. They close every morning, for two hours, for cleaning. I tell him I just want to wait inside. He looks at the money I've put down and then at my clothes and hair. Harmless, he decides, and gets up to open the door.

The foyer is cool and I walk past the darkened movie posters into the theater. Dim lights shine from the front of the auditorium, and I can see that the carpeting and seats are green. The high walls are covered with gods and goddesses, Egyptian, by the look of them, that I have never been able to see until now. They carry fruit, animals, and dishes filled with fire toward the stage. Over the stage are a long boat and the sun, and two elegant dogs crouching. It is all very well done, beautiful, I think, gilded except where the plaster walls have erupted in long ugly patches. The curtains are still drawn, and in the light I can see the screen is torn and stained, but in the dark I know it will be mended.

I find a spot in the first balcony, arrange my coat, and sit. A man is sweeping, but he soon finishes and I am left alone in the theater. Delicate sounds carry to me, soft rumbling and a fine hiss like a soothing voice whispering. The air is still in this massive room, but it can seem to be moving. It is easy to imagine in here. I scan the empty seats, row after row ready for the show to begin. The lights grow dim. They will be gathering now, waiting to get in, the men with the weak smiles and stunned eyes, lining up for the dark. I can see them in their coats, their wide-brimmed hats, walking up the carpeted hallway past the movie posters now dazzling, toward the steel doors with the gold handles, toward the quiet and dark. I see them in flanks, in long shambling columns, coming to where I wait. Let them come to me.

DEAN ALBARELLI

Honeymoon

M Y GRANDFATHER REMEMBERS walking down
Sackville Street with Michael Collins in 1916, so you might say
we've a history of nationalists in my family. I used often try to
picture him there with the Big Fellow when I chanced to be on
O'Connell Street. It wasn't easy, what with buses painted with
bright hailstorms of Smarties, and neon lights, and McDonald's.
Around the General Post Office I could get a fair glimpse of
what they might have appeared like. Collins, tall, boyishly mas-
culine, the eyes of people upon him. My grandfather would not
have matched him in height, but I'm sure he bore himself with
equal poise. I don't recall just how they happened to be together,
but it was so.

This day, walking past the GPO, I did not picture them,
but recalled walking there with my grandfather years before,
when I was about seven or eight. He had stopped to show me
the bullet holes and pieces of lead in the pillared columns before
the building, left there from Easter Week. I had rubbed my
finger into the holes gingerly, with respect; touching history it

186

felt like. I now wondered if such scenes would etch themselves as fondly upon the memory of my own son. I was to be married in a week, and questions of a family began to occur to me.

I passed a young punk rocker whose hair was dyed green and orange, of all colors. He had all the gear: tight black pants, bulky tennis shoes, safety pins, the haircut with the cultivated cowlick. He stopped outside a record store where the window displayed a hideous poster advertising a new album by the Sex Pistols. I couldn't help wondering what must his parents think when he steps into his tidy little home in Clontarf or wherever.

Farther south, I crossed the quay to the bridge near Daniel O'Connell's statue. The Liberator. The demagogue who balked in the fields of Brian Boru is more like it. Unable to call a British bluff. Grandfather called him The Deliberator for that. "Wasn't he the t'in edge of the wedge among our heroes, though," was what he would often say.

Around the base of O'Connell's statue sit four angels with long thick hair which, were they not mere stone, would most certainly be blonde. I studied the angel on the right as the morning crowd pressed by. From the time I was about four I had believed her to be not just an angel, but my guardian angel, that dear protectress who, as grandfather said, was always by my side. She was beautiful, and had a bullet hole in her left breast, a wound sustained in Easter Week.

Soon I reached the green gate of Trinity. I had only twice been within the hallowed grounds since taking my degree two years before. My mother has lived in Dublin all her life, and never once set foot in Trinity. My father nearly threw me out of the house when I decided to study English and history there, even though it was by then nearly seventy percent Catholic. I entered the front gate, where Oliver Goldsmith, self-consciously ugly, hides his face in a book. Edmund Burke looks across at what was once the Irish Parliament and, being a logical man, understands how it has become the Bank of Ireland.

I followed two culchies with thick Kerry accents—dressed straight off the dusty bargain racks of McBirney's—down into the Buttery and ordered a pint. Something about culchie clothes in the city always depresses me, especially in the pretentious atmosphere of Trinity, and I started thinking about this culchie's mother packing him off to Dublin, sending him so far from home with so little taste.

But I was feeling less sorry for the culchies than for myself this morning. I was to meet an American student who was selling his passport. It disturbed me to have been tapped for so menial a task, especially after spending six weeks in Syria, learning to "pick oranges," as the standard joke went. It was rather like a student receiving a scholarship prize, and later being told he must repeat his courses. Doubtless the lads at the office had fed Ferguson some tripe: "O'Toole's a school teacher; he's nothing to do in the summer. Let *him* pick up the passport."

From the description, I recognized the American's denim jacket with a silver studded peace symbol on the back. He kept looking at his watch, and after a short while he left. I followed him across the cobblestones, watching his back and remembering Ferguson once telling me that the symbol was really "the footprint of an American chicken."

It occurred to me that perhaps Ferguson was testing my commitment or toying with me to see if I'd balk by sending me on what was practically a messenger-boy job. Because while in Syria, of all times, I had begun to reconsider my involvement. Of course, Ferguson couldn't know that I was entertaining such thoughts. I hadn't mentioned them to anyone. Even so, ridiculous as it sounds, I had often heard the man discuss his belief in extrasensory perception, which he claimed to have often experienced. And even if he was just taking the mickey out of someone, or using the line to intimidate a man, there have been times when I've thought those bedroom eyes of his have read men's thoughts even as the thoughts occurred.

The American was glancing behind him, and I looked down

as we passed the ugly new Arts Block and a Calder piece called *Cactus*. I decided it was more likely Ferguson had sent me simply because I knew Trinity.

I walked across College Park, where the grass was stained with faint lines of white lime, which had marked the 800-meter track earlier in the summer. I forgot about Ferguson, but all those doubts that had begun in Syria sprang up again, like the blades of grass I was trampling. Especially doubts about the occasional weekend trips to Belfast. Someone else could do those jobs. They had to be done, but someone else could do them. There were dozens of headers who wouldn't mind the few extra quid they could pick up in my place.

The entire dilemma was ludicrous, really. I had always been so dedicated to the whole thing that I gave myself completely to anything they asked of me. (I'd even written part of a speech for Ferguson for the Easter Week rally a year before.) And having learned much in the way of destruction for constructive change, as it were, they sent me off to Syria to train with the elite. Who turned out to be a lot of smelly Arabs with Soviet guns and money, who never bathed, and leered over my fiancée. And there I began to sense that I wanted no part of this life. It was not the same organization my grandfather had known. It was tainted and tawdry; backed by opportunists, loaded with the hooligan element and naive neo-Marxists, and a few deluded romantics like myself.

It has always been that way with me; just when I become quite serious about something, or committed to it, or proficient at it, I lose interest in the thing. Here at Trinity it was distance running. I had good luck in my first season of cross-country. I placed in the top ten in every match, and by third year I was usually first or second for Trinity. And around track season my interest began to falter. I thought maybe it was just the atmosphere of the track, running eight loops around an 800 meter oval, over and over. I was sure the feeling would leave by the time cross-country began in the fall. But it didn't. And then the following spring I was captain of the track team, running worse than ever, and no longer caring a great deal about it, walking to the starting line without an ounce of adrenalin flowing in me. And then running circles.

The American was standing, hands pressed deep in his pockets, in a deserted dressing room of the Pavilion. He was nervous. I told him we knew, of course, that to get back home he would eventually have to report the loss of his passport. But he was not to do so until the following May. Since this was in August, it gave us a long time to make use of the book. Ferguson had told me we would want to be getting a man into and out of the States. I told the American that if there was an emergency in which he would have to leave for home, he was to contact us first. "Mind now, you tell anyone, and it's big trouble for you, understand?" He nodded his head so that his little wire glasses slid on his nose and said yes he did. His hand was shaking when he gave me the little blue book. I looked inside; there was his picture, coat and tie, with a sloppy signature across the edge of the photograph: Neil Blanchard. I gave him the fifteen £20.00 notes, which he seemed to pocket happily enough, glancing at and half thumbing the wad, but not bothering to count it.

I had considered earlier whether or not to give him all £300.00. With marriage and an expensive flat only a week away, I was tempted to change the price. He was nervous enough that he would probably have taken much less, but I abandoned the thought, said a solemn "Cheers," and left. It was as well not to have the money hanging over me. With my Catholic complex, I would probably get to the point of repentant nights on my knees if I were to pull it off, but I would have no knees if I did not. I only realized how much the idea had troubled me by my great relief at deciding not to retain any of the notes. I left him there and nearly added "Thanks," as I turned into the corridor messed with pellets of mud and bloody tissues from the rugby players. Of course, it was only wise to be abrupt and keep him frightened, but I wondered if my not thanking him was evidence of the general rudeness I had conditioned myself to in Syria. The Syrians were forever commenting on my "pleases" and "thank yous."

"Why do you always be so polite? Never mind to say 'thank you.' You are so Breetish."

Going out the back gate of Trinity, I met Professor Baxter, who had been one of my lecturers in Irish literature. He was a Brit, and a homosexual. His affected speech rather betrayed him. He liked to speak in the manner of Oscar Wilde and the Victorians. "Ah, Master O'Toole, and where did you acquire such an exquisite tan?"

"Hello, sir. I've been in the Mideast."

"Ah, yes, Joyce's region of fertility."

"Yes, sir, Plumtree's Plotted Meats and all that—I mean Potted."

He smiled his curious smile of a Saxon. I used to wonder if he found me attractive. I had forgotten the days when I had been the first to arrive at his tutorial, sitting alone with him in his office, anxious for the others to arrive, yet sharpening my confidence on that smile and his attentions. I always imagined that I was frustrating him. Joyce's region of fertility! After his lectures on *Ulysses* we would laugh at how he must know "bugger-all about fertility."

I returned with the passport to the office on Tara Street. Ferguson was there, and asked me to stay a moment. We went into his office. On the wall behind his desk there was a silk-screened poster of men in sunglasses and black berets that had been used for a rally in April. He sat down, took his silver watch off, and began winding it. "Would you like to go to Belfast again?"

"For what?" I asked, hoping he did not think I meant money.

"The stuff you and the girl brought back from Syria. The blessed try-ny-t of her immaculate conception," he said, winking at me over his pun.

Mary, my fiancée, had come to meet me in Syria near the conclusion of the six weeks I was there. She was only nineteen, and it was the first time she had ever been out of County Dublin. It was, perhaps, rather frivolous, but we had never been apart in the three years we had known each other. After several long distance phone calls during which she'd get weepy and try to convince me to come home early, I had finally encouraged her to leave the bakery for a few weeks and join me. I said it would be a sort of early honeymoon for us, but Mary is very Catholic, and took a room in a hotel next door to my own.

Mary was raised almost entirely by her father; her mother died in childbirth. Terence, the older brother, told me the mother had been warned not to have any more children after his own birth, and when she became pregnant with Mary, her death had been almost inevitable. Since then, Mary's father, Mr. Wolfe, had turned zealously to religion. He kept her life at home pious and sheltered. He was more than suspicious of me for well over a year after I met Mary. I could see how to play him, though. Just happening to run into Mary and her father at nine o'clock Mass on a regular basis helped him overcome his suspicions.

When I think of the years I first started seeing Mary, I always remember the two of us watching television with her father in their tiny living room. It's six o'clock, we're waiting for the news, and the Angelus bells come on with a picture of the Virgin Mother. Mary and her father cross themselves, and he looks peripherally at me to see if I'm doing the same. It's not something I'm accustomed to doing, so I make an ambiguous motion with my right hand to push my hair off my forehead, and then scratch my stomach. By now he's shifted his eyes away, so I can forget the lint on my left shoulder.

I continued to attend nine o'clock Mass on Westland Row, crossed myself to the tune of Angelus bells, and, more naturally, voiced my republican politics until Mr. Wolfe no longer regarded me with suspicion at his front door.

He was not altogether pleased about Mary's plans for

Syria, to say the least. In fact, at first he told her she could not go, but when he realized that wasn't going to mean much, he decided she might as well go with his blessing. His blessing, of course, was accompanied by Mary's understanding that this was not yet an official honeymoon. ("Please God, child, I needn't tell you that.") He knew pretty much what I was doing there, but he was an old republican himself once the lines were drawn. It was really because of him, I suppose, that my involvement always had such a romantic appeal to Mary. What did not appeal to me was that after two weeks in Syria, she had to take part in that dubious romance.

Before we returned home, I was asked by one of our people to smuggle, with Mary's assistance, a package of trinitrotoluene and cyclonite back to Dublin. There was very little for me to do actually. The Syrians who worked with us provided Mary with a false front, which was hollow and strapped around her back, to appear as if she were pregnant. I expected her to be terrified with that package nestled against her belly, but she was not. She was most disturbed by the possibility that someone might recognize her in that apparently expectant condition at Heathrow Airport.

If Mary was relatively calm, however, the entire return trip was ruined for me. I stared out at the plane's vibrating wings, and each of the few times I tried to fall asleep, my nightmare came to me. It was a dream stemming from something that had happened to me a year before, and it was always the same. I had been in Belfast, staying at a safe house where I was arranging to bring two men down to the south. One of them had been in the basement of the house, making up a package like the one Mary carried, when it went off. I had been on the upper level, and was unhurt. When I went downstairs, I saw the girl who lived in the house, lying on the floor beside the bath. She was wearing only a pair of jeans, no blouse. I could see her breasts quite plainly, all white and stretched slightly flat. A movement at her hip distracted me, and I saw her skin opened like a seam there, while parts of her insides oozed onto the linoleum tiles. It sickened me, but I just stood staring at her breasts. There were shouts in the street outside, and I knew I should have run, but I stayed and stared at her face and breasts for a full minute. In my dream this girl always became Queen Elizabeth, and, although I know fuck-all about anatomy, I was always able, in the dream, to identify her liver as it spilled out of the seam. Sometimes I saw her kidney and appendix, too, but more often it was just the liver.

I gave up on trying to sleep on the plane, only wanting to get to Dublin, where we could rid ourselves of the package. When I finally delivered it to Ferguson the next day, I ran from his office all the way to the bakery, where Mary kissed me in front of her father and gave me a bag of warm doughnuts. I thought then that I had heard the last of that package, but now Ferguson sat before me, still smiling over his pun.

I picked at a hangnail on my thumb, and avoided his eyes. "When?" I asked.

"Saturday night."

I smiled at him. "I'm getting married Saturday. I'll be having my own fireworks."

"You're a bleedin' ballocks," Ferguson said, pushing back in his chair. But he congratulated me. He sighed, and said he would find someone else to do the job. "Just be sure you're not honeymooning in Belfast Saturday night."

On Friday night I took the bus to Mary's house. When I got there, I could tell she had been crying. We watched the telly for a bit with her father, but since he obviously wasn't going to bed, and we couldn't talk with any privacy in the kitchen, I suggested we go out for a walk.

"What is it?" I asked as we crossed the front garden.

"Daddy," she said.

"Well, don't make me beg you, Mary."

"You know he thinks you're just great, Shane," she began.

"Shite, you mean he doesn't want us getting married now?" I scuffed at the gravel the old saint had so carefully laid out on his driveway a few weeks before.

"That's not it, Shane."

"Well, what?"

"He thinks maybe I'm not enough to you."

"A fine time to decide that."

"No, he just worries for me. He worries for both of us. But he said he wants me to be sure that I'll be a wife, and not just an outlet for you—a sanctuary." I could tell these were her father's words. "From the violence and all," she said. She seemed to be asking me something.

"And is that how you think it is?" I asked her.

"No, I don't. Should I?" she asked.

"Of course not. What else did he say?"

"Mainly just that."

"Tell me everything, Mary," I said. We always told each other everything then, although I had not told her about the dead girl and the dream.

"Well, you know what his politics are, Shane. He says he doesn't see an end in sight. But he doesn't think anyone really wants one. Anyone. He says half the provisional wing doesn't want a settlement, they just want to fight."

"Well, there's fuck-all glamour and romance to fighting, if that's what you and your father think, Mary."

"I know," she said, "but that's just what he's getting at."

"What do you mean, 'that's just what he's getting at'? Speak fucking English."

"He thinks maybe I'll just be a warm bed for you when you have to get away from all of that." Once again I could hear her father's phrasing. "Shane, he said I'm not much of an intellectual companion for you. He doesn't think I'll hold your interest very long."

"And you believe him, don't you?"

"No."

I couldn't help yelling at her. "Then why are you crying, Mary?"

"I don't want to believe him. I mean, I know I'm not as smart as you are, that I haven't read enough, I never went to college. But I think I'm a good companion for you . . . or is he right . . . ?"

"All right, I'll tell you, Mary," I said. "In a way your father's right. Being with you *is* a relief from all of that. And you do make it easier for me. But without you I would still do that—and without that I would still love you. I would," I said, but I felt less sure of myself now. I could see that in many ways Mary had become a habit for me. Perhaps if her father had said these things long before, I would have sensed my own suspicions. Several times I had regretted not being better acquainted with girls who had been to college with me. And even though intellectual women bother me, sometimes Mary's simpleness bothered me more. "Believe me, Mary," I said.

She stopped and squeezed my arm, brushing her cheek dry on my sleeve. "I shouldn't believe the Hail Mary out of your mouth," she said. "But I do." She had a whole arsenal of these great Dublin phrases, some of which I hadn't even heard from my grandfather.

We circled the block back to her house. Mary was bright and smiling when we got there, and she kissed me for a long time outside the door. Inside, her father was watching a talk show. "I've a whole telly full of channels to choose from," he said when we came in, "and this is the only thing on that's not utterly disgustin'."

"Oh, Daddy, you watch the disgustin' stuff most of the time anyway," Mary said.

"Sure, I haven't much choice, have I? With the old blinkers goin', I'm not able to read as I once did. I did read that article on television sex and violence in the paper this morning. Did you see the article, Shane?"

"No, not yet," I told him.

"Well," he said," it's disturbing, the effects it's having on the young people. And it's only getting worse, mind you."

"Well, I suppose all those steamy love scenes on the dirty shows counter the effect all that violence has," I said.

From the kitchen doorway, Mary shook her head at me.

Her father frowned. "Sure, it's not a thing to be laughed at, Shane."

"No," I said. I spoke politely to him for the rest of the night, but I felt on the way home that he had betrayed me, saying what he had to Mary on the night before our wedding. And yet I also felt that he was right about me. Or was it only his suggestion that made me doubt myself now? As the bus sneezed along, I tried to think instead about all that was to come the next day.

The conductor, a man my own age, had pressed his face up close to the side window, and said to the driver, "Look at that, they're kicking the shit out of your man." I turned and looked out, but the street was not well lit, and I could only see myself and some other passengers reflected in the window. But when we pulled away from a light at the North Circular Road, I could see a man sprinting rigidly, without expression, from the direction of one of the seedier pubs.

"Pull over here, Johnny," the conductor said. He stood on the steps and swung out the door. "Do you want a lift?" he called. The man slowed up cautiously. His hair was wild, and his shirt untucked. He mumbled something I couldn't understand. "That's okay," the conductor said, "come on."

He got on and sat at one of the seats facing the aisle in the front. The skin around his left eye was blue, and puffing out like a golf ball, and his shirtfront was stained with blood; he seemed not to notice that the stuff kept dripping from his lips onto the shirt, his shoes, onto the floor of the bus in little splattering drops. His pants were ripped at the knee, which was also bleeding slightly, but he seemed all right otherwise. I turned to peer back in the direction from which he had come, but there was too much glare.

When the man got off, I began composing a list of things I wanted to pack for the next day. The bus passed near the office on Tara Street, and I remembered Ferguson's warning. "Just be sure you're not honeymooning in Belfast Saturday night."

We did not honeymoon in Belfast, but on Inishmaan, the middle of the three Aran Islands. Having driven to Galway after the wedding on Saturday, we flew in a nine-seater to the island, a beautiful, if barren, maze of stone walls. As there were only four cars on the island, we walked a half mile to the bed and breakfast, accompanied by Joe Flaherty, who had charge of the airstrip.

He was quick to tell us that the purest Irish anywhere is spoken on Inishmaan, and we were embarrassed to say that, yes, we did have some Irish, as he put it, but not enough to hold a real conversation.

It reminded me of the embarrassment I suffered at St. Paul's, where Sister Teresa, who came from the Gaeltacht, pandied our hands when we failed an Irish lesson. "There's no reason why you cannot learn a second language, especially the official language of our nation. It's a disgrace for an Irishman to speak only a foreigner's tongue." Whack!

One spring day she had called us all to the window, and pointed to a man in a black suit, standing on the corner below. "Now you see, children, *that* is a Protestant."

We all stared at the mundane figure. Finally, Aidan O'Malley said, "But, Sister, he looks just like anyone else."

She nodded sagely and said in a whispering voice, "That's the frightening thing about it."

Joe Flaherty left us, turning off the narrow dirt road into his thatched home. Chickens hopped about his front garden, and a hen was nesting in a circle of large, oval-shaped stones. About fifty yards beyond Joe Flaherty's, we stopped at a large two-story house to which he had directed us. Mrs. Mulkerrin, a woman in her forties, with a slight mustache and a big bottom, came to the already open door. *"Dia duit,"* she said.

We answered, *"Dia's Muire duit,"* and she continued on in Irish until I asked, "Have you a room vacant?" Mrs. Mulkerrin switched to good, heavily accented English.

The house smelled of fresh bread and braised liver, which was cooking on an ancient stove in the front room. Mrs. Mulkerrin brought us to a bedroom upstairs, and said she would have her daughter make up the bed. Just above the wooden headboard, on the wall facing the door in the tiny bedroom, there was a framed picture of the Sacred Heart, torn from a magazine. By the front window, over a porcelain wash basin, was an old and faded print of the Virgin Mother. I had been outside of Ireland often enough to realize that the Sacred Heart was more or less our national organ. Sitting on the gray mattress, I leaned over to straighten the picture of the man who wears His heart on His chest. "There, now don't say I never did anything for You," I mumbled, and Mary gave me a backhand in the stomach.

After a dinner of meat, potatoes, and soda bread, we strolled the dirt roads of the island, the only apparent visitors, and certainly the only people holding hands. I could hear Mary's stomach rumbling, and told her she should have eaten a decent meal for once. She'd recently begun dieting, and I could see it was all because she worked with an American girl at the bakery who was constantly talking calories and health foods. She had given Mary a pamphlet with an index of calories that Mary began carrying everywhere. She could hardly be called overweight, but consulted her calorie list every time she ate now. At dinner she had said to me, "Now, of course there are no calories in water, but do you not suppose there are calories in plain tea? I should probably be counting tea for at least a few calories."

We had been sitting at the table in the room used mainly for guests' meals, and I was flipping through the Mulkerrins' guest book. "Mary, you look fine, don't be a bleeding fool,"

I told her, but just then I came to the name Neil Blanchard. I couldn't place it at first, but then I saw the home address and realized, the American student who had sold me the passport. He had been in the very house only three weeks before us. It made me uneasy, as if my privacy were being impinged upon; there are some things that just keep coming back to a person in a place the size of Ireland. I could hear Professor Baxter's voice, with his damnably affected theatrics, from the recesses of some Trinity lecture hall. "I am trying to escape the nightmare that is history," he was saying.

Mary stood now on a crumbling little stone wall and threw some hay to a few sheep we were passing. She said she wished we had more than a few days to stay on the island, tossing her hair back like some film actress. It certainly wasn't costing us much, but I reminded her how much her father would need her at the bakery, and that school would be starting for me very soon. I taught at an all-girls school, which hadn't much pleased Mary when I was first hired. But I would have to start planning my lessons soon; have to keep the girls intrigued.

"I'm still going to be jealous of all those little girls getting spoony over you," Mary said. I kissed her forehead, and we went into the island's only pub.

The night had become cool, and the men with their pipes gladly made a place for us near the small coal fire when we came in. I suspected they knew we were honeymooning. Joe Flaherty was sitting at the bar, and he'd guessed as much earlier when we'd spoken with him. The conversation in Irish made a pleasant background, although we could understand little of it. We ordered a pint and a shandy, and talked quietly, occasionally just listening to the music of their several conversations, frustrated at not understanding the laughter when a joke was made. After we'd been there awhile, one of the younger men winked at me. He was slicing chips of pipe tobacco from a small plug with his jackknife. "Ah, 't'wont be such good weather as thish tomorrow, but a good day to shleep late," he said.

I wasn't sure if Mary copped onto him, but it was she who finally tugged my sleeve and said, "We'd better get started back to the house."

The night had grown completely dark in the half hour we spent in the pub. We had forgotten that there are no lampposts on the island. The narrow road was entirely black. We walked to the Mulkerrins' house holding each other closely, unable to see ahead of us except when we passed a few homes that still had lights on.

Mrs. Mulkerrin's daughter had made up the bed with a fancy quilt of green, black and orange circle designs. I slid under the covers in my underwear and toyed with the bulky alarm clock, watching Mary while she modestly undressed. She had begun to remove her bra, but caught me staring, and smiled in embarrassment. I didn't look away, and she made an if-you're-going-to-stare-I-won't-take-it-off expression; then slipped it off anyway and jumped into the bed, covering herself quickly. A loud clanging beneath us had her jumping back onto the floor even faster, shivering in her underwear with her arms across her chest. I got down on my knees and could see that Mrs. Mulkerrin's daughter had tied a large brass cow bell to the bottom of our mattress. I crawled under the bed, onto the cold floorboards, to untie it. In the darkness there, working the thin string out of the bed springs, I was reminded of a night in Belfast, huddled in the darkness, lacing a fuse. My nightmare occurred to me under the bed there, but I would no longer have to dread it with Mary beside me. Even to wake up wide-eyed in the middle of the night would not be such a horror now; not when I would find Mary's warm body nestled against me, not when she would hold me, and whisper her calming words.

Lying on her side in the bed, Mary pulled a barette out of her hair and kneaded my shoulder blades. "I can feel where you were an angel," she said. I had told her the story my grandfather told me when I was small, that our shoulder blades were once our wings when we were angels in heaven. Mary told me I was a scrawny thing, and wrapped her arms tight around me, pulling me on top of her.

That night I saw, for the first time, Mary's small, freckled breasts. They so fixed my attention that, until she screamed, I didn't notice that she was grimacing in pain and fright. She pushed me off from her, and cupped her hand between her legs. I felt far away from her as she choked with light sobs and told me in a shrill whisper, "Shane, we're after doing something wrong; I'm bleeding."

Rain was streaking the window, and I heard drum rolls of thunder as a northward moving storm pounded the island.

MICHELLE HERMAN

Auslander

THE TRANSLATOR, Auslander, was at first flattered. She listened, astonished, for a full minute before the caller— Rumanian, she had guessed after his initial words of praise— paused for a breath, allowing her the opportunity to thank him.

"No, no," he said. "It is I who should thank you, and furthermore apologize for disturbing you at your home. Naturally I am aware that this was most presumptuous. I admit I hesitated a long while before I placed the call. Still, it was difficult to resist. When I read the contributors' notes and discovered that you 'lived and worked in New York City,' I felt it was a great stroke of luck. I must tell you I was surprised that your telephone number was so easily obtained from Directory Assistance."

Auslander laughed. "I've never found it necessary to keep the number a secret. I'm not exactly in the position of getting besieged with calls from admiring readers."

"You are far too modest," the Rumanian said. He spoke hoarsely but with a certain delicacy, as if he were whispering. "Your essay was truly quite something. Such insight! Your understanding of the process of translating poetry is complete, total."

"It's kind of you to say so," Auslander said. She had begun to shiver. The telephone call had caught her just as she was preparing to lower herself into the bathtub, and she wished she had thought to grab a towel when she'd rushed to answer the phone.

"I assure you I am not being kind," he said. "Your work impressed me greatly. It is so difficult to write of such matters with cleverness and charm as well as intelligence. I imagine you are a poet yourself?"

"No, not actually," Auslander said. Her teeth were chattering now. "Could you possibly hold on for just a second?" She set the receiver down and clambered over the bed to shut the window. Across the small courtyard a man sat at his kitchen table laying out a hand of solitaire. He looked up at Auslander and she stared back for an instant before she remembered that she was naked. As she yanked down the bamboo shade, the man raised his hand in slow expressionless salute.

"Oh, I fear I *have* interrupted you," the Rumanian said when she returned to the phone.

"Not at all." Auslander cradled the receiver on her shoulder as she dug through a heap of clothes on the floor. She extracted a flannel shirt and shrugged her arms into it. "Really, it was very good of you to call."

"Good of me? No, no, not in the least." He was nearly breathless. "Your essay was *outstanding*. Brilliant, I should say."

"My goodness," Auslander said. She sat down on the bed and buried her feet in the tangle of shirts and jeans and sweaters.

"Marvelous work. Profound. I do not exaggerate."

She was beginning to feel embarrassed. "You're much too kind," she murmured, and quickly, before he could protest again, she said, "Tell me, how did you happen to come across the essay?"

"Oh"—he laughed, a taut, high-pitched sound—"I read everything, everything. I haunt the periodical room of the library. Nothing is obscure to me. The quarterlies, the academic journals, they all fascinate me, utterly. And I admit also that I have a particular interest in translation."

"A university library, it must be?"

"Ah, my God! How rude of me!" There was a soft thump, and Auslander imagined him smacking his fist to his forehead. "I am so sorry. I have not properly introduced myself. My name is Petru Viorescu. I am a student—a graduate student—at Columbia University."

Auslander smiled into the phone. A Rumanian: she had been right. "Well, Mr. Viorescu, I'm grateful for your compliments. It was very thoughtful of you to call."

This was greeted with silence. Auslander waited; he remained mute. She was just starting to become uneasy when he cleared his throat, and lowering his hushed voice still further said, "Miss Auslander, I do not want to appear in any way aggressive. Yet I wondered if it might be possible for us to meet."

"To meet?"

"Yes. You see, what I want to propose is a working meeting. Or, rather, a meeting to discuss the possibility . . . the possibility of working." He spoke quickly, with a nervous edge to his voice. "In your essay you write of the problems of translating some of the more diffuse, associative poetry in the Romance languages—of the light, respectful touch necessary for such work."

"Yes," she said. Cautious now.

"You have this touch, of course."

"I hope so," Auslander said.

"You even mentioned, specifically mentioned, a number of modern Rumanian poets. This was a great surprise and pleasure to me. I should add that I myself am Rumanian."

"Yes."

"Your biographical note included the information that you are fluent in nine languages. I assume, on the basis of your remarks in the second section of the essay, that my own is one."

"Your assumption is correct."

"And you are familiar with a great deal of Rumanian poetry."

" 'A great deal,' I don't know about, Mr. Viorescu."

"You are feeling a little bit impatient with me now, yes?" He coughed out his odd laugh again. "Bear with me, please, for another moment. Have you in fact done any translation from the Rumanian as yet?"

Of course, Auslander thought. She struck her own forehead lightly with her palm. *A poet.* "Some," she said. A *student* poet yet. More than likely a very bad one. Unpublished, it went without saying. She sighed. Vanity! Only this had prevented her from assessing the matter sooner.

"I thought so. I would be most grateful if you would consider meeting with me to discuss a project I have in mind."

"I'm afraid I'm quite busy," Auslander said.

"I assure you I would not take up very much of your time. A half hour perhaps, no more."

"Yes, well, I'm afraid I can't spare even that."

"Please," he said. "It might be that ten or fifteen minutes would be sufficient."

Irritated, she said, "You realize, of course, that you haven't described the nature of this project."

"Oh, that is not possible at the moment." It occurred to her then that he actually *was* whispering. Always such drama with poets! "I do not mean to be secretive, believe me," he said. "It is only that I am unable to speak freely. But if you could spare a few minutes to see me . . . ."

"I'm sorry," she said.

"Please."

It was not desperation—not exactly that—that she heard in this invocation. But surely, she thought, it was something akin to it. Urgency. Despair? Oh, nonsense, she told herself. She was being fanciful; she had proofread too many romance novels lately. With this thought she felt a pang of self-pity. She had lied when she'd said she was busy. She had not had any real work since early fall; she had been getting by with freelance proofreading—drudgery, fools' work: romances and science fiction, houseplant care and rock star biographies. But that was beside the point, of course. Busy or not, she had every right to say no. She had refused such requests before, plenty of times. Those letters, so pathetic, forwarded to her by the journal or publisher to which they had been sent, asking her to translate a manuscript "on speculation"—they wrote letters that were like listings in *Writers' Market*, these young poets!—she had never had the slightest difficulty answering. But naturally it was easier to write a brief apologetic note than to disengage oneself politely on the phone. Still, it was only a matter of saying no, and saying it firmly so it would be clear the discussion was at an end.

Viorescu had fallen silent again. A manipulation, Auslander thought grimly. He was attempting to stir up guilt. And for what should she feel guilty? As if her sympathy were in the public domain! What did he think, did he imagine that publishing a scholarly essay in *Metaphrasis* meant she was a celebrity, someone with charity to spare?

"I'm assuming that your intent is to try to convince me to undertake the translation of a manuscript," she said. "First I must tell you that my services are quite expensive. Furthermore, you have read only a single essay which concerns approaches to translation and which tells you nothing whatsoever about my abilities as a translator."

"On the contrary," he said. "I have read two volumes of your translations, one from the Italian, one from the Portuguese, and a most remarkable group of poems in a quarterly, translated from the German. I apologize for not mentioning this earlier; I excuse myself by telling you I feared you would question my motives, the sincerity of my praise. So much flattery, you see.

But I assure you I am entirely sincere. I have not been as thorough as I might have been in my research—my time is limited, you understand, by my own studies—but I am certain I have seen enough of your work to know that it is of the highest caliber. I am well aware that the finest poem can lose all of its beauty in the hands of a clumsy translator. The work I read was without exception excellent."

Speechless, Auslander picked angrily at the frayed cuff of her shirt.

"And, naturally, I would expect to pay you whatever fee you are accustomed to receiving. I am hardly a wealthy man—as I say, I am a student. 'Independently poor' is how I might describe my financial status"—that curious little laugh again—"but this of course is important, it is not a luxury."

Auslander could not think of a word to say. She looked around at the disorder in her bedroom, a tiny perfect square littered with clothes and papers and precarious towers of books, and through the doorway, into the kitchen, where the tub stood full on its stubby clawed legs. The water was probably cold as a stone by now.

"All right," she said finally. "I'll meet with you. But only for half an hour, no more. Is that understood?" Even as she spoke these cautionary words she felt foolish, ashamed of herself.

But he was not offended. "That's fine," he said. "That's fine." She had been prepared for a crow of triumph. Yet he sounded neither triumphant nor relieved. Instead he had turned distracted; his tone was distant. Auslander had a sudden clear vision of him thinking: All right, now this is settled. On to the other.

They set a time and place, and Auslander—herself relieved that the conversation was over—hung up the phone and went into the kitchen. The bathwater had indeed turned quite cold. As she drained some of it and watched the tap steam out a rush of fresh hot water, she resolved to put the Rumanian out of her mind. The tenor of the conversation had left her feeling vaguely anxious, but there was nothing to be done for it. She would know soon enough what she had gotten herself into. She would undoubtedly be sorry, that much was already clear. It seemed to her that she was always getting herself into something about which she would be certain to be sorry later.

In truth, Auslander at thirty-four had no serious regrets about her life. For all her small miscalculations, all the momentary lapses in judgment that only proved to her that she'd do better to attend to her instincts, in the end there was nothing that really upset the steady balance she had attained. She had lived in the same small Greenwich Village apartment for a dozen years; she had a few friends she trusted and who did not make especially great demands on her time or spirit; her work was work she liked and excelled in. The work in particular was a real source of pleasure to her; and yet it was not the work she had set out to do. She had begun as a poet, and she had not, she thought, been a very bad one. Still, she had known by her freshman year at college that she would never be a very good one. She had been able to tell the difference even then between true poets and those who were only playing at it for their own amusement. Poetry as self-examination or catharsis was not for her—not enough for her—and knowing she would never be one of the few real poets, she gave it up without too much sorrow.

The decision to make her way as a translator of other, better, poets' work was one that hardly needed to be made: she found she had been moving toward it steadily for years, as if by intent. As early as the fifth grade she had discovered that languages came easily to her: the Hebrew lessons her father had insisted on were a snap, a pleasure; Yiddish, which was spoken at home, she taught herself to read and write. In junior high school she learned French, swallowing up long lists of words as if she'd been hungering for them all her young life. At that age she took this as a matter of course; it was only later that she came to understand that facility with languages was considered a talent, a special gift. By her sixteenth birthday she was fully fluent in French, Hebrew, Yiddish, and Spanish. By eighteen she had added German and Italian, and by the time she had completed her undergraduate education she had mastered Portuguese, Rumanian, and Russian as well. Her choice to become a translator, she knew, was a kind of compromise between aspirations and ability; but it was a compromise that satisfied her.

She knew her limits. This, Auslander believed, was her best trait. She did not deceive herself and thus could not disappoint herself. She always knew where she stood. She was aware, for example, that she was not a beauty. She was content with her looks, however, for they were certainly good enough ("for my purposes," she had told a former lover, a painter who had wondered aloud if she were ever sad about not being "a more conventionally pretty type"). When she troubled to make even a half-hearted effort she was quite attractive—neatly if eccentrically dressed, solid looking, "an indomitable gypsy," in the words of the painter. Her unruly black hair and eyebrows, her wide forehead and prominent nose, her fine posture—about which her father had been insistent along with the Hebrew classes—all of this made an impression. Her figure, another ex-lover had told her, was that of a Russian peasant—he meant her strong legs and broad shoulders and hips. The notion amused her (though the man, finally, did not; he was a biochemist with little in the way of real imagination—his stolidness, which she had at first interpreted as a charming imperturbability, depressed her after several months). She knew she was the kind of woman of whom other women said, "She's really very striking, don't you think?" to men who shrugged and agreed, without actually looking at her, in order to keep the peace. And yet there was a particular sort of man who appreciated her brand of attractiveness—men by and large a decade or so older than herself, intelligent and good-natured men who had a tendency to brood, even to be sullen, and whose wit was mocked by self-criticism. In any case, she was not "on the market." She had no call to compete with the slim, lively blondes or the dramatic dark young beauties who weaved like lovely ribbons through the city, brilliantly pretty and perpetually bored and lonely. Auslander watched them at publication parties and post-reading parties, in Village cafés and restaurants and bars, and she eavesdropped on their talk with mild interest: there was a hunt on in the city; there was always talk—she heard it everywhere—about the lack of available, desirable men. Auslander herself was not lonely, never bored. She liked having a man in her life, and frequently she did, but she was most at ease alone, and she grew uncomfortable when a man tried to force himself too far into her affairs. It made her nervous to have a man—no matter how much she cared for him —poking about in her things, clattering through cabinets and riffling through her books, cooking pasta in her kitchen, sitting casually in her desk chair.

Auslander's boyfriends—a ridiculous word, she thought, when the men she knew were over forty (though the men themselves seemed to like it)—always started off admiring her "independence" and "self-sufficiency." Later, they would accuse her of "fear of commitment," "obsessive self-reliance." Her most recent affair, with a poet named Farrell—a very good poet, whose work she admired greatly, and the first, and only, poet with whom she had ever been involved in this way—had dissolved after nearly a year into a series of nasty arguments: he called her inflexible and cold; she pronounced him infantile, morbidly dependent. In the end she slept with a young novelist she met at the Ninety-Second Street Y, and carelessly let Farrell discover it. He drank himself into a rage and howled at her, pounding the refrigerator and the bathtub with his fists, and hurled a bottle of shampoo across the room; the plastic split and pale orange globs spattered the walls. She watched in mute amazement, breathless with fear, as he flung himself around her kitchen in a fury, bellowing like an animal. Finally she slammed out of the apartment without a word, and when she returned an hour and a half later he was asleep on her bedroom floor, curled like a shell among her clothes. She spent the night sitting wide awake and shivering at her desk, and in the morning when he rose he only nodded at her and said, "Well, all right, then," and left.

She had not seen him since—it had been five weeks now— and she had found that she missed him. This itself was disturbing. If he was gone, she wanted him gone: done with. She yearned for clarity; ambivalence unnerved her. They had been a bad match, she told herself. Farrell was so demanding, and what did he want from her, after all? To be a different sort of person than she was? He needed constant attention and she couldn't give it to him. But there was no getting around the fact that she liked him. More than liked him. She was fonder of him than she had been of anyone in years—perhaps ever in her life. She wasn't even entirely sure why she had slept with the young writer except that she had felt suffocated. She'd needed to poke her way out, shake things up. But still she had taken a good deal of pleasure in Farrell's company before their battling had begun.

This had happened again and again, this cycle of pleasure and discontent. Auslander could not help but wonder sometimes if she was simply picking the wrong men. To hear other women talk, most men were afraid of involvement. Her friend Delia, a playwright, had confessed to her that the man she'd been seeing for the last two years complained constantly about feeling trapped. "He says he wants to be close," she told Auslander, "but then he admits that the whole notion of togetherness terrifies him." Why then was it that the men Auslander knew seemed only too eager to cast in their lots with her? Delia laughed. She said, "Oh, sure. You ought to try taking one of them up on it sometime. He'd be out the door so fast you wouldn't know what hit you. Take Farrell, for instance. Do you think he'd know what to do with you if he had you? He'd be scared to death."

Auslander wasn't so sure. Not that it mattered anymore. Farrell, she felt certain, was out of the picture for good. They had spoken on the phone a couple of times, but he was still angry with her, and the last time they'd talked—he had telephoned her, drunk, in the dead middle of the night—he had called her a "cold ungiving bitch."

It was of Farrell that Auslander was thinking as she readied herself for her appointment with Petru Viorescu. It wasn't that she was imagining a romance with the Rumanian. She expected that she would read a few of his poems, gently tell him she could not translate them, and they would never meet again. No, it was only that this was the first time in more than a month that she had dressed and tidied herself knowing that she was going to meet with a man. She had been keeping to herself since the explosion with Farrell, seeing only the occasional woman friend—Delia or Margot or Kathleen, all of whom lived nearby—for lunch or coffee. She had not even attended a reading or seen a play or a movie since that night. It struck her now that it was as if she had been in hiding. Hiding from what? she wondered, surprised at herself. Afraid that Farrell would sneak up behind her on the street or in a theater? And if he did? What did it matter?

Displeased, she shook off the thought and took a few steps back from the full-length mirror behind her bedroom door, considering herself. She grimaced. What a specter! Brushing and tugging and straightening, turning this way and that. There was something demeaning, Auslander thought, about thinking of one's appearance. Still, it was unavoidable. She tipped her head, squinting at herself. She looked all right. She had decided it would be wise to appear a trifle stern, and in gray corduroy slacks and a black sweater, boots, no jewelry, no scarves, her hair in a single long braid, she was satisfied that she had achieved the appropriate effect. Nodding to herself, she swept out of the room, snatched up her long coat and her gloves, and was off, even looking forward to the meeting now as a kind of mild diversion.

In the Peacock Café she had no trouble spotting him. He had the hollow, unhealthy look of a youngish poet—mid-thirties, she guessed, somewhat older than she had expected—and wore the uniform of a graduate student: shirt and tie, corduroy jacket and blue jeans. He was very slight. As she took him in with a glance from the doorway, she calculated that he was about her own height, certainly no taller than five-six at most. He sat smoking a cigarette and tapping a teaspoon against a coffee mug at one of the small round tables in the front of the café.

Auslander went in flourishing her coat and smacking her gloves together, her braid flapping behind her, and moved straight to his table and extended her hand. "Mr. Viorescu?"

He started, and half-stood so abruptly the mug clattered against the sugar bowl. "Ah, Miss Auslander?"

Auslander nodded and sat down across from him. There was an alert, tensely intelligent look about him, she thought— almost an animal-like keenness.

"You are younger than I had imagined," he said. His presence of mind seemed to have returned to him. He was assessing her quite coolly.

She thought of saying: You are older and shorter. But she only nodded.

"I don't know why I should have expected that you would be older—perhaps fifty." He grinned and tilted back his chair, folding his arms across his chest. His smile made her uncomfortable and reminded her that the meeting was not likely to be a pleasant one for her. "Would you like a cappuccino? Or an espresso perhaps?"

"American coffee, thank you." She decided not to remove her coat; she would make it clear that she meant to stick by her half-hour time limit. Viorescu continued to grin at her, and she was relieved when the waitress finally idled by to take her order. They sat in silence until she returned with the coffee. Then the Rumanian leaned forward and placed his hands flat on the table. "I know you are busy, so I shall come to the point immediately. Would you be interested in undertaking the translation of the work of a poet who is, I assure you, quite brilliant, a magnificent talent, and who has never been published in English?"

Auslander raised her eyebrows. "I see you are not of the opinion that modesty is a virtue."

"Modesty?" Momentarily he was confused. Then, at once, he began to laugh. "Oh, yes, that is very good, very good."

Auslander, herself confused, did not know what to say.

"I am so sorry—I should have realized. You of course imagined that I was the poet. Yes, I would have drawn the same conclusion." He chuckled softly. "Ah, but my God, imagine me a poet! A fond wish, as it happens, but without even the smallest glimmer of hope." He shook his head. "No, no, look here. It is my wife of whom I am speaking. The poet Teodora Viorescu."

"You're not a poet?"

"Not in the slightest." He lifted his hands from the table and turned them palms up. "As it happens, I have no ability in this area at all. In fact, I have thought to try to translate a number of my wife's poems. I believed I might manage it. But I find it takes a poet to do such work, or—you said you were not yourself a poet—a rather exceptional talent which I do not possess. It was a hopeless task, hopeless. The results were . . . earthbound. Do you know what I mean by this? The poetry was lost."

Auslander sipped her coffee as she mulled this over. Finally she said, "Your wife . . . I take it she is unable to translate her own work?"

"Ah, well, you see, this is the problem. She has not the command of English I have. She has had some . . . some reluctance to learn the language as fully as she might. Oh, she is able to express herself perfectly well in spoken English. As for writing . . . that is another matter altogether."

"Yes." Auslander nodded. "This is often the case."

"I had hoped you might recognize her name, though it is understandable if you do not. Her reputation was only beginning to become established in our country when we left. She was thought of then as one of the most promising young poets in Rumania. She was very young, you understand—nineteen—but still she had published a small book and her work was included in two quite prestigious anthologies."

"Viorescu," Auslander murmured. "She has always published under this name?"

"Yes. We married when she was seventeen."

"Seventeen!"

He shrugged. "We have known each other since we were children. I was the best friend of her eldest brother."

"I see," Auslander said politely.

"And in any case, over the last eight years you most certainly would not have heard of her. Since we came to the United States there has been nothing to hear."

"Is she writing at all?"

"Oh, she is writing, she is writing all the time. But she writes only in Rumanian. None of the work has been published."

"How is it that she has never before had any interest in having her poems translated?"

"Well, it is somewhat more complicated than that." He shifted in his seat. "You see, even now she insists she has no interest."

"But then . . . ." Auslander narrowed her eyes. "You're discussing this with me without her permission?"

He poked at his pack of cigarettes with his index finger, pushing it around in a small circle. His eyes followed its path.

"You must realize that I could not possibly consider the translation of a writer's work against her wishes."

He did not raise his eyes. "Well, here is the problem," he said. "I am very . . . I am very concerned about her. I fear . . . . She is not—how can I say this correctly? She is not adjusting.

She is languishing here. A poet needs a certain amount of attention to thrive. Teo is not thriving. I fear for her."

"Still it doesn't seem—"

"*We* are not thriving," he said. Now he looked at Auslander. "She sits awake at night and writes; the poems she puts in a drawer in the bedroom. She will not discuss them. She refuses to consider the possibility of their translation. She is angry—all the time she seems angry. Often she will not even speak to me."

"Well, this is a personal matter," Auslander said, "between the two of you only."

He continued as if she had not spoken. "Teo is rather frail, you see. She has headaches, she does not sleep well. Frequently she is depressed. I feel strongly that she cannot continue this way. She has no life outside her part-time job at the university. She has no friends, no one to talk with. She says I am her only friend. And it was I who took her away from her family and a promising career."

"She is sorry she left Rumania?"

"Not quite sorry, no. The situation there was untenable, impossible. Worse for her than for me. She is a Jew—only nominally, of course; it is virtually impossible to practice Judaism in our country. But this in itself made life difficult for her. No, we were completely in agreement about leaving. But here . . . she is always unhappy. Her poetry, her most recent work—it makes me weep to read it, it is so full of sorrow. The poems are spectacular: violent and beautiful. But it is as if she is speaking only to herself."

"Perhaps this is the way she wants it."

Again he ignored her. "I have thought for a long time about finding a translator for her. I believe that if she were able to hold in her hand a translation of one of her poems, if it were precisely the right translation—she would change her mind. But how to find the person capable of this! It was daunting to me; it seemed beyond my abilities. When I read your essay in *Metaphrasis*, however, I was certain I had found Teo's translator. I have no doubt of this, still. I feel it, I feel it in my heart. As I read that essay, it was like a sign: I knew you were the one. With absolute clarity I knew also that you would be sympathetic to the problem . . . the unusual situation."

"Naturally, I'm sympathetic. But what can I do? Without her approval I could not translate a word of her writing. Surely you understand that. What you're asking of me is not only unethical, it's unfeasible. Without the participation of your wife . . . ." She shook her head. "I'm sorry. It's impossible."

Viorescu's expression was impassive as he tapped a cigarette from his pack and placed it between his lips. As he lit it, he breathed out, in rapid succession, two dark streams of smoke.

"But I would still like to see some of her poems," Auslander said. She did not know herself if she were being merely polite or if he had indeed called upon her curiosity. In any case it seemed to her absolutely necessary to make this offer; she could not refuse to read his wife's work after all he had said.

Viorescu took the cigarette from his mouth and looked at it. Then he waved it at Auslander. "Ah, yes, but are you quite sure that itself would not be 'unethical'?"

His petulance, she decided, was excusable under the circumstances. He was disappointed; this was understandable. Calmly, she said, "I see no reason why it should be." She kept her eyes on his cigarette as she spoke. "Unless, of course, you would simply prefer that I not read them."

He smiled, though faintly. "No, no. I had hoped that in any event you would want to read them." From a satchel hung on the back of his chair he produced a manilla envelope. He laid it on the table between them. It was quite thick. The sight of it moved her, and this came as a surprise. Viorescu folded his hands and set them atop the envelope. "I have chosen mostly those poems written in the last year or so, but also there is a quantity of her earlier work, some of it dating from our first few years in this country. I have also included a copy of her book, which I thought you would be interested in seeing."

"Yes," Auslander said. "I would, thank you."

"It is, I believe, a fair sample of Teo's work. It should give you a true sense of what she is about. See for yourself that I have not been overly generous in my praise."

"You're very proud of her."

"Yes, naturally." He spoke brusquely enough so that Auslander wondered if she had offended him. "Perhaps this is hard for you to understand. Teo is . . . she is not only my wife, she is like my sister. I have known her since she was six years old and I was twelve. We were family to each other long before our marriage."

A dim alarm went off in Auslander's mind—a warning that confidences were ahead. This was her cue to change the subject, no question about it. But she remained silent. Altogether despite herself she was touched.

"Ah, you find this poignant," Viorescu said, startling her. Embarrassed, she nodded.

"Yes, well, perhaps it is. That we have been so close for so much of our lives is itself touching, I suppose. But we are not . . . . She is . . . . Ah, well." He shrugged and smiled, vaguely.

Auslander cautioned herself: This is none of your business; you want no part of this. But she felt drawn in; she couldn't help asking, "What were you about to say?" And yet as she spoke she groaned inwardly.

"Oh—only that something has been lost. This is maybe not so unusual after so many years, I think." He closed his eyes for an instant. "Something lost," he murmured. "Yes, it may be that she is lost to me already. Well, it is my own fault. I have not been a help to her. I have done a great deal of damage."

At once Auslander realized she did not want to hear any of this. Not another word, she thought, and she imagined herself rising immediately, bidding him good-bye and taking off—she did not even have to take the package of poems. What was the point of it? Did she honestly think there was a chance she might discover a hidden genius? Who was she kidding?

"It is very bad, very bad," he muttered.

A mistake, Auslander thought. Sitting here listening, offering to read the poetry of his wife—all a mistake. She could feel her chest tightening against what she suddenly felt was certain to be a perilous intrusion into her life. For it would get worse with every moment: confessions led to further confessions. *No more.* She wanted no more of Viorescu and his poet wife.

He pushed the envelope toward her. "Here, I can see you are impatient. I did not mean to keep you so long."

She picked up the envelope. "It's true, I should be going." She half-rose, awkwardly, and drew the envelope to her chest. "Ah—shall I phone you after I've read these?"

"I will phone you." He smiled at her, broadly this time. "I should like to thank you in advance for your time. I am very grateful."

Auslander felt uneasy. "I hope I've made it completely clear that I'm not going to be able to take Teodora on."

"After you have read the poems," he said, "perhaps you will change your mind."

"I'm afraid not."

"You have agreed to read them, after all."

"I am always interested in good poetry," Auslander said stiffly. "If your wife's work is as you say, I would be doing myself a disservice by not reading it."

"Indeed," he said, and now he laughed—his telephone laugh, that short curious bark. "I will phone you next week."

She could feel his eyes on her back as she retreated, the envelope of poems under her arm. For his sake—and for the sake of the unknown, unhappy Teodora—she hoped the poems were not dreadful. She did not have much confidence in this hope, however; the excitement that had begun to stir in her only moments ago had already left her entirely.

By the time she had passed through the cafés door and emerged onto the street, she was convinced the work would turn out to be inept. As she crossed Greenwich Avenue, her coat whipping about her legs, her head bowed against the wind, she was imagining her next conversation with Viorescu. She would be gentle; there would be no need to tell him the truth about his wife's work. If he deceived himself, he deceived himself. It was not her responsibility.

As it turned out, Viorescu had neither lied to her nor deceived himself. Teodora Viorescu's poems were extraordinary. Auslander, after reading the first of them, which she had idly extracted from the envelope and glanced at as she sat down to her dinner, had in her astonishment risen from the table, dropping her fork to her plate with a clatter, and reached for the envelope to shake out the remainder of its contents. A batch of poems in hand, she ate her broiled chicken and rice without the slightest awareness of so doing. She could hardly believe her eyes. The poems jumped on the pages, full of terror, queer dangerous images of tiny pointed animal faces, blood raining through the knotted black branches of trees, fierce woods that concealed small ferocious creatures. And the language! The language was luminous, electrifying. What a haunted creature the poet herself must be! Auslander thought as she at last collapsed against her pillows at half-past twelve. She had been reading for five hours, had moved from table to desk to bed, and she had not yet read all the poems Viorescu had given her; but she intended to, tonight. She needed however to rest for a moment. She was exhausted; her eyes burned.

For ten minutes she lay listening to the dim apartment sounds of night: refrigerator, plumbing, upstairs creaks and groans, downstairs murmurs. Then she sat up again, stacked her pillows neatly behind her, and set again to reading. When she had read all of the poems once she began to reread; after a while she got up and fetched a legal pad. For some time she reread and made notes on the pad, resisting with difficulty the urge to go to her desk for a batch of the five-by-seven cards she used to make notes on work she was translating. Finally she gave in, telling herself it was simply easier to use the index cards, their feel was more familiar, and with a supply of the cards beside her she worked until dawn in something of a feverish state, feeling like one of the poet's own strange night creatures as she sat wild-haired and naked in her bed, chewing on her fingers and the end of her pen, furiously scratching out notes as the gray-bluish light rose around her.

For days, anxiously, she awaited Viorescu's call. On the fifth day she checked the telephone directory and was half-relieved to find no listing; she knew she should not phone him. But she felt foolish, waiting. Dimly she was reminded of her adolescence—hateful time—as she stared at the phone, willing it to ring. After each of her ventures out of the apartment—her few forays to the supermarket and the library, her one trip up-town to return the galleys of a gothic romance—she hastened to her answering machine. The playback yielded up several invitations to functions that didn't interest her, a number of calls from friends, one from her mother, one from Farrell.

"Do you miss me, Harriet my love? Are you lonely?" Auslander breathed impatiently, fists against her thighs. Farrell's message was intended of course to make her angry. He never called her "Harriet" except to taunt her. Well, let him, she thought. She would not allow him to upset her. She had been less preoccupied lately with missing him; she had other things on her mind (and she'd like the chance to tell him that, she thought)—though the sound of his voice on the tape, it was true, sent a shiver of sorrow and loneliness through her. "Has it hit you yet that you're all alone? Are you enjoying it, as antici-pated? Or are you sorry? Or are you not alone—have you al-ready found someone else to resist loving?" There was a pause, then, harsher: "Don't call me back. I've changed my mind; I don't want to talk to you after all."

Eight days passed; then nine. On the tenth day—once again as she was about to take a bath, one leg over the side of the tub—the phone rang and she knew instantly it was the poet's husband.

He was cheerful. "So? What do you make of my Teodora?"

Auslander felt it would be wise to be guarded. "Well, she's something, all right. An original, no question."

"You enjoyed her work, then?"

She could not remain cautious; she was too relieved to hear from him. " 'Enjoyed?' Ha! She's a terror, your wife. The real thing, astonishing stuff."

Viorescu was cackling. "Yes, yes, it's true, absolutely true. She is one of a kind, a wonder, a gem!"

Auslander stood beside the bed coiling and uncoiling the telephone cord about her wrist as they went on to talk about the poems. She excused herself to get her notes, and then she was able to quote directly from them; Viorescu was delighted. She had just launched into some observations about one of the most recent poems when she happened to glance up and saw that the man across the way was standing at his window staring blankly at her. Good lord, she thought, he would begin to imagine she strolled around naked for his benefit. She sat down on the bed, her back to the window, and pulled the blanket up around her.

"Listen, Petru," she said, "I've been thinking. I really ought to meet Teodora."

He clicked his tongue. "Well, as you know, this is not such a simple matter. I am not sure it is possible at all right now."

"It may be difficult," she said, "but surely we can manage it."

"Tell me, have you given any further thought to the question of translating her work?"

"I've already told you I would not consider it without her full cooperation."

"But you are interested! Well, this is good news indeed. Of

course you must meet her. Let me think . . . . Why don't you come to dinner? Let us say, next Friday night?"

"Are you sure?"

"Yes, of course. But it would be best not to let her know immediately that you are a translator."

Auslander was discomfited. "Are you sure this is necessary?" she said. "If I'm not to be a translator, who am I? How did we meet?"

"Oh, I shall say I met you at an academic function. Teo never attends department functions with me."

"An academic function," Auslander echoed. She recalled then that she had never asked him what his area of study was. "What department is it that I am to be associated with?"

"Philosophy," he said with a short laugh. "That is my department. My specialization is Nietzsche."

"Wonderful," Auslander said. "You can tell Teo I'm a renowned Nietzsche scholar and I'll remain silent all evening."

"I can tell her that you are Hannah Arendt and she would not know the difference," Viorescu said dryly.

"Are you sure all this intrigue is necessary? Maybe you ought to simply tell her the truth."

"No. She would suspect a plot."

"Has she such a suspicious nature?"

"It does not take much," he said, "to arouse suspicious thoughts. Why take such a chance? We can tell her the truth after an hour, two hours perhaps, once she is comfortable in your presence."

For the second time, Auslander hung up the phone after talking to the Rumanian and found herself wondering what she was letting herself in for. Gloomily she paced around her bedroom—the man across the way, she noted as she went to the window to pull down the shade, was no longer looking out—and tried to convince herself that she was in no danger of becoming personally involved with the Viorescus. They needed a translator, she told herself; it was not necessary to be their friend. Still, she didn't like the circumstances; they did not lend themselves to a smooth working relationship. Even assuming that all went well—that Teodora was willing, that she could be reasoned with—the project was likely to be full of difficulties and strains, starting out the way it was. Already she had agreed to this preposterous masquerade! It was clear enough that between Viorescu and his wife there were problems, serious problems. Auslander hated the thought of these complications.

But the poetry! Auslander shook her head, tugged at her hair as she circled the room. *Oh, the poetry!*

She would have recognized Teodora Viorescu at once, Auslander felt. Had she passed her on Sixth Avenue a day or two ago, she was certain she would have thought: Might this not be the poet? Small and pale, with hair like a slick black cap cut so short her ears stuck out pointedly from beneath it, she felt her way through the room toward Auslander like a swimmer.

"I'm very pleased to meet you," Auslander said. "Petru has told me a great deal about you." She took the poet's small hand in hers. It was very cold.

"So you are Miss Auslander."

"Just Auslander is fine."

"Ah, yes, so my husband told me." She smiled. Her face was perfectly round, her eyes also—oddly—round. How white her skin was! As if she truly never saw daylight. And how grave she looked, even as she smiled. It was in the eyes, Auslander thought. Her eyes were the eyes of one of her own imaginary creatures: liquid-black with floating pinpoints of light, emitting a steady watchful beam.

During dinner there was small talk. The food was Rumanian, traditional, Viorescu explained. He seemed very nervous and spoke at length about ingredients and methods of cooking. Auslander avoided meeting his eyes; she was sure it was plain to Teodora that something was up. Teodora herself kept her eyes downcast and picked at her food; between the Viorescus barely a word passed.

Auslander helped Viorescu move the table back into the kitchen and pile the dishes in the sink; he tried to whisper to her but she waved him away impatiently. Enough of this, she thought. She returned to the living room to find the poet sitting on the windowseat, gazing out upon Riverside Drive. Auslander seated herself on the end of the couch nearest the window and said, "Please, Teodora, won't you tell me about your work? Your husband informs me that you are a fine poet."

"There is nothing to tell." She turned slowly toward Auslander. Her tone and facial expression were remote. Auslander recalled what Farrell had told her when she'd described a famous poet she'd met as "terribly cool and remote." "Wrong again, Auslander," he had said. "Not *remote*. Only massively depressed and riddled with anxiety—like me."

Auslander tried again. "Petru tells me you published a book in Rumania."

"Yes."

"And have you any interest in publishing your work in the United States?"

Teodora glanced over at her husband, who had entered the room silently and positioned himself by the bookshelves opposite the couch where Auslander sat, and spoke quietly to him in Rumanian. Auslander heard only snatches of what she said. "Unfair"—she heard this word several times—and "You should have told me." Once, clearly, she heard the poet say "unforgivable," and then—her heart sank—she heard unmistakably the Rumanian for "translator." Viorescu did not speak. Finally Teodora turned again to Auslander. "I am sorry if we have put you to any trouble. I do not wish for my work to be translated into English." Abruptly she stood and left the room.

Auslander started to rise, but Viorescu said, "Please, Auslander. There is nothing we can do."

"What do you mean 'nothing we can do'?" She was astounded. "I thought you were so eager to convince her."

"I believed she might be convinced. Apparently I was wrong."

"But you didn't even *try*."

"It would be pointless. She is very angry at having been deceived."

"Why didn't you just tell her what I was here for in the first place?"

"You must realize that it would not have mattered either way. She is obviously beyond—"

"You're giving up. I can't believe it. You do this whole . . . ." She sank back into the couch and looked up at him in amazement. "And giving up so easily!"

"Easily!" He laughed hoarsely. "I have been trying for years to talk her into having her work translated. I am giving up now *finally*." He shook his head. "There is a story—do you know it?—about a famous philosopher who decided, after long consideration, to become a vegetarian. For many years he lived as a vegetarian. He spoke and wrote of it, of course, since under the circumstances such a decision could not be a private matter only. He spoke brilliantly, in fact, and movingly, on the moral logic of his choice. Then one day he sat down to his table and began to eat a steak. His students, as you would imagine, were quite agitated when they saw this. Why the change? they cried. What had happened? And the famous philosopher said, 'Ah, well, it was time to give it a rest.' "

"There is no relevance to this story, Petru," Auslander said wearily.

"Oh, I quite disagree, Auslander, my friend. But in any event don't you find it a charming story?"

"I have other things on my mind," she said. "Tell me. Why *doesn't* Teo want her work translated? What does she say when you ask her?"

"She says, 'Because I say so.' "

"But that's a child's logic."

"No. It's a parent's logic, rather. The child asks, 'Why not?' The parent says, 'Only because I say not.' "

"Well, then." Auslander shrugged and stood up. She was angrier and more disappointed than she could have predicted. "I guess that's it. Shall I mail the poems back to you?"

"Are you in a rush to be rid of them?" He smiled at her. "No, my friend. Let us not altogether give up. May I telephone you tomorrow?"

"What's the point?"

"Oh, I shall talk to her tonight. Perhaps it would be wise to tell her you've already read her work, extend your compliments. It will depend on her spirits."

"But I thought . . . ." Auslander stopped herself. There was no sense trying to follow him. "All right, fine. Call me."

"Tell me something," he said as he walked with her to the door and helped her into her coat. "Are you absolutely certain that if her work were translated it would be publishable here?"

"Oh, without question," Auslander said. Then a thought came to her. "Why? Do you think it will help if Teo knows this? Because if you like, I can make a few calls tomorrow, ask around, get a feel for it." Instantly she regretted this offer. Who on earth could she call to discuss the work of an untranslated Rumanian poet? Without work to show, what could she expect an editor to say? It was nonsense, absurd.

"That would be very kind."

"I should go now," Auslander said, her hand on the doorknob. As she went down the hall to the elevator, she reflected that it was a miracle that she had escaped without having made any further promises.

On the IRT heading back to the Village, she removed from her Danish schoolbag the envelope containing Teodora's poems. She was not sure why she hadn't told Viorescu she had the poems with her—evidently she wasn't ready yet to part with them. She flipped through the pages until she found the one she wanted. From the front pocket of her bag she took out a pen and the packet of index cards she had begun to keep on Teodora's work, and she sifted through the cards, stopping at the one headed "In the Cold Field, In the Troubled Light." She ran her eyes quickly down the card; besides the title, she had already, automatically, cast a number of lines into English as she made her notes. She sighed and turned to the poem itself. Then, pen in hand, using the canvas bag as a lap-desk, she began the translation.

He did not even bother to say hello. "She wants no part of it," Viorescu announced. "She will not discuss it."

"What did you tell her? Did you explain—"

"I pleaded, I made promises, I was a madman." He laughed miserably. "She made me sleep on the couch."

"That's none of my affair," Auslander said sharply.

"I want to apologize for all the trouble you have taken."

"Yes, well, here's a surprise for you," she said. She took a deep breath and then told him about the poems she had translated last night, working until four o'clock, until she couldn't see clearly anymore.

"My God, that's . . . . Is this really true? How marvelous! Please, will you read them to me?"

For half an hour she read Viorescu his wife's poems. She had rough versions—very rough in some cases—of eight poems already; one or two were quite polished, almost perfect.

"But this is wonderful! Incredible! Oh, we *must* convince her. Do you think . . . what if we did as I had thought to begin with . . . ."

"I don't know. If you were to simply show her these translations she might get very angry. She might—quite justifiably—feel invaded."

"She might feel complimented."

"She might. You would know better than I."

Auslander was not altogether sure of this, however. His track record did not seem to be the best.

Several days passed. Auslander continued to translate the poems. There was no logic in it, she knew; she had almost no hope by now that Teodora would agree to have this done. She was translating the poems because she wanted to; there was no other reason. She was working at it late on Saturday afternoon when there was a knock on her door. Surprised, her first thought was of Farrell. Nobody ever dropped by without calling. Farrell himself had done so only once, and he would surely only do it now if he were drunk. Cautiously she went to the door and stood listening.

"Auslander, are you there?"

It was Petru Viorescu. She snapped away the police lock and swung the door open. He looked terrible.

"Petru! What on earth's the matter?"

"May I come in?" He brushed past her and heaved himself into her desk chair. He looked around. "What is this room? Bathroom, study, kitchen?"

Auslander closed and locked the door. "What's going on? You look like hell."

"I want to tell you something. I need to discuss this with someone. I am going to lose my mind."

"Is it about Teodora?" she asked anxiously. "Has something happened?"

"Oh, something has happened, yes, but not what you imagine. You think she is so fragile! You are afraid that she has tried to commit suicide, that she has had a 'nervous breakdown'. No," he said. "She is made of iron, my wife." He laughed, but then after a second he placed his head in his hands and began to weep. Auslander stood back, uncertain what was expected of her. Finally he stopped crying; he looked up at her and very calmly told his story: He had met a young woman, someone in his department. He was in love; there was nothing to be done for it.

"I don't understand," Auslander said. "When did this happen? Just this week?"

"Months ago," he said. "Months."

"But I don't understand," she repeated. "Have you . . . ?"

"I have not slept with her, if that is your question."

"But then . . . . Have you told Teo about this?"

"Of course." He seemed offended at the implication that he might not have.

"But why? You haven't done anything. What is there to tell? You are . . . you have a crush, Petru, only that."

"No, no. It is not a crush. I am in love."

Auslander was at a loss. "Well, what do you want to do?" Then immediately she said, "Never mind. I don't want to know."

He began to weep again. Auslander wanted to scream. Suddenly a suspicion came to her. "Tell me something," she said. "How much does this business with the other woman—"

"Ana," Viorescu said.

"I don't want to know her name! How much does it have to do with Teo's refusal to have the poems translated?"

"How much does anything have to do with anything?"

"Don't speak to me that way, I won't stand for it," she snapped at him. "Answer me truthfully." She began to pace around the kitchen. "What's going on here? What is this all about? When did you tell Teo about this woman?"

"Months ago," he said. "As soon as I knew. I could not keep my feelings secret from her. We tell each other everything, we always have; we are brother and sister, inseparable."

"But you fancy yourself in love with someone else," she said sarcastically.

"One has nothing to do with the other. You must yourself know that."

"You're not planning to leave Teo?"

"No, I am not going to leave her. The question is whether she will leave me."

"But why has it come to this now, if she's known all these months? What's changed?" At once Auslander had the answer. "Petru," she said, "did the idea of having her poems translated somehow backfire on you?"

He shrugged.

"Did you come up with the notion of getting me to do this in the first place as a way of . . . of placating her? Giving her something of her own? Did you think that having me translate her poems might make things all right between the two of you?"

"This is partly true, yes."

"You could have just bought her flowers," Auslander said bitterly. "It would have saved a lot of trouble."

"I have bought her flowers," he said. "And in any case the trouble, it seems to me, was worth it. No? You don't agree? You understand that this was not the only reason I wanted to have the work translated, do you not? I have been discussing the matter with her for years, years. Long before I knew Ana, long before I met you. Years!" he said angrily. "She will not listen to reason. And what is a poet without readers? I have been her only reader for too long."

Auslander continued to stalk the kitchen, twisting her hands together as she paced. For a long time she did not speak. Finally she sighed and said, "Well, now there are two of us."

"Yes," Viorescu said. "Yes, exactly. Now there are two of us."

The call from Teodora the following night woke her.

"I am sorry to be disturbing you at so late an hour," the poet said. "But I will not be long. I wanted only to say one thing. I understand that Petru has been troubling you with problems of a personal nature."

Auslander was too startled to respond.

"I apologize for this," Teodora said. "I want you to know that I have asked him not to trouble you any further."

"Oh, really, it hasn't been all that much trouble," Auslander said.

"In all events he will not be calling you again."

"Oh, that isn't—" Auslander began. But it was too late; the poet had already hung up.

Auslander did not for a moment seriously consider the possibility that she would not hear from Viorescu. Thus she was not in the least surprised when three days later he called. There was a note of hysteria in his voice, however, which alarmed her.

"What is it, Petru? What's wrong now?"

"She wants to leave me! She says she has had enough, she is fed up. Auslander, please, I need your help. Will you call her? Explain to her? Please?"

"Explain what?" Auslander said. "I don't understand it myself."

"Please. She is at home now. I am in the library. You could call her right now and she could talk to you freely, she is alone."

"I'm sorry, I can't."

"But she wants to leave me!"

"Petru, I can't help you with this. It should be plain by now that I can't. There's nothing I can do."

"Yes, there is. But you refuse! You refuse to help!"

Auslander could not think of what else to do, so she hung up the phone. She stood staring at it. It began to ring again instantly.

She lifted the receiver. "Please don't do this," she said.

"Jesus, Auslander, you're right on top of it tonight, aren't you. I haven't even started doing anything yet."

"Oh, Farrell. I thought you were someone else."

"I wish I were."

"Please," she said, "not tonight. Look, I don't mean to be rude, but are you calling to give me the business? Because if you are, I don't think I'm up to it."

"No, actually I thought I'd take my business elsewhere." He sighed. "You're not laughing, love. What's the matter? Is something really wrong?"

"No, Farrell," she said flatly, "nothing's really wrong."

"Well, shall I tell you why I called? See, I've got this idea. What if I gave up drinking? How would that be?"

"How would it be how?"

"Come on, Auslander. You've always complained about my drinking. What if I stopped?"

"I don't know." Suddenly she felt like crying.

"Hey, what's going on with you? Are you really all right? You sound awful."

"I'm all right," she said. Then, after a second, "No, I'm not. I guess I'm not. I don't know."

"Is there anything I can do?"

She shook her head before she remembered that he couldn't see her. "No," she said. "Not a thing."

"Well, what do you think? Do you think it would make a difference? In our relationship, I mean. Do you think it would help?"

"Look, Farrell," she said, "if you want to quit drinking, then quit drinking. You know perfectly well that I think you ought to. I've said it enough times. But if you're going to do it, do it for yourself, not for me. I don't want to be responsible for the decision."

"Oh, sure, that's right. How could I have forgotten? You don't want to be responsible for anything or anyone, do you."

"Farrell, please."

"Please what? I am making a perfectly reasonable gesture toward straightening things out between us, and you're just tossing it right back in my face."

"That's not what I mean to do."

"No? What do you mean to do, then? Tell me."

"I don't know."

"You don't, do you."

"No." She realized she was gripping the phone so hard her fingers ached. "I don't."

"Tell me something, will you? *Do* you miss me? Ever? Do you even think about me?"

"Of course I think about you. I think about you a lot. I wonder about how your work is going. I wonder how life's treating you."

He laughed softly. "Oh, Auslander, my love, you should know. Life's not treating me at all—I'm paying my own way."

Into bed with her that night she took the envelope of Teodora's poems and all of Farrell's poetry that she had in the apartment —all the poems of his that she had in typescript, all the magazines that had his poems in them, his four chapbooks, even some stray handwritten lines on pages torn from legal pads, which he'd left scattered about the apartment on nights he couldn't sleep. She read all of it, every line, Teodora's and Farrell's both, read until she felt stunned and overburdened, and fell into a sleep that was a kind of stupor. Under the blanket of poems, dreaming, she turned and tossed in her sleep; poems crackled and fluttered, flew off the bed, alighted on the floor.

It was months before she heard from Viorescu again. He called to tell her that Teodora had killed herself. He had returned from the library late at night and found her. There was no note. "She left nothing," he said. He spoke of the funeral and of Teodora's family. Several times he wept, but very quietly. Auslander listened without saying anything. When he had said all he had to say, she waited, expecting to hear herself tell him that she was sorry, but she remained silent.

For a moment they were both silent. Finally Viorescu said, "There is something else I must tell you. Teodora destroyed all of her work—all the poems she wrote from the time we left Rumania. I have searched the apartment; she was very thorough. Every copy of every poem is gone."

Now Auslander was able to make herself speak. "I'm sorry," she said.

"You are not surprised, I imagine."

"That she destroyed her poems? No, I suppose I'm not."

He hesitated. "You understand that you now have the only copy of her work."

"Yes."

Again they were silent.

"You want the poems translated," Auslander said.

"This is not the time to discuss this, of course," he said. "But after a reasonable amount of time has passed, yes."

"Yes, I see," she said.

"And in the meantime you will be careful, will you not?"

"With the poems? Of course."

"Well, then . . . . We will speak."

"Yes."

As she went to her desk and removed the envelope from the center drawer, where it had remained undisturbed for months, Auslander thought briefly of Farrell's poems, which that same morning months ago she had set on the top shelf of her bedroom closet. She saw them in her mind—the bundle of poems secured by a rubber band, surrounded by the accumulated clutter of years: stacks of letters; shoeboxes full of photographs, postcards, cancelled checks; spiral-bound notebooks dating back to graduate school. Then the image vanished and she sat down at her desk; she flipped open the oak box in which her index cards were filed and removed the cards on Teodora—the notes and the dozen translations she had done. One at a time she laid the cards on her desk, as slowly and precisely as a storefront fortune teller, spreading them out carefully in a fan, one corner of each card touching the next. When she had come to the end of the cards, she shook the poems themselves out of the envelope. Now the desktop was littered with poetry. For a time she sat looking at all that she had spilled out there. Then she scooped up everything and stood, hugging the papers and cards tightly to her chest. She crossed the kitchen and with some difficulty unhooked the police lock. In the hallway she hesitated for an instant only; then she moved quickly. With one arm she held the poet's work; with her free hand she pulled open the door to the incinerator chute. It was a matter of seconds; then it was done.

ANN PATCHETT

All Little Colored Children Should Play the Harmonica

S A M P S O N, Skipworth, Slonecker, Small, Smiley. Smiley, Grover T. There are still four people ahead of me on the list, I've got awhile to wait. The *s*'s, we're way the hell down there so we gotta hear everybody before our turn comes around. At first I thought I was miserable, but after the thirty-fourth audition (Claire Beth Fibral, who said God told her she could play the flute), I decided it was poor old Miss Neville who was having a rough go of it. She calls out a name on the list and hands over a piece of sheet music, asking if they can make any sense of it, most everybody says no. Then she asks them if there is anything in particular they think they could play. This is where she makes her big mistake, if you ask me; just cram something in their hands and talk about it later. Every kid says they's just sure they can play the so and so. The girls all say they can play the flute, the boys say the bass. They is all lying.

Some group of old white men decided all little colored children should play musical instruments, that it would keep their minds off breaking out store windows or sitting in front of the Five and Dime looking uppity. That's why we're all here now,

Miss Neville says that's legislating. I think they must have legislated this one up in spring, when it was cool outside and music sounded real pretty. But this here's August and even the flies are looking for a house with the fan on. It's Miss Neville who's got to decide who's gonna play what. She's gotta listen to every kid in Central Valley Junior High blow or bang or strum on something before she can assign them a place in the school orchestra. Ain't no telling how long she's been the music teacher here, most everybody's got a story or a guess. Harvey Rachlin says his older sister was in Miss Neville's orchestra when she went here, and his sister is a grown-up woman now, with a baby and everything. Some people say that Miss Neville stays at school all the time, that they let her sleep under the piano or something. I can't figure her out; I crawled up on the bleachers to watch her for a while and she looked like she was listening to all of them. You can tell by her face that she thinks every kid that comes up might really be able to play. Then when she really hears them her face gets kinda sick, like they were all hitting her in the stomach. I would think that going through an audition once would be more than any regular person could suffer, I don't know what it would be like year after year.

They've got the whole school mashed into this one basketball gym. The ninth graders get folding chairs, which they make a very big deal of. The rest of us get bleachers or the floor. I got this nice little spot between the door and the risers where nobody can step on me. From where I'm sitting the whole world is knees and ankles, not one person in there who cares a rip about keeping his socks pulled up or his shoe laces tied. You never think about feet until you're down there with them. Miss Neville calls out a name and then I see a pair shuffle onto stage and wait a minute, then shuffle back to their place, which has almost always been snatched up.

I don't want nothing to do with their spitty old instruments. No way am I gonna spend four years sucking on some piccolo that somebody sucked on before me. It had been my intention to keep Roy Luther out of school, sorta separating my class time from my free time, but this is an emergency.

Me and Roy Luther hooked up when I was six years old, so we've been together a little more than half of my natural life-time. My daddy, Mr. Nigel T. Smiley, runs the numbers where he works in the bakery making fancy doughnuts. He used to let a couple of us kids sit in the back room with his business friends, we made the place look honest. One day I was hanging out on a cherry crate playing with this special aggie that had been my birthday present. This man comes over and says that it was a real fine marble, that he'd never seen a shooter quite like it. I say, Yessir. He says he'd like to have that marble for his little boy. I didn't look up, I was scared he was gonna take it. He says, wouldn't I like to bet him something for that aggie? He pulls out this silver bar, the size of three Havana cigars. Then I look up, it was the most beautiful thing I'd ever seen.

"We'll shoot us out some craps, boy." The man says to me, "I win, I take your marble home to my boy; you win, you get to keep this here harmonica."

Man, I'll tell you I wanted that thing. I didn't know what it was or how to use it, only that I'd die right then and there if I didn't get it. I nodded my head. The man dips one of his fingers into a tiny pocket on his vest. He must have just been eating Cracker Jacks or something cause when he pulled it out there were two dice hanging on it. The other guys, mostly soldiers that hung out during the day started coming around, checking out the action and laughing at me cause I'm the sucker. Just then, a big metal door smashes open and Papa walks in from the front room. Kids used to tease me about my father being white, cause he was always plastered with flour. Nobody ever said anything to him about it.

"What you doing with my boy?"

"Just a friendly game of craps, Nigel. Your little shark here's hot after my harmonica." He shook up the dice to show he meant business.

Papa looked down at me. "You gambling with this man?"

I was pretty little then, I just nodded my head yes. One giant, floury hand come swinging down through the air and clept me right above the ear. I went sailing off my cherry crate and slammed back against some drums of cooking oil. What everybody says about seeing stars ain't true. I saw big, furry spiders.

"How many times I got to tell you kids? You never, ever gamble with a man without letting me check out the dice. Jesus you is a fool." Pape plucked the pair of spotted cubes out of the other fella's hand and rattled them around. "Loaded." He shook them in my face, "Loaded!" I thought he was gonna hit me again, but he walked into the other room and got a fresh pair. Everybody knew Papa used clean dice. He gave the new set to the man. "Now you talk about gambling with my son."

The man shook his head like a little black bunny rabbit. "Just joking with you, Nigel, just trying to teach the boy here a lesson, hee hee. He can keep his dirty old marble."

"You gamble with my boy, Mister." Papa picked me up with one hand and shook me like a sneaker with a rock inside. "You let the man roll first, Grover."

His roll came up two specks, Papa says Snake Eyes. I gathered up the dice and threw them out again. A howl went up. A two and a five, sweet, sweet seven. Roy Luther must have been the man's name, because it was engraved on the side of my "Hohner Marine Band." I thought it had a good, solid sound to it. I knew right away this was going to be my special thing. All the other kids in my family got something special. There's the oldest and the youngest, and the twins that get all their clothes to look alike and get their picture taken a lot, and my brother Wilson who has his very own fish, and Delilah who twirls in the marching band, and Albert who skipped two whole grades just for being smart. Up till now I never had a thing that made me me. I'd walk into a room and Mama would call me two dozen names before she could place who I was. That first night I was sitting there staring at Roy Luther when the twins come up and try to take him away. Mama tells them to scat, "That's Grover's thing," she told them. "Leave it be." I slept with Roy Luther between my head and shoulder, so I'd be sure to wake up if someone tried to make off with him. Me and Albert share a bed, he thinks it's him I don't trust, but I couldn't let it go. Albert slept facing the wall after that.

There was a good three years I didn't have too many friends. My brothers and sisters told other kids they didn't know me, even Mama made me stay a good piece behind her when we went out. My thing wasn't so much being a harmonica player as it was being a bad harmonica player. I played all the time, grinding up and down that same old scale any place I could catch my breath, in the bathtub, under the dinner table. I was as bad as Original Sin. It was like learning to talk all over again, except this time there was no one to listen to. My hands didn't know anything about playing harmonicas, they knew about marbles and baseballs, and my mouth was a gum-chewing mouth. There wasn't no music in that mouth when things started out.

Back then, I took Roy Luther to school. Every five minutes or so a new sound would come into my head and I would raise my hand, asking if I could visit the washroom or get a drink of water. If the teacher said yes I would dart outside and try blocking up a different set of holes, blowing harder or softer than the day before to see how it sounded. Somebody'd always rat on me and Roy Luther would spend the rest of the day sitting in the principal's desk drawer.

I got used to the way it was always cold, tasting part like a tin can and part like the old Lifesavers and ticket stubs I kept in my pocket. As much as I loved the sound, I loved just putting it in my mouth, letting it hit against a filling in my tooth and running a shock clear through my eyes. It got to where I couldn't walk through a door without someone saying "Grover, go way!" I'd shinny up into the sugar maple and stay there. First the birds all flew away, then after a while they got used to me, I even learned a few of their songs. One morning I was playing outside the kitchen window before breakfast, I heard Mama say, "Listen to the nightingale, will you? Glory but that ain't God's finest bird."

And that's when things started turning around.

I sat under the front porch and played a fire engine and my little brother ran outside, hooping and hollering for everybody to come watch the fire. Then he spent the whole day looking for one. I sat in the alley behind the white grocery store and played "What'll I Do?" so soft you could barely hear it, and just about everybody that walked out of the store was humming that song without knowing why.

It was like one day I was the stink bug somebody stepped on and the next day I was a fistful of wisteria. Mama stopped sending me outside all the time. I could play the things she heard in church on Sunday. When the radio went out I was the chief source of entertainment in the family. I got to sit in the red leather chair and blow my brains out till I got dizzy or my tongue went thick; once I got going I could feel the vibrations go past my jaw and head for my stomach. The whole family spread out at my feet, except for Papa, who would listen from the other room. On those days it could rain ice or be a hundred and five in the shade and everybody was happy. I could play the popular stuff and make them dance till they fell down. I could play the blues and break them in half.

Suddenly nobody remembered that I'd ever been bad. Now folks say, "Grover! Hey, Grover T., that sounds real fine, come play in my store," or, "Hey son, come sit in my diner where it's cool." Like we was all best friends or something. Mr. Thompson used to say I wasn't even to think about walking down the street where his soda fountain was; now he calls me over all the time, tells me I'm good for business. I go, he gives me free lemon cokes.

After school I went to the community library and tried to teach myself how to read music. The place had two or three books called "How To." I'd sit there for hours looking at the henscratches, trying to make sense of it all. Finally I figured out that each line was two spaces on the harmonica, and that the black spots were where my fingers should go and how long I should leave them there. I'd run down to the bathroom with the book inside my sweater and give it all a try. The guy who stacked the books caught me a few times, said I was a real stupid kid, then he'd show me how to do it. He said he had a girl once who played the harmonica, said that's why he dumped her. You play a long time and your lips go funny on you he told me.

On Fridays, Papa had me come down to the business to play while the men waited to find out who won the races. It seemed to calm them down a whole lot. They all wanted to hear the new Benny Goodman stuff, everybody liked swing. A bunch of their sweeties waltzed in and said I was awfully good. One of them said I was cute as hell, and I was only ten back then. Everybody made a circle around me and started laughing and clapping their hands. Papa told me to get him a cigarette from the front room. One of the women held my arm, told me to stay put, that she had plenty of smokes. Papa looked down at me, way down, like I wasn't any bigger than a lizard. He said go get him a cigarette. I did. He told me to light it so I did that too. He said he was glad to see I could do something useful for a change. The one with the peach-colored dress that swung way down in the back, the one who said I was cute, asked couldn't they have another song, maybe "Coming in on a Wing and a Prayer"? I looked up at Papa, he liked that song a lot. But he said it was a fool's song, that it was a good one for me cause any fool could play the harmonica. Then he ripped Roy Luther out of my hands. I felt all dizzy, like I couldn't breathe. He might as well have ripped off my face. All of the sudden I remembered I wasn't nobody, just another little nobody colored kid at the bottom of the barrel. Then I heard him blow, Lord, you'da thought they was killing a cow, *slowly.* His hands were so big and dry they couldn't move to change the scale. Nobody laughed, he wasn't the kind of person you'd laugh at. He didn't say a word, just gave Roy Luther back to me and left. After that, we didn't talk too much about music.

Miss Neville calls out my name. I am number sixty-nine and she looks like somebody's hit her in the stomach hard. She's this little bitty old white woman with her hair knotted to the back of her head in a vice.

"Grover T. Smiley?"

"Yessum."

She hands over a piece of sheet music, "Can you make any sense of this?"

I glance over it; it's something I already learned, a real easy piece. "Yessum."

She looks up a little bit, I'm only the third person to even say I knew what it was. "What would you like to play Grover? Do you know the bass?"

"No, Ma'am, I brought my own."

The kids in the assembly hall aren't listening, most of them are asleep or whispering. Miss Neville sits down at the edge of the table and folds her arms across her chest. "Alright then."

"You want me to play this, Ma'am?" I hold up the music. I was hoping she'd say no cause I know stuff that's a lot prettier than this.

"That will be fine."

I pull out Roy Luther from my pocket and put him in my mouth real quick. If you go too slow, somebody always says, "Oh no, not the harmonica. I thought you could play a real instrument." I jump right in, without even getting a good breath. Miss Neville looks up, first to stop me and then to listen. After the first few bars the kids that were asleep wake up and the kids that were talking get quiet and everybody sits up real straight, like it was gonna make them hear better. Roy Luther has that sort of effect on people. I finish, it was an okay job I guess. Everybody claps real politely, like they were at a picture show. Miss Neville takes my arm.

"Do your parents know about this?"

She let everybody else go on. Carl Smith through Herman Zweckler got to miss their audition all together. Roy Luther and I were taken to the principal's office and asked to wait there.

Miss Neville comes in looking all pink and flustered. That's one thing you can say about white people, they're always changing color on you. She smacks this stack of sheet music in front of me and says, "Can you play this?" When I know she thinks I can't. I don't know what to do, if I should tell her no, that I can't read a note of the stuff and the other thing was just a freak of God, or that I can, which I could. Mama says to always tell the truth, Papa say to go with the flow. The piece on top is one of my favorites, Schumann's "Scenes from Childhood." I say yes.

Miss Neville tapped her foot real fast and looked at me like she thought I was crazy. Finally she threw her hands in my face and said, "Well then *play* for God's sake!"

I never heard a teacher take the name of God in vain before, it made me like her. I folded my lips into my mouth to get them ready and then pulled up Roy Luther. He tasted like my house keys. Harmonicas remind you that everything in your head is all hooked together, playing is a lot more than the mouth, it rolls into the back of your neck and through every tooth individually. My eyes don't read music anymore, it goes straight to my tongue and fingers, each pressing on the two different sides like they was trying to break through for company. My head likes this piece a lot. The notes sound real good in the little office and I start to forget all about Miss Neville and the school orchestra. I just keep my eyes on the paper and play. It's a real pretty song.

When I get through, Miss Neville is looking up at the ceiling real hard, like there's something important up there. I look up too. She turns around, all watery and pale again. She thinks I'm making fun of her by looking up, but she lets it go. "That was lovely, Grover."

I knock the spit out of Roy Luther and thank her kindly.

She swats at her eyes with the back of her hand. "Have you been playing the harmonica a long time?"

"Six, seven years."

"That's just fine."

"You want to hear something else? Some swing maybe?"

She looks like she's come back down now. "I'll have to contact your parents at once, your father has a phone where he works doesn't he?"

Papa didn't like being bothered at work. "You gotta call my folks?"

"Certainly, yes."

She rang up Central and got connected. Papa didn't like being bothered at work.

"Mr. Smiley? Yes, hello, this is Miss Neville down at Central Valley. I'm calling about your son. No, Grover. No, there isn't anything wrong, quite to the contrary."

This was news to me.

"It seems we have stumbled upon a rather remarkable musical gift . . . yes, I do think this is important. Did you know about the situation? About his music?"

I motion for her to hold the line, she put her little hand over the receiver. "Tell him it's about Roy Luther."

She looked confused so I nodded at her, the way Mama does us kids when we're not sure if we're doing something right. "Mr. Smiley? Grover says to tell you it's about Roy Luther . . . you know about that? Well, he demonstrates an amazing aptitude for the instrument. I would like to have a conference with you and your wife at once, to make arrangements to put Grover in a special program, perhaps even a special school. I've never seen a talent like this, Mr. Smiley. It is a force to be reckoned with."

I was sent home early with a "Gifted Child Form," and told that it should be completed and returned the next day so that plans could be made. The form was pretty easy stuff, name, age, place I was born. One space needed my middle name. I thought about it, I'd always just written Grover T., nothing more than that. I asked my folks about it, they said there were lots of kids, they couldn't remember no fool *middle* name. I wrote the T in the blank. It looked kinda stupid sitting there by it-self. I wrote in Truman, because he's the vice president and seems like a real friendly white guy. On my form for gifted children my name was Grover Truman Smiley. It looked pretty good. Papa signed the form without reading it, said he didn't want no more *music* teachers calling him at work. I said I was sorry.

I found Miss Neville in the principal's office typing away. I gave her the form, which she clipped onto the thing she'd been working on.

"I've been doing a lot of planning for us, Grover." She didn't look at me, she just worked at her desk, shuffling and making notes in a little pad. Somehow it all looked real important, the way she was putting it together so carefully.

"I didn't mean to be a bother, Ma'am."

This stopped her dead. She laid all the papers back down and took hold of my hand, you could tell she wanted to be real nice. "You won't ever be a bother, Grover. You are the most important person in this whole school to me."

I looked at the floor, there was a little red ant making his way toward the bookshelves.

"Do you know how long I've been a music teacher?"

"No, Ma'am."

"A very long time, and I've had a few good students. Not very many, but enough to make it worth my while."

She let go of my hand, I was glad and stuffed it in my pocket. She went beneath her desk and brought a wallet out of her purse. "I've kept photographs of all of them. I felt like they were my children." She unfolded this strip of plastic and out stumbled about five little colored children, one of them's got a violin and the next is standing beside a piano. They all look like regular kids, they's all smiling. "Every one of these children had a chance to be very fine musicians, to do something important with their lives. And do you know what happened?"

"No."

"Well, Charles Hunt," she pointed to the kid with the piano, "he got a job in his uncle's filling station, and my prize pupil, Cynthia Rachlin, she married a checkout boy at the A&P and had a baby."

It was old Cindy Dobbs, Harvey Rachlin's big sister.

"And all the rest of them did about the same. They all had a chance and gave it away. I didn't become a music teacher to force children with no musical ability to join an orchestra, I simply wanted to find the ones who could make something of themselves. This," she held up the papers, "is my letter to the governor, it's all about you and . . . and . . . ."

"Roy Luther."

"Yes, I've told them how talented you are and what I think we should do about it. They'll listen to me."

"You wrote the governor?" I rocked back on my heels a little. I remember seeing his picture in the post office. He was the only person besides famous criminals who got his picture there. "You think he's going to want to hear me play? You think he's got a favorite song or something?"

Miss Neville licked the envelope and pressed on a stamp with the heel of her hand. "I'm positive you'll play for the governor someday, you might even play for the president of the United States." She smiled at me for a second and then her face got all busy again. "Of course, you won't be playing the harmonica then, you'll have learned a real instrument."

I thought I must have heard her wrong. "Ma'am?"

"Grover, you certainly don't expect to become great while playing a bucolic instrument."

I wasn't even sure what she said, but I knew what it meant.

I could feel myself getting lightheaded, the same way I did the night Papa tried to play. I never talked back to a teacher, come to think about it, I'd never talked back to anybody. I wasn't looking to cause trouble. All I ever wanted to do was play, maybe someday get that job in the bakery that every kid in the world wanted. Miss Neville was going to mail the letter.

"If it's alright, I think I don't really want to play for the governor after all." It sounded pretty polite to me.

"I wouldn't worry about it too much."

"Do you think I shouldn't be playing the harmonica?"

She let out this big breath and turned around, she didn't want to miss the postman. "I think you've done a wonderful job with what you have. I think all little colored children should play the harmonica if it would help bring them to the point you're at now. But people get older and they move on to different things. That's where you are now, that's why I'm trying to help you."

I drew in my breath, which is a lot. "No. No thank you, Ma'am."

She was just as surprised as I was. "I beg your pardon?"

"They're talking about giving me a job at the theater, playing before the Sunday matinee. I'd like that, playing my harmonica for people." I tried to look at her, but decided best that I go before I lose my nerve. I darted past her out the doors and down the front steps. I could feel her watching me run down the street with Roy Luther flat inside my hand, her holding onto the letter.

By the time I got to Mr. Thompson's soda fountain I was all out of breath. I stood there for a long time, just fogging up the glass. Every now and then I'd take my thumb and make a mark showing I was here. I wondered if she'd mail the letter, but I was pretty sure not. She'd find somebody else for her wallet quick enough.

Mr. Thompson caught sight of me standing on the sidewalk. Any other kid he would have run off, but he calls me inside and asks if I'd please play him a song. Old Cindy Dobbs was sitting at the counter with her baby and gives me a nice smile, asks how I'm doing. Mr. Thompson says, "What do you feel like humming up today, Grover?" Suddenly I knew that everything was good, so I tell him, anything he's wanting to hear. They decide on "Don't Sit Under the Apple Tree With Anyone Else But Me." Then he draws me up an extra large lemon coke, but I ask him, wouldn't he please give it to Mrs. Dobbs, cause I'm not so thirsty. I slip in Roy Luther, he tastes like butterscotch Lifesavers and warm nickels. I play so loud that people come in off the street to listen. It's the best feeling in the world, when you're playing one the people really like, especially when it's a happy song. If you ask me, nobody gives the happy songs half enough credit.

EMILY LISTFIELD

Porcupines and Other Travesties

H ER NEEDS STICK out all over, like a porcupine's needles, keeping men away. I do not like her. I do not even pity her.

The way she wraps her arms around men who do not want her. I need a man, she says again and again, I need a man. And the men look over her head pressed up against their chests, look over her head at a woman who is looking elsewhere.

Her desperation, like the premature gray that courses through her unbrushed hair, flies in all directions, static airwaves saying, I need, I need, I need, I am afraid of getting old, I want a child, Will you take care of me? Please, please, please. She does not pretend to like independence. It is not something she ever wanted, it has been thrust upon her and she groans under its weight.

She looks drawn, parched, her skin cracking, bony, lined. Moisturize, I want to tell her, Moisturize, I was told, It is so important as one starts to age, say the ads, Moisturize, said my mother, handing me a bottle of yellow liquid for my sixteenth birthday, and I did, I do, Moisturize, moisturize, yes ma'am.

. . .

Two women lie sunbathing, oiled, deeply tanned. They smell of coconuts. One is about forty, the other is younger. The older one, with a gold ankle bracelet, a ring on her toe, a string bikini, talks about her relationship with George. After listing his numerous merits, she says, "But he's only twenty-five."

"My god," says her friend, "I didn't know that. It's fantastic. I adore it, I just adore it."

"Why?"

"Because it's freedom, that's why. I adore it, I really do adore it." Her voice is shrill. It is the shrillness of hope wearing thin. Soon it will be an unbearable voice. She will be the only one who can stand it.

I had a boyfriend once. He had sharp cheekbones and dark skin and big brown eyes. They took him away and put him in an expensive sanatorium. Something to do with schizoid tendencies.

I imagined him there, gaunt, his cheekbones sharper, his eyes shinier, bigger. When he came home, though, he was all pale and puffed out, like the Pillsbury doughboy.

"All they give you is starch to eat," he said, "and there's nothing to do all day, no exercise."

We were teenagers then. I was waiting to go crazy too. It seemed inevitable. A lot of things seemed inevitable at seventeen. Good things, bad things, adult things. But not loneliness. We thought it was something you outgrew.

They are separating, he and his wife. They have separated and unseparated and separated and unseparated before. "There's no going back this time," he says. I don't know what he said the times before.

And so now they are separated. This is the truth. I've checked. And he doesn't want to be alone. Neither do I, but I am giving him time. He doesn't ask for it, he doesn't even think he wants it, but it is the only thing I can give him. Weaving without a break will break the weaver. I know. I've tried. "Don't weave me in just to pick up another strand," I tell him. "Time, time," I say.

In time, he will come around, I think.

He comes around now, but he has weaving on the mind.

Three girls are on a train going from Providence to New York. They are eighteen and work together as waitresses in a hotel. They are on their way to the big city for a week's vacation.

They swap room service stories. They read *Cosmopolitan* and drink beer. Who will be the first to get married? they wonder aloud. Who will it be? Who will it be? Each hopes the others will name her. Who will it be?

Nobody likes lonely women. Rotting flesh stinks. Ashes to ashes, dust to dust. Go on home, honey, go on home and forget all about it.

Nadine is from the south, black and from the south. "That girl is homeward-bound," says Nadine about a woman no man in his right mind would want. Black or white, makes no difference, homeward-bound girls come in all colors.

Nadine didn't get married 'til she was forty-two. Now don't go getting the wrong idea, it's not that Nadine was homeward-bound, not Nadine, she just took her own sweet time about it.

I went away with a boy who turned out to be insane. This time, I should have known better. He had tattoos and no home.

He sat on the bed of our hotel room, throwing the switchblade into the wooden door six or seven feet away. It went fast and would stick and then he would get up and pull it out and go back to the bed and throw it again. Again and again. I cannot describe the sound a switchblade makes as it snaps open. You have to hear it to know. Again and again. I didn't do anything. I couldn't very well pretend to be reading.

When he grew bored with his game, he went over to the

desk and cut himself a piece of cheese. "Here," he said, motioning to me with the knife. "You're the woman, you clean this."

"What are you, crazy?" I said. This was not the proper response. He grabbed my arm and held the cheese-smeared knife to my throat. "You'll clean more than that," he said. And I did. Damn straight, I did.

He slept with the switchblade under his pillow. He was a heavy sleeper. I lay rigid until dawn when I carefully picked up my bag and ran.

Only one letter managed to catch up with me at the next American Express office. "These are not the times of Zelda Fitzgerald," it said. "You can't just go running off like that. Come home."

We sit at the bar, our stools close together, talking intently. We have much in common, our coloring, our haircuts, our sexual preference, though not our sex. We are both currently in what are called open relationships and we find ourselves spending more nights together at the bar than we used to.

He puts his arm around me and says something that makes me laugh. He laughs with me and then we stop laughing and resume whatever serious talk we have been having, probably something to do with convincing each other of the values of open relationships.

To my left is an old man with a big face, pockmarked and toothless and flecked with red, a drunken drunkard's face. He stares at me and stares and stares at me. I ignore him. But my friend is getting upset. "Will you please stop staring," he says.

"I'm juz trying to figger out who's using who," the man says, slurring and accusatory.

We laugh at him. Our laughs, though, are a slightly higher pitch than before.

On buses, I scan the seats, looking at women's left hands. Is there a gold ring there? Are they married?

Cabs are no relief. If, for some reason, the driver is not inclined to tell you about his children, he is sure to want to discuss your marital status.

"Are you married? A pretty girl like you should be married."

"Are you married? No? Well, you must have a lot of boyfriends. Just one? What do you want to have just one for? A girl like you should have lots of boyfriends. You're too young to settle down."

The truth of the matter is that I really don't care how much time I spend with him. I don't mean I don't care about him. It's just that I don't have much time, and I don't always know what to do with it.

"I need a secretary," I tell him.

"Give me a break," he says.

"I need a vacation," I say.

"So go," he says.

It could be that he doesn't care much either. We have more in common than we care to admit. Our not caring binds us in comfort, making it easy to spend time together.

"I can't tell you what I'm doing next Friday," he says.

"I can't tell you what I'm doing tonight," I say.

"Well, I guess whatever happens, happens," he says. "She always had to know where I was all the time."

I don't ask. I don't particularly want to know. It's easy when you're not in love. It makes it so easy.

Three women find themselves living together. None of them had planned it this way, but nonetheless, here they are, sitting on the bed, polishing their nails, gossiping, feeling as if they are suddenly in the sorority they had no desire to join so many years ago. They are keeping each other company.

Each has been alone and not alone and now alone again.

It is what, more than anything else, they have in common. They talk most about the times when they were not alone, the good times, the hard times, but not alone times. It has not always been this way.

Three pretty women all in a row. "You all must be having some wild time," says a man they know. In fact, they watch television and talk about when they were not alone and plot strategies to be not alone again. This is just an intermediary period. They take up smoking and buy a case of wine.

I go to a country club dance with her. It is the price exacted for a weekend's visit. She must go so I must go.

Her father, after a day of sailing and martinis, stands in his red pants, his paper-white hair, under the yellow and white striped tent, coming on to her friends. If he is not exactly coming on to them, he is certainly kissing them longer than he should.

Her mother, lean and elegant, prefers to be the center of attention. She grabs a man's khaki hat and puts it on her head. "Yippee," she yells and claps her hands.

"Let's get out of here," my friend says. It is a quiet car ride back to the family house. "I'm never going to get married," she says as we wait for a light to change.

It must be bad when watching a couple kiss on a lousy sit-com hurts. It must be bad.

In the dark, I reach for the enamel pill box sitting on my night stand, distinguish between shapes and the sensations they will bring, make my choice. I don't need water. I just need some rest.

"What are you looking for?" I ask him. An old habit.

"I'm not looking for anything," he says.

"Everyone's looking."

"Not me," he says, "I'm all looked out."

. . .

Lonely lady number one buys a puppet. A yellow, long-haired, beady-eyed monkey. She sticks her hand in it and wraps its arms about her shoulders. They gaze into each other's eyes, whispering sweet nothings for their ears only.

I do not like her. I am nothing like her. I am just taking my own sweet time.

SUSAN MINOT

Thanksgiving Day

GUS AND Rosie Vincent waited for their six children to crawl out of the station wagon and then slammed the doors. The Vincents were always the first to arrive.

They would pull up to the house in Motley, Massachusetts, where their father grew up, and crunch across the gravel, and in the doorway was Ma with her dark blue dress pleated from collar to waist and they would give her kisses, then file in to dump their coats in the coatroom and right away the first thing would be the smell of Pa's cigar. He waited in the other room. Every Thanksgiving they descended upon him and every year it was the same.

The three girls wore matching plaid skirts with plaid suspender straps. Caitlin and Sophie, who looked alike, had on hair bands of the same material. Delilah, the youngest daughter, was darker, with a short pixie. She said it wasn't fair she didn't get to have long hair too. The three boys came after, Gus and Sherman and Chickie, in gray flannels. Chickie's were shorts, since he was the baby.

For Sophie, the best thing was getting to see the cousins, especially the other Vincents. Bit, the only girl cousin, was Sophie's age, ten. And Churly was the oldest of everybody; he was fourteen. Churly and Bit arrived with Uncle Charles and Aunt Ginny. Sophie hesitated because sometimes you didn't give them a kiss. On Aunt Ginny's cardigan was the turkey pin she wore every year. The other cousins were the Smalls. Aunt Fran used to be a Vincent before she married Uncle Thomas. They had three boys. The oldest was Teever Small, who drooled.

Once everyone was there, the children had to put their coats back on for the annual picture. Bit had a white rabbit muff that Teever Small grabbed at, trying to flirt. "That's enough of that," said his father, but Bit had already snatched it back. Sophie felt how soft the fur was, thinking about the dead rabbit; the muff was in the shape of a rabbit too. The grown-ups shuffled everybody around, then stood beside Sophie's father, who had the camera. They crossed their arms against the cold, talking to one another and watching to make sure the kids didn't move.

"I'll be doggone," said Uncle Thomas. Sophie stared at his bow tie. "Will you look at that."

"A bunch of young ladies and young gentlemen," said Aunt Fran, smacking her orange lips. She had white hair like Ma's, except hers was short.

"Knock it off, Churly," Uncle Charles said.

Sophie turned around. Churly was smirking. He had a head shaped like a wooden golf club, with his long neck, and a crew cut like the other boys. Sophie looked back at the house and saw Ma inside, watching through the French doors.

After the picture was taken, Rosie Vincent told her children to say hello to Livia, and the cousins tagged along. The hall to the kitchen was dark, the floor with a sheen from the glow at the end. The kitchen was pale gray, with no lights on, and a white enamel table in the middle. Livia gave them pinched kisses, her eyes darting around the room, checking on food, on the children. She was huge and huffing in her white uniform. The kitchen smelled of Worcestershire sauce and turkey. "Are you behaving yourselves now?" She held up a shiny wooden spoon. When she was cooking, everything on Livia sweated, the steam rising behind her from the pots on the stove.

"Not me," Churly said. "I always try to be as naughty as possible."

Caitlin laughed while Sophie looked at Livia's face, which meant business. Livia sat down. "Now what are the seven blessed sacraments?" she asked, addressing Gus and Rosie's children—Catholic, thanks to their mother. Livia tipped one ear forward the way Sophie had seen the priest do in confession. Sophie fingered a tin Jell-O mold shaped like a fish, and Caitlin busied herself by tucking in Sherman's shirttails. No one answered. Livia rattled them off herself, slicing apples so the blade came right to her thumb without even looking. The cousins drifted off into the pantry as Livia thought up new questions—all having to do with catechism.

The dining room table had already been set. The cranberry sauce had a spoon sticking out. Bit stole some mint wafers, reaching past the blue water goblets into the middle of the table, and gave one to Sophie. "It's okay," said Bit, noticing Sophie's expression.

"I saw that," Churly said from the doorway. Sophie blushed. He came in and whispered, "All right, you guys . . ." and she saw how his eyes were like those light-blue paperweights that had white lines of glass streaked from the middle. He leaned past them and plucked a candy out of the cut-glass boat. "Delish," he said. "Don't mind if I do."

In the living room, the grown-ups stood stirring drinks at the red-leather bar stand; then they sat down. Sophie's mother was the only one without a scotch or a Dubonnet. There was nothing to do while the grown-ups talked except to look around at each tiny thing. Three walls were covered with books, and over the mantelpiece was a portrait of Dr. Vincent, so dark and shiny that the lights reflected off it. One side of the room was all French windows, with dead vines at the edges. The windows overlooked the lawn. Beside the fireplace was a child's rocking chair with a red back, an antique. Gus had gotten to it first and was sitting there, holding onto his ankles, next to Ma's place on the sofa. They had the hard kind of sofas with wooden arms and wood in a curve along the back. You could tell it was Ma's place because of the brown smudge on the ceiling from her cigarette smoke.

The girls examined their grandmother. Her shoes, the pair her granddaughters liked the best, were pale lavender with pink trim and flat bows, her fancy shoes.

"Gussie," said Aunt Fran, the one person in the world who called Sophie's father that. She said it as if it tasted bad. "How'd you like the game?" The last time they had seen each other was at the Harvard halftime in October when they were stretching their legs under the bleachers. Gus, with his children, said, "Good day to you," as if he saw his sister every day, which he didn't, each walking in the opposite direction.

The grown-ups talked about the sports the boys were playing.

"Churly's on the debating team," said Uncle Charles. He was the oldest Vincent son.

"I certainly am," said Churly, the only one of the children taking up a seat. "Anyone want to argue?"

Under a lamp was a picture of Ma before she married. She was holding a plume of roses at her waist; her chin to the side, her dark eyes and dark hair swept up.

The grown-ups were talking about the woman next door who died after she cut her finger on a splinter from a Christmas tree ornament. Ma said how appropriate it was that a pheasant appeared out of the woods at Mr. Granger's funeral.

"But *she* was the one who loved to shoot," said Aunt Fran with her Adam's apple thrust out.

"Terrible story about their son," said Sophie's mother. Her thumb rubbed her knuckle while the conversation continued.

They talked without looking at each other, their chairs all facing in. Aunt Fran addressed her remarks to the one spot in the room where no one sat or stood. She and Uncle Thomas were having a pond dug in the back of their house and by mistake the workers had struck a pipe. Aunt Fran and Uncle Thomas told the story at the same time, interrupting each other.

Uncle Charles said, "It's like a zoo at my house." When he made jokes, he barely cracked a smile. Bit was lucky, she got to have a pony and three dogs and sheep. "Our sheep just stand there in the rain," said Churly.

Uncle Charles said the chickens hated him. And now they had a turtle, with a chain attached to the loop on its shell so it wouldn't run away. "It chooses to sleep where I'm accustomed to park my car," he said.

"A what?" said Pa, angry at having to strain.

"Turtle," yelled Uncle Charles.

"Where's our turtle soup then?" Pa said and some of the family chuckled. Sophie didn't think he was kidding. He sat there still as a statue, his hands gripping the mahogany claws of his chair.

Caitlin was up at the bar with Churly, pouring a ginger ale. Sophie got Bit and Delilah to go to the owl room, and the boys followed. There were glass owls and a hollow brass owl with a hinge so its head lifted off, two china owls with flowers, owl engravings, and a needlepoint of an owl that Caitlin had done from a kit. They had a game they played by closing their eyes and then going nose to nose with someone and saying "One, two, three, Owl-lee, Owl-lee," and opening their eyes, imitating an owl. Delilah and Sherman were playing it.

Stretching down the corridor were group silhouettes of Vincent ancestors, black cutouts of children with ringlets, holding hoops, or men with bearded profiles. There were Pa's team pictures from Noble & Greenough and his class pictures from Harvard. All the faces in the photographs had straight noses and white eyeballs and hide-gray complexions. In one, Pa lay on his side, lengthwise, in front of everyone else. Sophie tried to match him with the Pa back in the living room. You never saw Pa smile, that was common knowledge, except in one picture the Vincents had at home, of Pa with the Senator. His job had been to write speeches, and, according to Sophie's mother, he got a dollar a year to do it. In the picture, his grin is closed, like a clown's. There was Pa in an army uniform—but Sophie knew the story of that. Pa missed the war, sailing to France on the exact day Armistice was declared. At the end of the hall, Sophie came to the picture of Pa's brother, the famous doctor who discovered the cure for a disease whose name she could never remember. He had died a long time ago.

When they drifted back into the living room, Uncle Charles was recalling when the lawn froze and they could skate over the sunken garden.

"Not true," said Pa, gurgling. "My lawn was never an ice rink."

"Sure," said Sophie's father. "Everything was frozen solid."

Pa said, "Never happened in my lifetime."

Uncle Charles clamped on his pipe with his back teeth. "Oh yes it did, Pa. You must be losing your memory." His voice was squeaky.

"Ma," demanded Pa.

With her perfectly calm face, Ma said, "I do remember it, yes." She looked at Pa and said gently, "It was when you were away."

"Nonsense," he said. "I never went anywhere."

The children's table was wobbly. This year Sophie got to sit at the big table, and Caitlin and Churly, too. Bit said she was glad to stay at the children's table where she wouldn't have to use good manners.

When the plates came, they had everything on them already, even creamed onions whether you liked them or not. Pa looked down at the food in front of him.

ing hoops, or men with bearded profiles. There were Pa's team pictures from Noble & Greenough and his class pictures from Harvard. All the faces in the photographs had straight noses and

"Gravy, Granpa?" shouted Aunt Fran. Half-frowning, he regarded her. She swung a silver ladle over his turkey, bringing it up with a flourish. "Yummy," she said in a booming voice.

Everyone at the table used loud voices—family behavior. When Sophie went out to go to the bathroom, she stood for a moment in the hall between the Chinese portraits and listened to the clatter behind her, the hollow echo from the high ceilings, Aunt Fran's hooting, the knives clicking on the china, her mother's voice saying something quietly to the little table. Sophie could tell Uncle Charles from his whine, and her grandmother was the slow voice enunciating each word the way old people do because they're tired of talking. Sophie went up close to study one Indian picture—you could see the tongue of the snake and the man's pink fingernails and even the horse's white eyelashes. Ma said they used one cat hair at a time to paint it. In the bathroom was the same brown soap shaped like an owl. The towels she used were so stiff it was like drying your hands with paper.

Sophie came back as Aunt Fran was saying, "He's a crook."

"Now stop that," said Ma, lifting her chin.

"Who is?" asked Churly, brightening.

"Never mind," said Ma to her knife and fork.

So Churly asked, "What'd he steal?"

Ma said, "They've started reshingling the house in North Eden." The Vincents went to Maine every summer. A drawer in one of the side tables was always kept pulled out—a red velvet slab with rows of arrowheads, ones that Pa had found on Boxed Island in Maine. You played Kick-the-Can on the sloping lawn after supper. When Churly was it, Sophie would let herself get caught. One time, playing spy, they saw Ma on her balcony with her hair all down, falling down her arms like a white shawl. Sometimes Ma and Pa were like ghosts. You'd see them pass behind a window in their house, or snapping out a light and vanishing. In the daytime, Ma's hair was twisted into a knot at the back.

Aunt Fran was wondering whether there didn't used to be a porch around the house out at Cassett Harbor, the old house. Uncle Thomas shouted, "That's right. Mrs. Lothrop said they'd have the Herreshoff teas on that porch."

"The correct term," said Ma, "is piazza."

"It must have been quite a view," said Sophie's mother.

"It's where you'd sit with your beaux," said Ma.

"We tore down the piazza," said Pa. Sophie was surprised he was listening.

Aunt Fran said, "I thought it burned down."

"Yes." Ma's nod was meant to end the discussion.

"How'd it burn down?" Churly asked. His long neck went up and his ears stuck out. Sophie felt herself flushing.

Pa said, "It–was–torn–down." His shoulders were round and low and his chin hovered inches above his plate.

Down at her end, Ma said, "The remainder was torn down, yes." Pa glared at her. His bottom lip drooped, as white as the rest of his face.

"How'd it burn down?" Churly asked eagerly.

Ma pulled some empty dishes over the tablecloth toward her. "You finish," she said. She stood up and carried some things to the sideboard, then glanced over the table to see what else to take. She piled small dishes on the turkey platter in front of Pa and went to lift it.

"Don't touch that," he said. He didn't look at her, or at the platter, but stared at the middle of the table.

"I think you're done," said his wife.

Sophie's mother pushed her chair back. "Let me . . . ." Her napkin bloomed like a white flower when she let go of it on the table.

"I'm not through," said Pa. "I want to pick." He didn't move.

"Now, Pa," said Aunt Fran. "We've got Livia's pies coming."

"Damn Livia's pies," he said. "Only occasionally you will disguise a voyage and cancel all that crap."

The little table fell quiet.

"I'm all ready for dessert." Uncle Thomas looked perky. "You ready for dessert there, Churly?"

Churly nodded, then looked to see what Pa would do next.

Caitlin and Sophie started to take their plates, but their mother gave them a stay-put look and made several quick trips through the swinging door.

Pa growled, "I've been eating goddamn custard all Monday."

Aunt Ginny asked, "What kind of pies do we have? Each year they had the same: apple, mince and pumpkin. Everyone began saying which kind they wanted. Ma sat back down.

As they ate their pie and ice cream, Pa kept mumbling. "Bunch of idiots . . . . Going to knock it off like a bullhorn . . . . Newspaper, *then* cigar . . . ."

"No dessert for you, Pa?" Uncle Charles asked.

"I wouldn't set foot in there to piss," said Pa Vincent.

Ma went down and whispered into Pa's ear. No one could hear what she said, but Pa answered in a loud, slow voice, "Why don't you go shoot yourself?"

In the kitchen, Sophie and Caitlin watched Churly tell Livia.

She fidgeted with pans and finally set them in the sink. "Your grandfather just needs his nap," said Livia. She studied the children's faces to see if they understood this. She was frowning. Her gaze drifted off and she turned her mammoth back to them, kept on sudsing things in the sink. She muttered, "He'll be wanting his . . ." but they couldn't hear what.

In the living room, the grown-ups were serving coffee. On the tray were miniature blue enamel cups, a silver bowl holding light-brown-sugar rocks, and chocolate mints in tissue paper envelopes.

Ma and Aunt Fran came down from upstairs where they had taken Pa.

"Everything all right?" bellowed Uncle Thomas. His wife scowled at him.

Ma took her place on the sofa. "Fine," she said. "Fine."

Rosie handed her a cup with a tiny gold spoon placed on the saucer. Delilah, her arm draped across her mother's knee, felt brave. "Was Pa mad at us?" she asked. Caitlin glared at her.

"Hah," shouted Uncle Charles, half-laughing, "he wasn't mad at me."

Sophie's father said, "He didn't know what he was saying, Delou." He was over by the window.

Ma sipped at the rim of her cup. Gus Vincent touched the curtain with one finger and gazed out. Rosie busily poured more coffee.

Looking at Delilah, Ma said, "He was not mad at you, dear."

Aunt Ginny looked up, surprised. "The turkey was delicious," she said.

"Oh shut up, Virginia," said Uncle Charles.

Sophie looked at Churly and noticed his ears sticking out and all his features flattened out, stiff, into a mask.

Uncle Thomas said, "Super meal, super." He jiggled the change in his pocket, waiting for something to happen.

"You can thank Livia for that." Ma set down her saucer. Sherman was in the rocking chair at her feet, lurching to and fro.

"Yes," said Rosie Vincent, "but you arranged it so beautifully."

Ma folded her hands. Her expression was matter-of-fact. "Actually, I don't think I've ever arranged anything beautifully in my whole life."

The grown-ups exchanged looks and for a moment there was no sound except for Sherman creaking in the rocking chair at Ma's feet. He got up, all at once aware of himself, and scurried to his mother. The chair went on rocking. Ma stared at it. Rocking empty, it meant something to her.

So she reached out one lavender shoe to still it, and did just that.

Debra Spark is the author of the novel *Coconuts for the Saint* (Faber & Faber, 1995). She teaches at Colby College.